The Loyalist Legacy

Book Three of the Loyalist Trilogy

Elaine A. Cougler

Peache House Press

Peache House Press

Certain characters in this work are historical figures, and certain events portrayed did take place. However, this is a work of fiction. All of the other characters, names and events as well as all places, incidents, organizations, and dialogue in this novel are either the products of the author's imagination or are used fictitiously.

Copyright © 2016 by Elaine Cougler

All rights reserved.

No part of this book may be reproduced or re-transmitted without the express written consent of the author.

Cover by Spica Book Design.

Text layout and design by To The Letter Word Processing Inc.

The back cover photo of the author was taken by Paula Tizzard.

Createspace ISBN 978-1539451280

Acknowledgements

CREATING THIS HISTORICAL TRILOGY and especially this third in the series has had its challenges but also its absolute joys and moments of great gratitude. My beta readers are at the top of the list of those whose help I very much appreciate. A group with varied backgrounds, each member found excellent ways to improve my work. They are Barb Cope, Sandra Leeuwestein, Jacqueline Engelen, Elaine Ballantyne, Ruth Stephenson, Nancy Tulloch, Betty Mathers, Millie Gremonprez and John Cook. Thanks to each one of them.

Museum and historical site curators, as well as a number of librarians, have pointed me toward books that I might not have found but for their interest in my project and their thorough understanding of the resources they have. Very old texts that I found online, placed there through various endeavors, allowed me to read from the comfort of my computer chair first-hand accounts of the times and places which are my subject matter. I am thankful these old sources have not been lost but have been made accessible to the world.

I thank all the wonderful readers of the first two books whose encouragement kept me going to finish this third in the series and whose unstinting support and praise has fed my fire. Especially I give thanks to the many who have gone and continue to go out of their way to help me get the word out by inviting me to speak, by writing reviews, and by telling all and sundry about my books.

As always I must speak of my family, both immediate and extended, for their unwavering support in so many ways. My husband joins me on my research travels, gives me honest answers when I use him as a sounding board, and always listens intently as I think aloud about how some new research might fit into my novels. I am truly blessed.

Also by Elaine Cougler

The Loyalist's Wife

The Loyalist's Luck

For William Garner and Catherine Cain Garner

and

For Chelsea Blom and Benjamin Cougler

All of whom inspired this book in different ways

The John Garner Family

John Garner* (Butler's Ranger)
Lucinda Garner nee Harper (his wife)
Their Children:
1. Harper John Garner
2. William Garner* m. Catherine Cain*, daughter of John Cain* (Butler's Ranger); four children named William, John, Eva, baby Catt (died)
3. Robert Garner (twin) married Mary Anne, an American; four children named Mary Anne (died), Thomas, Elizabeth, Russell
4. Thomas Garner (twin) (died in War of 1812)
5. Helen Garner married Timothy Greenstone, an American soldier; three children named Thomas, John, Ernest

Chippewa Family

Migisi (husband)
Kiwidinok (wife)
Their Children:
1. Baby (killed)
2. Solomon (adopted)
3. Boy
4. Girl

*names of real people

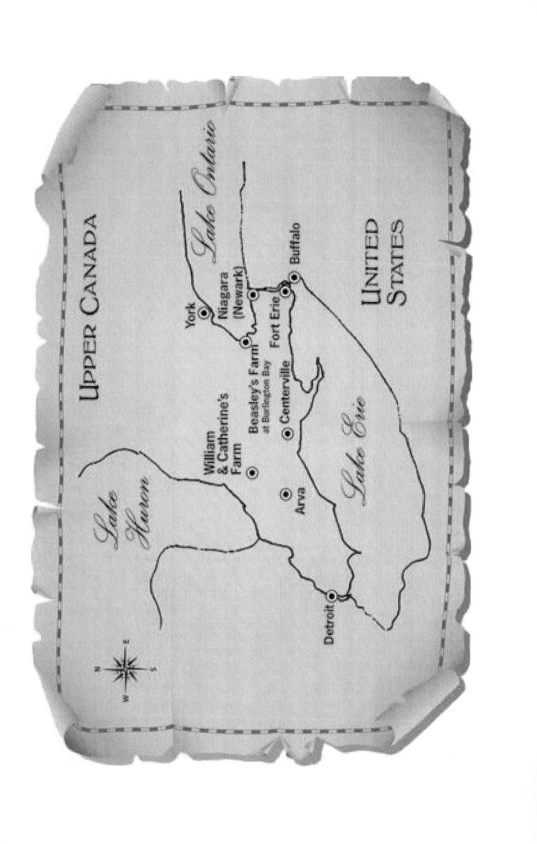

Contents

Part I: Loyalists on the Land

Chapter One — Nissouri Township, District of Oxford; April 1818

Chapter Two — April, 1818

Chapter Three — Niagara; September, 1817

Chapter Four — Nissouri Township; May, 1818

Chapter Five — Niagara; May, 1818

Chapter Six

Chapter Seven — Nissouri Township; June, 1818

Chapter Eight

Chapter Nine — Richard Beasley's House on Burlington Heights; June, 1818

Chapter Ten — Nissouri Township; Fall, 1818

Part II: Across the Niagara River

Chapter Eleven — Buffalo; Fall, 1818

Chapter Twelve — Buffalo; Winter, 1818-1819

Chapter Thirteen — Winter, 1819

Chapter Fourteen — Nissouri Township, District of Oxford; September, 1824

Chapter Fifteen — Chippewa Indian Reserve; December, 1824

Chapter Sixteen — Robert Garner's farm; Spring, 1825

Chapter Seventeen
Chapter Eighteen
Chapter Nineteen
Chapter Twenty

Part III: The Rising Rebels

Chapter Twenty-One	Nissouri Township; Fall, 1831
Chapter Twenty-Two	
Chapter Twenty-Three	Spring, 1834
Chapter Twenty-Four	
Chapter Twenty-Five	Spring, 1837
Chapter Twenty-Six	June, 1837
Chapter Twenty-Seven	Toronto, 1837
Chapter Twenty-Eight	October, 1837
Chapter Twenty-Nine	Norwich, 1837
Chapter Thirty	William and Catherine's farm; July, 1838

Part One
Loyalists on the Land

Chapter One

Nissouri Township, District of Oxford
April, 1818

CATHERINE STOOD AGAINST the wooden table and pounded the grayish dough into a glutinous sticky mass. With each stroke her anger rose. She picked the bits of batter from her fingers and pushed them into the dough with more force than usual. And heeled her hands into the ball once more. Slapping it into the meager flour bits on the table, she saw the loaves begin to take shape and, in spite of herself, breathed a little easier.

William Junior glanced up from his numbers at the other end of the table. She felt his eyes on her and the question he dared not ask. Not until she simmered down anyhow. The loaves slipped easily into the greased pans and she smoothed the tops before spreading a cloth over them and lifting the whole lot to the warming shelf above her great black beast of a stove. William's stylus scraped on the slate. She turned to face him, this child who would rather perfect his letters than play jacks in the corner with his brother and sister.

"Go ahead, William. Ask me." She forced a smile and was rewarded with a softening of his features.

"Why did Daddy go? Who is Uncle Robert? What will we do if the Indian comes back?" He took in a quick breath. "You're so angry, Mama. Why?" The stylus dropped to the table but he paid it no mind. His head tipped up toward her as though the very angle of his holding it could slice into her thoughts and make her answer.

"Slow up, my son. One day all your questions are going to get you into trouble." She tousled his dark hair and felt his tension ease. Her own did, as well. "Uncle Robert is your father's brother who lives far away. In the United States. We told you that, William." He didn't need to know why she was so angry. Only a child, even though he was her eldest, he didn't have to shoulder the worries of their world just yet. Far be it from her to pass her burdens and fears to his thin shoulders even though he was almost eight years old.

"But Mama, I saw you punching that dough. The whole table shook. I couldn't make my letters straight." He stood before her, up to her chest, his green eyes wide. He needed an answer. She reached for him but he edged back.

"Come outside with me, away from your brother and sister." She brushed past him and grabbed the door handle.

Sunlight swept across the expanse of the lowlands on either side of their river making a golden path right up to their porch. Thames, the river was called, named by Governor Simcoe after the main shipping channel in London far across the ocean. John, her father-in-law, had told her about his trip to Detroit with the Governor so many years ago. She could see him now sitting in the rocking chair by that giant stove in the house by the mill. His face shone and his voice rose and fell with each new detail in the story. She shook her head and tucked a stray strand of hair under her cap. What had happened to them? No word in almost two years.

Up the hill on the other side of the river tall maples, oaks, elms and beech trees still covered the land; this was the year William planned to turn that forest into fields. Two hundred acres of wheat and corn swaying in the autumn sun—his dream had become hers, except now he'd ridden off to Niagara with his brother.

On this side of the river brown stumps filled the landscape all around their house, the coarse nubs of last year's corn stalks flowing between them through mud and mire and the odd lump of dirty snow. Spring should be here but no slips of green nor buds on bushes yet heralded its coming. Only the robin's call from the one tree William left near their house coaxed Catherine from her black mood. The door opened behind her and young Will joined her at the railing.

"You remember your father's parents? And Uncle Robert's?"

"Of course. They stayed with us after the war. On our farm."

"Yes."

Young Will faced her. "What about them?" His mouth dropped open. "Are they...dead?"

The fear in his voice melted her anger. Facing him she placed her hands on his shaking shoulders. "No. Well...that is...we don't know."

The boy's eyes took on a sombre cast as he peered into her own and tilted his head once again. "But you're angry. Why?"

"That's only me, Will. Angry at something I can't change." She turned and pointed across the river. "I just hope he comes back... in time to make a start on clearing all that land. We have to make a life here, my son." She slipped her arm around his shoulders and pulled him, unresisting, to her. "I didn't want you to worry."

She worried all the rest of that day as she drove herself and her children to prepare a huge kettle of stew, sauce from last fall's dried apples, johnny cake and whatever else she could think of to feed the host of men coming on the morrow. William had wanted to get a start on cutting trees while the ground was still hard and last week had ridden the rough roads to the few neighbors up and down the concessions. He needed their help and they would come, as he had often gone to them. This time, however, William was gone and the neighbors would arrive on the morrow to find her taking her husband's place.

CATHERINE ROUSED THE CHILDREN before daybreak and sat them at the rough table in the center of their squared-log house. They shovelled down the porridge she'd made from the last of the oats they'd managed to grow the summer before. They would need a good breakfast today; she planned to keep them helping the whole time while she did William's job in the woods.

"Will." She raised her voice above the giggles and laughter. "I'll need you to watch wee John and Eva. Mind you don't wander off." He nodded. "I'll be taking your father's place. Working the saw." Her hands stopped their cleaning up and for a moment she studied them. What would they look like by the end of the day?

"Mama! I hear a horse!" Wee John jumped from his place on the bench at the table and ran to the window. "A man, mama! He's coming in!"

She quelled her rising stomach and shushed the children. Without a word she opened the door and waved to the approaching figure before stepping back inside to don William's heavy coat and her boots and scarf with William's heavy gloves.

"Finish your food, children, and clean up the dishes." She leaned their way and fixed her eyes on them. "Remember...your best behavior today."

Outside, the icy daylight crept over the stumps and a pale pink glow to the southeast hailed what might become a sunny day. Frosty wisps of words filled the air as the gathering men greeted each other. She stepped toward the small circle. They parted immediately, their faces questioning yet kind.

Peter Logan, their nearest neighbor, spoke first. "Is your husband sleeping still, Mrs. Garner?" The others chuckled.

"I am sorry, gentlemen. He's gone to Niagara to help his parents."

The men's smiles turned to frowns.

"They've disappeared. William had to go."

"You're here alone?" Mr. Logan asked.

"I'll take William's place today, gentlemen." Sharp intakes of air stopped her a moment. "It's what William wants." She turned to Mr. Logan and raised her voice. "Where do we start?"

Mr. Logan led them and their horses away from the cabin, through the frozen field of last year's stumps, and down to the river. The men piled their saws and ropes atop William's raft, lashing them tightly before helping Catherine in her heavy coat onto the bobbing vessel. The rope they attached at two corners. Her eyes fixed on the swirling waters, Catherine spread her feet wide for balance. She was determined not to cry out but her stomach was knotted all the same as the mounted men started across the river, her raft in their midst.

Usually the river was quite fordable here but in the spring run-off the waters flowed higher and higher until the horses were no longer walking but swimming. The bay on her left rolled its eyes white, jerking against the controlling bit as its rider struggled to keep upright. The black water reached almost up to the top of his leg and the horse's back. He held a musket high with his free hand. Why did he bring a gun? Catherine wondered, but focused on her own troubles.

The raft tipped and tossed, thrust as it was into the main flow of the river, and she soon had wet feet and her skirt dragged more and more against her legs. She tried to stay standing and leaned so heavily on the one upright board that on a particularly violent thrust of the water it cracked and she fell backward on to the flooding planks. Her fingers found a large knothole and she clung to it until the raft found solid ground on the other side of the river.

One by one they dragged horses, tools, and themselves up to the top of the bank.

"We need a fire," one of the men said and he and Mr. Logan disappeared into the trees. Catherine sat on an old log and squeezed water out of her drenched skirt. She took off her boots and dumped out what she could, wrung out her thick stockings and wished the sun were warmer. In no time, however, the men had a fire going, a pot of tea on the boil, and she began to revive.

"We've waited too long," Mr. Logan said at her elbow. "Should've cut and hauled before the ground started to thaw."

"Oh, no. Now we're over here we'll start today." Catherine pulled on her stockings and boots. "Besides, Mr. Brown promised to come along the trail with his oxen. We need to begin." She jumped to her feet with more spirit than she felt and faced his frown with her chin thrust upward.

He didn't move. Beside him, though, Mr. O'Brien got to his feet. He smiled at her and reached for one end of a long crosscut saw. "I can't use this alone," he said. No one moved. He dragged the saw over to the wide trunk of an ancient maple, positioned it as best he could by himself and turned back. Catherine took one look at the others and stomped over to grab the other end. Together they placed the huge blade against the gnarled bark and began to score the tree.

Catherine had never done this before but Mr. O'Brien's words guided her. As the saw jerked back and forth ripping and grinding into the silent morning, the two of them found a rhythm and she began to breathe harder but in a way easier. When they hit a knothole and the saw jerked to a sudden stop, sounds of two other saws cut the morning air and sunlight streaked between the leafless trees.

Throughout the morning the saws and axes worked their way through the standing timber, the rasping sound stopping for long periods as the men and Catherine positioned themselves and felled the almost sawed-through trees. At first they left the fallen giants where they landed but when Mr. Brown came driving his team of oxen from the east through the trees toward them, Mr. Logan and his partner dropped their saw and helped drag the trees to a spot overlooking the river. Here they started two piles, one of logs to be kept and sawn and the other of those to be burned once they'd dried, probably next year.

Catherine hardly dared look at her hands under the heavy gloves. With each pull of the saw she gritted her teeth, determined to keep up with Mr. O'Brien. Fatigue filtered through her hands and arms up to her shoulders and into her very belly. Pushing and pulling the saw took all her strength but she was barely keeping the wretched thing steady while her partner did all the work. He noticed it, too.

"We will take a moment, Mrs. Garner." He dropped his hands from the handle of the embedded saw and stood straight but Catherine hardly saw him. She yanked on her end, realized the saw was stopped, and allowed herself to wonder why.

"Come. Come." Mr. O'Brien pulled one of her gloved hands from the handle and the other slipped off, too. Both were stiffened into clenched hooks as though she still held the saw. He led her to a fresh-cut maple stump bigger than her table and motioned for her to sit. From his bag he pulled his own stoppered jug of hot tea.

"No cup," he said as he passed it to her.

She took the jug in her bare hands and managed to get it to her lips, afraid all the time her hands would let her down and she'd drop the thing in the dirt. The first sip of warm tea, sugared more than she liked, but strong, oh so strong, slipped down her throat with all the balm of her mother's hand on her fevered forehead, and she relaxed into the warmth. Her fingers loosened up. The jug felt secure. She raised her eyes to Mr. O'Brien.

"Thank you," she whispered.

In a few moments the others gathered around her stump. Why have they stopped? Her belly rumbled. They were hungry.

Back across the raging river they swam the horses, this time with Catherine riding behind Mr. Logan, her hands clinging to his slim waist, her nose pressed into the sweaty folds of his felt coat. On solid ground again Mr. Brown helped her down. She almost fell but he steadied her and her feet stepped toward the porch where young Will stared at her. Somewhere she found the strength to smile and his features relaxed.

"Johnny hit Eva, Mama," he said.

"Shush. You're fine," she answered and dragged into the cabin to set the food on the table.

After the boisterous meal with the three children first shy and then excited to have so many at their table, the men pushed back their chairs and began to make their way outside to their horses. Catherine quickly gave young William instructions and donned her sodden coat to follow after the men.

"No, Mrs. Garner." Mr. Logan turned from his horse, the reins in his hand. "You'll not be going with us this afternoon."

"But I must take my husband's place." Her voice carried in the cool air. "You need me."

"No, Mrs. Garner," he replied. "We do not." He ran his right hand over his horse's rump. Clasping the reins in his left hand along with the saddle horn, he hauled himself up and sat high above her. "We'll be working without you this afternoon." He glanced around the yard. "You've enough to do here." He kicked his feet into the horse and led off down to the river.

Catherine stood a moment, ran forward a few steps and stopped. The men urged their mounts into the water once again but none looked back. Catherine went back into the cabin.

A HORSE NEIGHED OUT ON THE ROAD. William had built the cabin to face the river but that meant their door was not on the road side and anyone coming down the road had to wheel in and drive around the cabin to get access to their front door. She ran to the one window facing the road and saw a wagon pulled by a heavy team edging to a stop on the rough road. Apparently the driver didn't want to risk towing his heavy load of all manner of pots and chairs, pails and picture frames, buffalo robes and banging tools onto their soft and slippery property.

"What is it, Mama?" Will's voice was loud even though he was right beside her.

She ran for her coat from the hook by the door. "Stay inside," she called over her shoulder and banged the door behind her.

Chapter Two

April, 1818

THE ROADS BACK to Fort Erie had not improved since William and Catherine's harrowing journey almost two years before. Mud holes frozen over in the early hours of the day turned to slop in the spring sun and on rainy days like this one became death traps for all who stumbled upon them. Along the way patches of dirty snow dotted the track and hid what dangers lay beneath. Still bare, with no buds at all, the maples and birches and elms reached their tentacles over the mounted men in threatening gestures; grey clouds blotted out any weak rays from the sun.

William and Robert walked the horses most of the time for fear of hidden holes and downed logs that might break a horse's leg and leave them stranded. The brothers took turns leading, but even when treading where the leader had gone the danger was paramount. The distance Robert had traveled in five days on frozen roads now took considerably longer with the spring thaw. The strain was unbearable.

William took his turn following his brother, both men stiff and silent as they rode past fields of stumps, great stands of forest, and cabins spewing smoke into the gray-blue sky. Occasionally they noticed someone outside and gladly stopped in response to a friendly wave but, pressed for time, they pushed on toward their father's mill. At night they were fortunate to find hospitality with strangers and slept in more than one straw mow, smelling fresh-sawn wood in a recently built barn.

Everywhere the landscape breathed new life out of past woes with piles of charred lumber and branches waiting for the dry winds of summer before they could be burned, right alongside freshly built cabins and even the odd house complete with a front porch. The war was over but its mark was writ upon the land as surely as if scorched by a branding iron. How long before the settlers would recoup their losses, William wondered?

On the seventh day the two finally rode south from Fort Chippawa, along the Portage Road extension, toward the place where they had spent their boyhood. It seemed a lifetime ago. William's thoughts ran to the battles and the forced marches and the heat and the rain and—he swiped his hand over his taut face. He forced his mind to look elsewhere, at rides with his father to the shop at Fort Erie, to that wagon trip back to his farm on Lundy's Lane when Catherine had told him about the baby, and—the story crept back into his thoughts—that night he rode all the way from Queenstown, taking his brother's battered body home for a decent burial.

"What's going on in that head of yours?" From beside him Robert reached over to grab his reins. "Are you deaf, man?"

"Why are you yelling?"

"I've been trying to get your attention, but you've surely lost your hearing." Robert shook his head and lowered his voice. "We're almost there." He pointed to the break in the trees ahead where the long lane started.

William's head cleared. The laneway was covered with snow patches over bare ground with nary a hoof or a boot track in sight. He sniffed the air. No smoke. They rounded the huge maple tree they'd climbed as boys and cantered right up to the abandoned mill. The brothers sat and gazed about. Even the birds were shocked into silence. Out on the river ice floes knocked about in the rushing water.

....

The Loyalist Legacy

Beside the grey stone structure hulking before them, a stone foundation, weathered framing on only two sides, and wide oak planks formed the first floor of the new house.

"This is what I saw three weeks ago."

William nodded toward the house. "In two years they haven't got any farther than that." He dropped his eyes to his hands and jerked up again. "Where were the neighbors?"

"Couldn't say. And I couldn't go asking, now could I?"

The two tied their horses to the railing by the loading dock and clomped up the steps into the mill. All was dark and dusty, the thin strands of light streaming in through the open door showing nothing of interest. Something scurried in front of William's feet. He jumped back. Robert laughed and slapped his brother's shoulder.

"There's nothing here but critters and dirt. Let's leave."

William moved to the stairs. "Let's just look, shall we?" His feet clomped on the solid steps and, in a moment, Robert followed.

The second floor was as still as the first, though both men covered their mouths against the dust they stirred up. In the small office where Robert had stayed a few days with his parents after the war, two moldy plates met their eyes. "Mama hasn't been here for some time," Robert said.

"And they left in a hurry." William picked up a cup and righted it on the table. "See the stain? Mama would never have left that."

"They took the bedding." Robert smoothed the striped tick. "Left this, though."

"Didn't plan on being gone long?" William looked at his brother whose wild hair almost blotted out the dark freckles on his red cheeks. He hadn't changed much, except for the lines deepening around his squinty eyes as he sat on the bed, his hand brushing the tick beside him.

"We've got to find them!" Robert leapt to his feet and pushed by William through the door and down the wooden steps, his boots clattering and stirring up more dust.

William coughed and rubbed his eyes. "Slow down!" he yelled and ran after him. Robert was taking over as he so often did when they were children.

At the bottom of the stairs, though, his brother stopped. He stood still, his hands reaching high in the air and the end of a rifle barrel sticking through the door. William couldn't see any more but stayed his steps, hoping the intruder hadn't heard him, and wondering what he might do.

"Get out here!"

Robert's boots scraped across the floor as he moved closer to the open door. The rifle barrel grew longer. Hands appeared, clutching the weapon. And then arms. Knowing the man's face would be next, William sidled to his right, hoping to hide. His brother was out the door blocking his view but also that of the intruder. Why did he leave his own rifle on the horse? He glanced around in the gloom but no weapon was apparent.

Suddenly Robert's high-pitched laugh and a deeper guffaw broke the silence.

"Get out here, William! It's nothing but a crazed old Scotsman!"

He edged toward the door and stepped into the full sun. Robert's long arms were wrapped around someone a head shorter, the man's gun now clutched in a gnarled hand against Robert's back. They stepped apart.

"William!" Mr. McKie, their old neighbor, hobbled toward him and wrapped him in a desperate bear hug. Mr. McKie's arms still had a lot of strength in them.

The three stood a few moments basking in mutual smiles and stories until the talk moved on to John and Lucy.

"Where are they?" Robert asked. He told of enlisting William in the search.

"A'm sairy, lads. Sorry. A dinna ken..." He pointed at his rifle.

"No, Mr. McKie. Don't be sorry. You were looking after our da's mill." William gestured around the property. Robert put his arm around the older man's shoulder and squeezed.

"They're well...both o' them...but 'tis a long story, lads. Perhaps..."

William took one look at him and suggested they sit inside out of the wind. In the end they decided to ride back to Mr. McKie's warm farmhouse where they could talk and get a bite to eat. When they arrived, Mrs. McKie smiled her joy at seeing them and immediately put a sliced ham, half a pork pie and applesauce on the table.

Soon they were all drinking tansy tea and sharing tales of days long gone, the sad stories shoved to the back of the conversation as though by wishing they could all pretend that nothing the slightest bit unfortunate had happened in the war. Two years and more had passed since its ending and William was glad to see the new buildings on the McKie land. He thought of the rebuilt barn next to the new house where they laughed and ate and the huge wood stove heated both the room and their hearts.

Mr. McKie pushed his chair back. "You'll be wantin' to know the story, lads." A pall settled on the room. Mrs. McKie wiped her reddened hands on her apron and sat again at the pine plank table. William laid his fork straight alongside his dish emptied now of bread pudding. He didn't like to break the mood but needed to know where his parents were and why they were not in their home. He cleared his throat.

Robert, like the impatient boy he had always been, spoke first and asked where his parents were and why they were not at the mill and when they had left and if the McKies had any knowledge at all about them. "Tell us everything," he finished.

"Bin helpin' us all, he has." Mr. McKie looked at each of them in turn.

"Ah, get on with it, Stuart." Mrs. McKie's ample arm waved across the table before she turned to the brothers. "We best tell ya straight out, boys."

"There's bin a deal of troubles with the roads 'n' property lines, boys. Yer father bin writin' words ta help us all." He nodded at William. "Ye mind how he's a way with words."

"And he knows them lawyer types," Mrs. McKie piped in.

"Strangers bin poachin' land all about and when the owners come back, someone else is livin' on their land."

The couple went on to explain how John ran afoul of the new men. Some of the poachers were tied in with a group of privileged folks in York connected to the higher ups and appointed by the Governor.

"They say this Governor Gore opens everyone's mail!" Mrs. McKie couldn't keep still.

William turned to her blazing eyes and then motioned for her husband to continue.

"And the Assembly representatives canna tich the monies. An' we elected them, every one!" Mrs. McKie said.

"But why?" Robert leaned toward her husband.

"Tis the Governor!" shouted Mrs. McKie.

"But how can they do that? Don't people complain?" asked William.

"Yer da found out Jock Strachan be leader of that wily group of the Governor's...'n' he's got secret spies all up and down the land." Mr. McKie paused as though considering what to say next. He leaned in, glanced at the door, and went on. "That year...when it were so cald with frost every month o' the whole summer—"

"Yer da had not one load of grain fer the mill!"

"Sh, woman. Let me talk." He leaned in again. "Yer da got up a paper, a petition, it was. We all signed."

Robert spoke up. "What did it say?"

Mr. McKie put both hands on the table and laced his fingers together before him. He cleared his throat, took a sip of his hot drink and told the story. The petition, he said, asked for help for all of Upper Canada's starving Niagara citizens who had no flour and no vegetables, and whose cattle, with no fodder to last the winter, had simply perished. Hay did come on ships from Ireland but at $45 a ton no one could afford to buy it. Had seed potatoes not arrived from Nova Scotia, no crops would've been grown the next year either. John had written the substance of the petition and collected the signature of almost every person in Niagara, which he then sent to Governor Gore.

"That's not illegal." William couldn't keep silent.

"No," added Robert. "There must be something more to it."

The Loyalist Legacy

Mrs. McKie offered more tea but for once held her peace, glancing first at her husband and then at the two brothers.

Mr. McKie didn't answer. The grandfather clock ticked on as Mrs. McKie sat again at her end of the table.

"No, but 'tis no matter to the likes o' Strachan and the Governor."

"But what happened?" Robert jumped up so fast his chair slammed backwards onto the floor. "You must tell us!"

Mrs. McKie looked away from her husband at the end of the table. "One morning last summer, in August it was, we woke to sich a bangin' on the door, the mister sprang for his gun. Didn't put on a stitch. Nekkid he was, on account o' the—"

"Hush, woman!" He pointed his gnarled finger at her. "Let me tell it." He sighed and began to talk.

William and Robert sat again and listened to Mr. McKie's halting voice grate out the tale. Lucy was at their door, disheveled and utterly distraught. The couple barely recognized her. Her bonnet was in her hand, so filthy she must have snatched it from a mud puddle. Her cheeks were streaked with sweat although morning had barely come. She fell into the room and ran past Mr. McKie to the arms of his wife where she poured out the story of the constabulary coming in the night and arresting John. She thought they took him to Niagara, but didn't know any more than that.

"What then?"

"That's jist it, William," Mrs. McKie said. "We thought she was goin' home."

"But nae, it weren't the case at all."

The McKies had traveled to the mill as soon as he could get his clothes on and she could grab a little food to take along but they arrived to find the mill completely deserted. Lucy wasn't there. The door to the mill stood wide open. Inside dishes were upturned on the table and the bed was stripped. Other than that, little sign of anything untoward was evident. On his way out Mr. McKie secured the door and together the two of them headed back home. The next morning he rode to Niagara but couldn't find any sign of either John or Lucy. When he entered the jail and started asking questions, the lout holding the keys and blocking the entrance to the cells threatened to lock him up.

By this time darkness had come. He found a bed of straw for the night in a stable and the next day headed home in heat so oppressive neither he nor his horse could keep moving for any time at all. More than once his head collapsed over the horse's mane and the animal just stopped. Finally, he climbed down, tied the horse to a tree by a small stream and fell asleep. Two days it took for him to reach home, an exhausted, defeated man.

William and Robert said their farewells and promised to report back with what they might learn at Niagara. They hurried to Fort Chippawa and along the Portage Road to Queenstown where they stopped for the night in the Inn. One or two patrons knew William. Socializing, however, was not their purpose. They gobbled their late meal and hurried to their room. In the morning when the only person stirring was the girl scrubbing the floor, they struck out for Fort George and Niagara.

The last time he had been in Niagara, the jail was in a different building, one that had burned in the horrific fire of December, 1813, when the Americans occupying Fort George ordered the burning of the town. Only one hour they had, his mother and all the other inhabitants, before the enemy soldiers torched street after street.

The two brothers spoke little as they cantered along the straight streets admiring the buildings already up and those still under construction. Brick and stone seemed to be the material of choice, probably because of the speed with which the fire had destroyed their wooden homes five and a half years before.

"There it is!" Robert indicated the sign. "Niagara Court House and Jail." He urged his horse on.

"Hold up, Robert!" William grabbed his brother's reins. When Robert slowed he went on, "What shall we say? Think of Mr. McKie's trouble here."

They decided to take a different tack and slowly dismounted in front of the jail where they tied their horses to the rail in front of the new building. The sun was barely up in the east but the sky was already blue with pink clouds rimming the horizon. William noted the slight frost still in the air and rubbed the stiffness out of his fingers. The only sound was their boots clomping along the broad wooden sidewalk to the solid door of the jail.

Robert went first into the darkness. William followed. The small room was black as coal. They stopped dead, unable to see anything.

"Close that door!" A deep voice growled the order.

"We can't see," Robert answered and would have gone on but William put his hand on his brother's arm. "Steady," he whispered. Raising his voice he went on. "I'm William Garner and this is my brother, Robert…" The jailer moved into their sight. "We have a question for you."

"Garner you say your name be?"

"Yes."

"You wouldn't be kin to that skunk we got in the cells, would you?"

William swallowed. "He is our father."

"And he's certainly not a skunk!" Robert said as calmly as he could manage.

William raised his hand to stay his brother. His eyes were accustomed to the dimness now and he could see the jailer held a rifle. "May we see him, sir?"

For a long moment the man stood still, fingering his raised rifle. It wasn't exactly pointed at them but William knew it could be in a heartbeat. He smiled at the man.

"Come this way." He turned and opened the door behind him, stood aside and motioned for the brothers to enter. From his pocket he pulled a jangling ring of keys with his right hand while still carrying the rifle in his left. William followed and Robert came after him, for once silent as they stepped into a dim hall lit only by the light from one window behind them. On the left another bit of light shone through a large archway and lit the stone floor beneath their feet. They followed the jailer into the room but didn't see the solitary cell. Holding his light high, the jailer lit the broad barred alcove that was little more than a closet with bars on it. A slumped form on the bed moved.

"Git up, you! Ya got visitors!" The jailer jammed his key in the lock and stood back to let them in.

"I've brought food, father," William whispered.

"And news," Robert added.

Behind them the cell door clanged shut. William jerked around but was too late. The key scraped in the lock.

Chapter Three

September, 1817

LUCY KNEW THE WAY to Niagara where those smelly ruffians dressed as soldiers had taken him. Never, though, had she driven the thirty miles alone and for a moment she held the horse back at the end of the McKie's laneway trying to decide what to do next. Her children were scattered like dandelion fluff and just as hard to catch hold of as they struggled to raise their own families. William was far away in Nissouri, Robert and Helen across the river and the other two had met their Maker years before.

She wouldn't think of them.

Lucy was, once again, on her own. Well, she had managed to escape alone more than thirty years before and she would do it again, now. She glanced back at her hurried packing in one corner of the wagon. Blankets, pillows—she'd brought one for John in the hopes she was successful—a satchel of clothing and another of some foodstuffs from the cupboard. It wasn't much.

The lines, both stretched tight, twisted through her weathered fingers. They shook just a little as the horse struggled to go on. Maudie, named after another horse, which all those years ago had taken John a good way with the Rangers, stamped her feet. In the warming September day, Lucy could see steam rising above the horse's head and she tensed when the animal tossed her head against the bit.

She loosened her hold and pulled the left line. Maudie lurched forward. Lucy shifted her body on the seat, wedged her feet against the footboard, and set off. The sun was still low in the sky. Could she reach Niagara this day? She would certainly try.

QUEENSTOWN LOOMED JUST AHEAD as the sun's warm rays gradually inched up her back and left side until suddenly the heat disappeared and the late summer clouds above took on a rosy hue. She had to make a decision. Her hands ached and she had lost feeling in her legs and other parts of her anatomy touching the hard seat of the wagon. Behind her, flowing pinks, purples, and darkening blues reached into the sky. She turned back to the road ahead and in a few moments pulled into the inn William had often visited during that last war.

In the morning boots pounding outside her door woke her. She rose and thanked Mrs. Smithers for giving her the last room (Lucy suspected it was the woman's own room) and hurried Maudie from her hay to continue their journey. She would go to Aaron, she decided. Such a good friend he had been to them both when she and John lived here during the last war and she longed to see a friendly face.

LUCY LAY ON THE LUMPY BED as the snow beat against Aaron's newly installed glass windowpane and tried to keep the tears from coming again. John had told her to forget about him. He worried that her constant running back and forth from the inn to the jail would aggravate her paining joints. "Go back home, Lucy," he'd said week in and week out the past three months.

"But I can't!" Her voice echoed in the bare room. How she ached to have him with her. She rolled over once again, taking care with her right knee. Her latest patchwork quilt at least kept her warm and reminded her of better times.

In the morning she would try to get the jailer to let her bring food to John. His hands were so bony and his trousers so loose, she knew they weren't feeding him much at all. She would make that jailer listen to reason!

The rebuilt Angel Inn, burned with almost every building in Niagara that December of 1813, this morning bustled with travelers and local hangers-on, all slurping their steaming bowls of porridge and gulping tankards of ale as though they hadn't eaten or drunk for days. Aaron was back in the kitchen dishing up orders while Lucy rushed as best she could from table to table, side-stepping the boots protruding into the aisles and the arms flung out to emphasize some important point in a customer's harrowing story.

Her mind was on her plan this morning. That jailer would listen or she would—well, she didn't know what she would do but she would convince him to let her give John the bowl of porridge she would carry with her. Maybe she'd take two and bribe the jailer with his very own. Ah, that's a good idea.

"Watch what you're doing, woman!"

She tripped and fell right into the table, upsetting the bowl of porridge she carried all over the men's food. "I'm so sorry, gentlemen!" With her cloth she wiped up the mess. "I'll get more. I wasn't thinking...Please forgive me." She couldn't stop talking and felt the heat spread from her face all down her front, adding to her embarrassment.

"Madam, do not worry." The well-dressed man's voice soothed as he spoke. "This is just a trifle. Do not concern yourself."

She looked up. The speaker was the ruddy-faced, white-haired man she'd noticed when he came in. He smiled at her. He still had most of his teeth. The table put back to rights, she picked up her cloth and curtsied quickly. "Thank you, sir," she whispered in a voice so soft she wondered if he could even hear it.

But he did. "Landlord! Give this woman a shot of brandy. She's pale as a ghost."

Lucy started to shake her head.

"On my account!" Turning to Lucy the man continued. "Sit with us a moment, madam."

Aaron placed a small glass on the table and nodded his head at Lucy, a wide smile creasing his wrinkled face. The gentleman pulled out the chair beside him and motioned for Lucy to sit. Her nerves all a-jangle and feeling none too steady on her feet, she slipped into the chair and took a sip of the brandy. Fire shot through her until she thought her face must now be the color of the sunset that night she'd stopped in Queenstown. She began to cough and sputter. No one spoke.

Her brain seemed to have forgotten all words and had no notion of calming down. She suffered through what seemed an hour of complete loss of control until—ever so slowly—the coughing stopped. Her eyes, however, would not lift from the splattered drops of brandy on the table before her. The man's white hand clutching his own handkerchief slid across the table and wiped up the mess. Still no one spoke.

Lucy took a deep breath and looked up. "Thank you, sir." His eyes smiled as did his mouth and she found herself relaxing. She was looking into the face of kindness.

For the next few days Richard Beasley, for so he called himself, ate often at the Inn where he had a room and Lucy lost her embarrassment in serving the man and his guests. Sometimes he ate alone and engaged her in conversation. She did not like to ignore him even though she always had work to do and precious little time to do it if she was to get over to the jail. Finally, Mr. Beasley asked why she was always in such a hurry and where she went every day.

"I must visit my husband. Take him food."

Before she could move away Mr. Beasley asked just where her husband might be.

She set the load of dirty dishes down on the blackened table and locked her eyes on the slight cleft in his chin. The words slipped out. "He's in jail." She steeled herself against what she might hear but all she saw was kindness in his lined forehead and suddenly darkened eyes. "They're holding him for nothing!" Her voice rose to fill the small room. "He's a good man!"

Mr. Beasley demanded Lucy sit. She poured out the story of John's arrest, his apparent crimes and her complete inability even to get the authorities to feed her husband decent food. As she talked Mr. Beasley sat back in his chair and listened, sometimes nodding, at other times completely in another world, a far off look in his eyes.

"He's done nothing but speak up for our neighbors against the Governor's unfair tactics. I don't know much about it but John would never do anything illegal. They haven't even charged him with anything." She gripped the corner of the table with one hand. Her other swept back and forth across the nubs in the fabric of her skirt out of sight of this man's hard glare. *Why doesn't he speak?* She stilled both her hands and positioned them together in her lap. And waited.

Aaron rushed by with a bowl of steaming porridge in one hand and scones and jam in the other. He slapped the food on the table across the room and, wearing a fixed smile, swept past her on his way back to the kitchen. The door swung open again. Rich coffee aromas from the huge tin pot he carried filled the room.

"More coffee, sir?" Aaron stopped momentarily but Mr. Beasley waved him away.

"I know quite personally of the machinations practiced by those higher ups who ignore what few freedoms we do have and simply put their own cronies in office to keep the status quo. When I reclaimed my property on Burlington Heights all the trees, gardens, orchards, and fences were gone. My years of work building a home were as if they had never been. And when I complained to the Governor's minions all I got was backs turned in my face." He lowered his voice and leaned across the table. "Gore won't even let our own elected Assembly control the public purse!"

The distraught man went on. He told of secret spies who reported back to Jock Strachan's group any dissatisfaction they uncovered. Neighbors told tales on neighbors in their desperation to try to keep ahead of the Governor's far-reaching hands. Why, the man even opened the mail of his citizens!

"And this is why my John is in jail? The spies have reported on him?"

Mr. Beasley leaned back in his chair. "Most likely, dear lady." He dropped his head. "And there's very little we can do."

"But who is this Strachan? And why does he have such powers?" Lucy kept her voice low, as she had noticed a table in the corner where two men seemed to be looking her way every so often.

"I do not wish to alarm you, Mrs. Garner. Please, disregard all I've said." He waved his arm at Aaron. "Innkeeper! More coffee, please."

Lucy refused his offer of coffee and hurried back to the kitchen to help the beleaguered Aaron. Gradually the morning crowd in the Inn thinned leaving more time for her to think as she cleared and cleaned behind them. Mr. Beasley had referred to a select group forming around the Governor and this man called Strachan. Their intentions seemed to be to hold power for the entitled few. People like her and John had never had any say before but now she desperately needed it. John was in jail!

DOWN THE UNEVEN STEPS she followed the burly jailer who, once more, led her into a large room with a stone floor and a two-foot window at one end which faced outside. The jailer placed his torch in the wall sconce lighting up almost all of the area except the one small cell to the left of it. Nothing moved behind the broad iron bars there. Across the outer room a quick rustling drew Lucy's frightened eyes and she almost dropped her small tray. Wooden casks and squared boxes stood against that wall and bits of straw and dark pellets scattered the whole floor.

All was quiet again. The oily smell of the torch filled the room. Lucy sneezed. And turned back to the forbidding bars of the cell. Clutching her tray she moved closer, trying to see into the darkness. She knew John was there but he made not a sound. Her breath stopped as the jailer clanged the huge key, found the hole, and released the lock. A strangled moan pierced the air and Lucy pressed forward as the jailer banged the door open.

John lay on the cold floor with only a thin strip of ragged muslin covering a bed of loose straw. She tried not to breathe in the foul smells but as she leaned over she realized that most of the odors came from him. In the shadows herself now, she could see better and placed the small tray on the floor beside her husband.

The cell was barely six feet long and maybe four feet wide, just a little larger than a grave. She looked back to demand a chair from the jailer but he had disappeared up the stairs. *Anxious to eat the porridge I brought him*. She pulled her skirt tightly around her and sat as close to the straw as she could. John's eyes were open now, watching her inch into as comfortable a position as she could find.

"Lucy." His voice was a mere whisper.

"I'm here, John." Her eyes filled and her throat constricted. "Sh. I've brought food." She reached for the bowl, dipped the spoon into it and brought it to her own lips. It was barely warm.

"Die...let me...die." His words barely reached her as close as she was. She sucked in a quick breath.

"No, John. You must eat."

The spoon went between his thin lips. For a moment there was no response but then his mouth moved and Lucy felt the tiniest tightening on the spoon, which she answered with the reflexive motion of pulling it up and out of his mouth. She blinked back tears and reached for more porridge, her own mouth opening and closing in a matching rhythm with John's. He ate the whole bowl.

She told him about Mr. Beasley as he drank his tea sitting on his straw bed against the wall. The cold floor beneath her seeped into her clothing and her knees ached with the bending position she was forced to hold in the small space but she hardly felt those pains as she saw John perk up. In the dim light of the torch she couldn't see his eyes clearly enough to tell but she heard the hope in his words. He was talking again. And feeling. And living. Even if he was still locked in this stone vault.

When Lucy left that day, she walked with a sure step behind the jailer's clomping boots up and out of the dreadful cell room, calling a cheering goodbye to John. In the light of the hall above, the jailer agreed to let Lucy visit every day and to bring food as long as she looked after him as well. So thankful, she even smiled at the jailer. Once outside, though, the cold slammed into her with brute force as she walked the short distance back to the Angel Inn and reality, swiping at tears.

In the months that followed little happened to improve John's lot except for the steady diet of healthy food Lucy carried to him every day through snow and sun, sleet and calm. He seemed to get better quickly but then stopped improving. His joints plagued him but Lucy could think of little to ease his suffering except rubbing on rosemary oil, a task she did for him almost every day. The jailer refused to allow her to leave the stoppered bottle with John, though, so it became one more thing she had to carry back and forth.

John's thinness distressed her; he never seemed to put on weight no matter how much pork and porridge he ate. He looked forward to her visits and was always standing at the flat bars when she arrived, a smile on his face and that small light of hope in his eyes that shone in the lantern light.

As the winter slowly warmed to spring, the air in the jail room improved. The jailer, who had become almost friendly, allowed the window in the outer room to be opened a crack for a few hours each day and though the place was colder the smell had almost disappeared. Lucy took to sweeping out the outer room and John's cell every few days which action he said cut down considerably on the sounds of scurrying in the night. She began to hope.

Mr. Beasley had left the Angel Inn for the moment, going back to Burlington Heights to proceed with restoration of his lands but he promised to keep working on his efforts to free John. He also promised to come back as soon as he could with news but Lucy held little hope he'd have time for their small problems. Nevertheless she walked across the street to the courthouse with a bit of a spring in her step now that the snow was completely gone and the streets almost dry.

This day the jailer wore a broad grin and fairly jumped out of his chair to hold the door for her. *Why is he so happy?* She gave it little more thought, anxious as she was to take John the stew and tart she had for him.

"Come along, ma'am," the jailer said in a higher voice than he'd ever used before. "I've a surprise fer ya."

She wondered what that might be as she hurried after him down the wide steps to the cells below. He had already placed the torch in the wall and turned toward her, a toothy grin on his whiskered face, when she rounded the corner.

"Mother!"

"Mama!"

The two voices hit her simultaneously. She swung her head to the sound and almost dropped her heavy tray. Standing shoulder to shoulder against the bars were John, William and Robert.

The jailer reached to steady the tray. "Surprised ya, eh?"

He seemed to think she'd be pleased but all Lucy could think of was two more of her men were behind bars. The jailer squeaked open the door and hands reached for the tray and then her, catching her as she slumped to the cold floor. She wanted to pass out and never wake up from this nightmare but the door clanged shut and John pulled her onto the straw where they sat side-by-side, William and Robert across from them leaning against the wide bars.

Nissouri Township

May, 1818

YOUNG WILL WIPED THE SWEAT from his forehead and grabbed another potato chunk. He and Catherine had spent every night cutting up the seed potatoes, making sure each piece had a nub of new growth that would become a new plant. Beside him she pressed her own pieces into the trench one after another, her left hand reaching into the sack that hung down in front of her as her right pressed the piece into the hole with its eye pointing up.

Every day they hitched up the horse to their prized one-furrow plow. With Will in front leading the horse and Catherine behind steadying the plow they drew long creases in the fresh earth curving around the stumps as William had the year before. With the furrows lined across the land the two hurried to empty their sacks and fill in the trenches.

Other years William had shouldered the burden alone while Young Will played happily with the younger children, minding them for her as though he'd done it forever. He did have a soft touch with Johnny and Eva. And her chores didn't include the planting. She'd never even thought of plowing herself, but now she knew what was needed. In spite of her constant worry over William—and his brother—she was determined to get the planting done.

Wee John and Eva, seven and almost six, played in the shade of the newly leafed maple by the cabin, their happy shouts and giggles mixing with the robin song she heard every time she paused to catch a breath or wipe off her brow. Will stopped and stared at her.

"What is it, my son?"

"A horse."

She looked across the river where the many tree trunks drawn into a haphazard pile and the tall brush piles almost totally obscured the mouth of the trail. (She had no idea how to get the cleared spaces plowed over there.) She shrugged her aching shoulders and looked back to the poor excuse for a road beyond the house. Crisscrossed log fences stretched north to south along the full frontage of their property, built the first year they were here because William insisted on doing his duty to the local government as soon as he possibly could. Sure enough a horse neighed and their colt answered back. Someone was on the road.

She hurried across the broken ground to the house for her rifle. William's mother, Lucy, had trained her to shoot, thank goodness, and now she grabbed the weapon from the high hooks on the cabin wall just inside the door.

"Sh, Eva. There's naught to worry about, little one." She brushed her hand over the wee girl's hair and hurried off the porch and around to the front of the cabin.

The wagon came closer. She lowered the weapon to her side and walked out to meet the visitor. "Children," she called. "Come and see what Old Tom has for us."

They were immediately beside her, jostling and laughing, anxious to see what treats the man might have. The last time he had come he'd given them each a lump of hard candy so red it left sticky marks on their hands and they had enjoyed sucking their fingers until it was cleaned off.

Old Tom, he told the children his name was, but Catherine felt uncomfortable allowing them to call him that. She didn't even know his last name, though, so Old Tom was what he got. How he managed to drive his heavy horse and wagon over the town-

The Loyalist Legacy

ship roads and beyond was a mystery, yet she knew her spread-out neighbors were just as happy to see him as she and the children were.

His grizzled beard and ragged hair belied a sharp wit that had them all laughing in no time. He crawled into the back of his wagon and searched out a small crate full of goods he'd brought from the store in Centreville for Catherine. He insisted on carrying it right into the cabin and leaving the children to poke and prod the rest of the wares on the wagon.

Johnny climbed into the back as soon as the adults disappeared around the corner of the cabin in spite of brother Will's admonishments. For a seven-year-old the wagon held its own buried treasure and he was determined to poke into it all.

"Come down, Johnny," Will called, but Johnny ignored him. One corner of the wagon was stacked high with crates and sacks on a sturdy table covered with a large oilcloth. Johnny couldn't see underneath. He grabbed a broom handle and poked.

"Ow!"

Johnny jumped back and hollered for Will who climbed over the side of the wagon. He grabbed the broomstick and edged it under the table again. This time no words came out but a whimpering cry seemed to fill the wagon. Johnny looked up at Will with wide eyes. Will patted his brother's shoulder and edged closer. He pulled the oilcloth back. Even in the bright sunshine the little cubbyhole was dark, but staring out of the tight space were the whites of two eyes pinpointed with black dots.

"Boys!" His mother and Old Tom rounded the corner of the cabin. "What are you doing up there?" Mama's voice shocked both her sons but the crying from under the table rose to a loud wail. Will didn't know what to do. His brother's face was crumbling. His eyes looked ready to spill over and Will wasn't any too steady himself. He jerked his head back and forth between his approaching Mama and the wailing child under the table.

"Which of you is making that infernal racket?" She shouted at both boys.

Johnny started to cry. Will couldn't stand it any more. "Mama, look!" He pointed under the table.

Catherine hoisted herself up on the wheel hub ready to reach over and grab her sons but when she looked where Will pointed she saw the source of all the wailing. "Boys, come down."

Beside her, Old Tom lifted first Will then Johnny out of the wagon. Before she could climb up, Old Tom hiked himself up over the side. He reached under the table and pulled out the child now making so much noise the rest of the children covered their ears and Catherine wanted to do the same. Old Tom picked the boy up and stood there on the wagon holding him against his grubby shirt, rubbing his hand up and down the child's poorly clothed back until he stopped wailing.

"Pass him to me," Catherine said.

The boy's bare arms went round Old Tom and he burrowed deep into the scraggly beard.

"Come along, lad," Tom whispered. "You're safe with us."

Will, Johnny and Eva stood so near their mother she had to push them gently aside to take the boy from Old Tom who, despite the child's reluctance, passed him over. He went into her outstretched arms. He was almost no weight in her arms but he smelled. When she struggled to set him on the ground his ragged shirt came right off and he twined his arms across his protruding ribs. His hair was matted and covered with scabs.

"What is he, Mama?" Will whispered at her side.

"What do you mean, son?"

"He's...his face...his arms. Mama, he's all black!"

Catherine and Old Tom laughed and gradually the children did, too. They grabbed hands to form a circle. Old Tom joined them for a moment. The wee boy once more began to cry. The adults dropped the children's hands and both leaned over the sniffling child.

"I have to get on my way, ma'am," Old Tom said. Catherine coaxed the child to take her hand but Old Tom straightened up and edged back with Will, Johnny and Eva.

The Loyalist Legacy

"Come, child," she said. "Come. We'll not hurt you." The tiny hand in hers, she sat him beside Will. "Keep watch over him," she said and slipped the boy's hand into Will's. "Play a game, while I get some fresh bread in the cabin. He looks fairly starved to death."

She smiled at the two of them and motioned for Old Tom to follow her around the corner of the cabin again. Inside, she went to the sideboard and cut a generous slice of yesterday's loaf, covered it with bacon grease, and turned back. "You'll have to take him with you."

"No, no, ma'am. I can't take him. Long road, rough, no place fer a wee mite like him."

"I can't keep him. William hasn't come back from Niagara and I've the work of both of us to do. Will just isn't old enough to take his father's place. No. I can't keep him."

"What am I to do with him?" He hesitated a moment. "Not everyone will be as kind as you, ma'am."

"You don't know that."

"Oh, I've seen things...you'd be shocked to know, ma'am." He shook his head and turned toward the door. "If his skin was white—"

"What difference does his skin make?" Surely that couldn't matter. "He's just a baby!"

"Well, I can't take him and that's that." He grabbed the door handle and stormed out.

Catherine picked up the bread and a cup of water for the child and hurried out. Her children were taking good care of the boy. "What's your name?" She sat between him and Will. "Come on, child. You must talk. Tell me, please."

He leaned against her and whispered something unintelligible.

"Beg pardon?" She turned his dark face up to hers. The terror in his wide eyes shocked her but she melted at the tiny turned-up nose over thick lips pursed tightly together. "You mustn't be afraid, child. Your name?" She, too, whispered and his features relaxed ever so slightly.

"Solomon."

"Such a big name for a small boy." Will laughed on her other side. She leaned back so that Solomon could see Will. "This is Will. And that's Johnny and Eva. Children, this is Solomon." They each nodded at the child but said nothing.

"I'll be off then, ma'am. Good luck." Old Tom called to her from the wagon where he sat high on the seat, the lines taut in his hands and the horse jerking against the bit. She thought of running over but before she could even stand up he cracked the lines and the horse trotted down the dusty road.

"Here, child." She broke off bread for Solomon and watched him devour it, his eyes on the piece in her hands the whole time. She gave him more, and water, too. Her own eyes fell on her trio, Will between the other two, holding them close. Eva's head sunk into her chest so that she could barely see her mother and the boy but, snuggled against her big brother, she watched. Johnny stared outright and Will wore his usual perplexed frown.

"Lovely warm day, children." She looked from one to another. "Time for spring baths."

Her two youngest began to whine but Will soothed them, saying he'd go first and show them how easy it was.

"You can all go in together," Catherine said. "You, too, Solomon." His face was positively stricken and he looked like he might bolt at any second. She held tight to his hand. "Or perhaps you can have it all to yourself?" He gave her just the barest nod of his matted head. He was so filthy she didn't want to put him in first, so the other three would get that honor.

After their initial reluctance the children helped her make the fire in the yard and carry water from the river. Solomon stood apart, watching. Once the water was warm enough Catherine doused the fire and helped her three into the huge cauldron where they laughed and splashed until soap got in Eva's eyes and she wailed like the very devil as Catherine washed it out.

"Time to give Solomon a turn," Catherine called. She'd brought clean rags from the cabin; the children quickly dried and got back into their clothes. She took Solomon's hand and helped him remove his ragged pants before climbing into the pot which seemed all the bigger now that just this tiny boy squatted in the tepid water.

He would not let go of her hand, nor would he sit on the bottom. Instead he almost sat on her arm he was so close but she managed to rub him all over with the lye soap and even gave his head a thorough but careful sudsing. When she got him out and dried she put some old clothes of Johnny's on him. The shirt hung almost to his knees and she had to roll the pants up so he could walk. She left him barefoot.

Later she and Will got back to the planting. Johnny looked after the two younger children although Catherine kept her eye on them whenever the furrow led back to the cabin. All seemed well. She and Will hustled to fill as many furrows as they could before the sun sank in the west. Finally their baskets were empty and the holes filled in. She headed for the cabin, wishing she could have a bath herself but she made do with a good wash at the pump and went inside.

She tried to put Solomon in bed with Johnny and Will but the bed was too small. Little Eva cowered in the corner when she suggested Solomon share the little girl's bed so she put him in her own. That would do for now. Eventually all was quiet in the cabin and she slipped into the cool spring night to sit on the porch and watch the stars. For the first time that day she wondered about William and Robert. The earthy smell of the plowed land filled her senses and moonlight lit up her furrows. For just a moment she smiled at the thought of the tiny boy snuggled in her bed. Old Tom should have taken him, and part of her wished he had, but deep within she was glad he hadn't.

Inside again she lifted the box of foodstuffs to the table and opened the seal. The candle high in her hand she peered in. For Heaven's sake! Everything she had ordered was there: flour, raisins, candles, brown chunks of sugar and, she supposed, all the rest of the items on her list. Just one problem came to her. The storekeeper had dumped all of it in together!

Chapter Five

Niagara, May, 1818

"MAMA, WE'RE ALRIGHT." Robert leaned across to take Lucy's hand and she looked toward him although his features were faint in the dim light.

Squashed into the tiny cell they shifted to find comfort even though such a state was impossible. How her three men had spent the night she could only wonder. Nevertheless she was glad they had each other for company. William and Robert looked well enough and John breathed steadily beside her, a far cry from his alarming state of a few months ago. But she had to get him out of here. And her sons, too.

"Why are you two locked up?" She looked from one to the other. "What have you done?"

"Nothing, Mama, nothing. That infernal jailer—"

"Robert, hold up a moment." William brushed his hand over his brother's arm. "We arrived late yesterday, Mama, and Robert's right, that jailer locked us up for no other reason than we are our father's sons."

"And a wondrous sight it was to see them," John whispered. He straightened himself against the wall. "Although not to have them join me, locked up for no—" A phlegm-filled cough seized him.

"I brought oatmeal, John. And fresh milk as a special treat." She stopped. "Not enough for all of you. Have they fed you?" Now she had three to bring meals for. And the jailer, too. "Eat it now. While it's still warm, John." She passed the bread to her sons who assured her they were not hungry and handed it to their father who refused to take it.

"We all share," he said.

When the jailer came back the empty dishes were stacked on the tray in the corner and gloom had settled over the quartet in the cell. They'd told each other all the news, tried to make a plan to get released, and now sat in thoughtful silence, each one throwing out a word or a hopeful idea every so often.

"Time's up, ma'am." The jailer slammed the key into the lock, eying each of the men in turn as Lucy slipped through the barely opened door. He slammed it shut and turned the key. "I'll be back," he said.

With one more glance and a semblance of a smile for the three of them she trailed after the jailer, her feet soft on the stones but his boots scraping every step of the way out of the dark. She picked his dish from the desk and added it to the tray.

"You said you'd be back." She paused. "Downstairs. You said you'd be back. What did you mean?"

The man laughed but stopped when he looked at her. "I'm going to take your sons out of the cell and put them up here." He pointed to the empty cell against the far wall. "More room." His beard moved ever so slightly and she saw he tried to smile. For once he looked right at her and she saw a brief flash of kindness.

"Thank...you."

He pulled open the door and she fled past him into the sunshine, the dishes rattling on the tray, her hands threatening to drop the whole load.

Somehow she managed to carry her weight helping Aaron at the Inn that evening but once the press of patrons slowed the two of them ate a quick bite at the corner table. As the crowd cleared, with Aaron jumping up to take their money and wish them Godspeed, Lucy languished over her pork stew. Her hand hardly moved the spoon to her mouth and when it did she ruminated over each bite until Aaron's voice broke her reverie.

"Lucy. What happened today?" He waited. "Lucy." He reached over and touched her arm. She tore her gaze from the scratch on the pine table and shivered. Her back straightened up as did her head and the room came back into focus. Here was Aaron, yet again trying to help.

"They're in jail, too…my sons."

"No! How can that be? Which sons? I mean what are their names?"

"William and Robert."

She recounted her discoveries that afternoon, her joy and sadness at seeing her boys with their father, and her utter frustration with the whole situation. Though Aaron commiserated, utterly appalled at the goings-on and Lucy's helpless situation, he offered few ideas on how to solve it. As the candle burned low and the dishwasher slipped out the side door to go to his own home, Lucy sought solitude and her bed. Barely making a sound she stood, lifted a limp hand to give a half wave, and went off to her room behind the kitchen, leaving Aaron to clear their dishes. For once she didn't even think of helping.

THE WARM WEATHER RETURNED but Lucy barely noticed. If her men couldn't see the sun, she felt guilty enjoying it although, truth be told, she really didn't like the heat all that much. Some days her visits to the cells were a relief, especially the ones to John, still down in the cellar of the Town Hall.

Meetings held in the large room upstairs meant William and Robert moved downstairs with their father, a brief chance to visit welcomed by them all. The jailer had come to trust these Garner men as he moved them up and down; he rarely carried his rifle with him on these moves. Once downstairs the three men could hear the shuffling feet and chairs sliding over the wood floor above. They even caught a few of the words although not enough to discern what was being said.

On one such meeting day voices rose loud and stayed loud and when the jailer brought Lucy for her visit, William and Robert peppered him with questions until he escaped back up the stairs. John had not heard much of the ruckus but in the cell above his sons had.

"Talking about the governor, they were," Robert said.

"And they were none too complimentary," added William.

"I thought I heard old Mr. McKie's voice," Robert said.

"I doubt he would come so far." John's voice, low and slow, surprised Lucy. Their sons stopped talking as she leaned over to place her hand on his forehead.

"It's a town meeting. Everyone at the Inn was speaking of it this morning. But I don't know much about it." She took John's hand. "I'm afraid I just didn't pay any attention." She barely felt his fingers squeeze her own.

"Find out about it, Mama," William whispered. "If they're talking about this damnable governor and his cronies, maybe we'll get some justice."

"For all of us." Robert's voice was low, too. "Even us rebels." He chuckled.

"I'd forgotten, Robert. If they learn you fought for the Americans, they're like to hang you." She sank back against the wall. "Oh my lord, what a pickle we're in."

THE TAPROOM BACK AT THE ANGEL INN was full to overflowing that night. Voices lifted above the melee as Lucy and Aaron struggled to serve the large crowd. Farmers they were, and shopkeepers, all riled up over the goings-on in the colony and especially over the latest rumors about the group some took pleasure in calling the Family Compact. The clergy reserves, originally set aside for the use of any church which might want to build on them, had caught the eye of the Compact who were all Church of England and pushing to shut out other churches.

"Trying to steal it, they are!"

"How can they?"

"With the help of the Governor, that's how!" This last shout almost bowled her over as she squeezed her full tray past the man's flailing arms. The Inn reeked of bodies and ale and was boiling hot even without the cold pot-bellied stove in its midst. Just as she placed her tray on the table someone stepped on her foot but she managed to keep her balance. A hand steadied her; she nodded at the man, emptied the tray and prepared to fight her way back to the kitchen.

"Over here!"

She didn't turn. Another tray waited in the kitchen. As the night went on and the ale flowed more freely, patience wore thin.

"Mrs. Garner! Here!"

She spun toward the voice. Mr. Beasley. She pushed through to his full table and smiled at the sight of him. "What can I get you, sir?"

"Hold on a moment. How are you, and is your husband free?"

She dropped her eyes.

"Ah. I feared as much when I did not see or hear of him at the town meeting today." He looked away from her and across the table. "I've someone here you know."

"Mr. McKie, I'm so pleased to see you. Tell me of your lovely wife—"

"Enough of that, Mrs. Garner. No time. We've news for you." Mr. Beasley motioned for her to sit but she didn't dare, the shouts for service were so loud.

"I'm sorry..." she looked from him to Aaron's beleaguered face searching her out.

"Of course. We are content to wait, dear lady."

"What can I bring you, sir?" She took his order and slipped through the throngs to the kitchen with a light step and a lighter heart.

THE ROOM WAS QUIET NOW but stale smoke still wafted in the air and the lingering odor of men who knew how to work a full day permeated the almost empty place. Three tables still held men but Lucy ignored two of them and slipped none too gracefully into the chair Mr. Beasley held for her at his table. Mr. McKie sat to her left and Mr. Beasley to her right. Aaron came by on his way to clear empty tables. She reached out to him.

"Do you mind, Mr. Beasley, if my dear friend listens as well?" The man shook his head and Aaron dropped his towel on the empty chair behind him before sitting opposite Lucy.

"Can we trust you, sir?" Beasley's normally pleasant voice blurted the words and added a special emphasis on the last one.

"John and Lucy Garner I would protect with my life, sir," Aaron said quietly. "And I believe you are of the same ilk...or you would not be sitting here." He looked at Lucy and back at Beasley. "Am I correct, sir?"

"We've all the same goal here, Mr. Beasley," said Mr. McKie.

Lucy breathed a sigh of relief. How lucky she was to have such friends. In the next half hour the four talked over John's situation and the plan to free him. At first, hearing of her sons' incarceration, Mr. Beasley and Mr. McKie discussed only the added complications of freeing them as well, but gradually they decided two more able-bodied men would be a great help.

"Now you know this will all take time to put in place, Mrs. Garner?"

Mr. Beasley spoke softly but she was glad of the now empty room, as his words seemed to echo to the ceiling and back. "Not too long, I hope." She glanced around the table before she spoke. "John was weak today again, weaker than I've seen him. I don't know how much longer he can survive in that dank hole."

The men shared a look. "We'll get him out, Mrs. Garner," Mr. Beasley said. He sat forward and stared at his tightly clenched hands before him on the table. His thumbs tapped a soundless rhythm and he seemed to be watching them for some sort of inspiration. Mr. McKie, with his silver hair—what there was of it—brushed tightly against his head and his grey-blue eyes flitting around the table, said nothing. Even Aaron had no smile as he met her glance.

The candle guttered. Aaron pushed back his chair, got another from the shelf and held it against the flame, the light from the first shining bright as the second took hold. When it did they all seemed to relax again.

"I've learned why they're holding him, Mrs. Garner." Mr. Beasley's voice crept out of the shadowed silence and pounced on them all.

"What is it, sir? You must tell us." Lucy was tired of all the secrets and the holding back and the waiting and wondering. The other two said nothing. Perhaps they already knew. "Please, sir."

"I have little good news for you, Mrs. Garner. Those in power are determined to make an example of him. His clever meddling to help his neighbors against those cretins in power has got him in trouble. They've noticed him. Even the governor knows his name."

"But John ha' done naught illegal, sir." Mr. McKie banged his fist on the table. "He's only sought justice for us all."

"They don't care," said Aaron. "Want to make an example and stop us from fighting them."

"You mean they're using him? To scare us? Every one of us who settled here these last thirty or forty years?" She couldn't believe it. "Surely they must see how unfair this is." But she knew they didn't.

THE JAILER SNUFFED THE CANDLE on his rough table, plunging William and Robert into almost total darkness. The man's snores began as a low breathy whistle and built to a loud wheezing rumble, keeping both William and Robert awake in the depressing darkness. Only the high window down the corridor glowed with light and it was far from their reach.

"A starry night, Robert."

William waited for a reply but for once Robert was silent. "What is it? Surely you're not sleeping with all that racket?"

"No. My head is full to bursting with thinking of the whole situation, of Father's illness, of just how helpless we all are. Even Mama can't do a thing. Any fool can see how worried she is. Why her hair has turned snow white!"

"I've been thinking."

Robert leaned closer although their small cell meant they were already on top of each other most of the time.

"The man trusts us—"

"Either that or he's a damn fool." Robert tried to whisper but his frustrated anger won out.

"He trusts us. We could use that...and escape."

"And what about Father?"

"We'll get him out, too, of course."

"Or he's going to die in here," Robert finished. "But how will we do it? We've no weapons."

"Only one jailer and all four of us."

The next day, back down the stairs the brothers went to join their father in his tiny cell. William studied the jailer's movements the whole time. Not ready to try anything yet, he avoided Robert's eyes until they were safely locked in with their father. When Lucy returned that afternoon they told her their plans but she urged them to wait until Mr. Beasley had everything arranged on the outside.

Two more weeks passed before Mr. Beasley returned to Niagara with the news that all was ready. That day Lucy went to the jail with more than food. With a smile on her face, she gave the jailer his share and tripped down the steps behind him to John's cell. As usual her sons were with him.

A half hour later the jailer returned. The dank cell was strangely quiet.

"Come along, Missus." The jailer rattled the key in the rusty lock and squeaked the door open trapping Robert against the wall. William reached his hand out to help her to her feet. She slipped on the straw-covered floor and fell back beside her John, banging her head against the bricks.

The jailer crashed into the tiny space pushing the door tighter against Robert. William lunged for the man and rammed him into the cell door opening. Lucy came to life and grabbed the lantern. Robert smashed the door into the jailer who fell backwards out of the cell, William's weight pinning him to the floor. Robert clapped his hand over the man's mouth as footsteps sounded on the stairs.

Lucy ran past the melee to waylay whomever might be coming. The steps became muffled on the stone floor as someone came around the corner. She recognized the man in soldier's uniform with a grey bandanna covering his face.

"In here," she said, the lantern streaking into the outer room where her sons held the jailer between them, his eyes wide. Robert held the man's one arm twisted around behind and from the side William gripped him around the neck, his hand clamped over the frightened fellow's mouth. The man whom she had bribed with many meals these last months gasped for air.

John pulled himself up against the bars and Lucy rushed to him. Aaron brushed past her in the tight space. "Let me," he said. He slipped John's arm over his shoulder and followed Lucy from the cell. William and Robert pushed the jailer in but before they could tie a neckerchief over his mouth, the man shouted. "I can help you." He twisted away from William's hand. "A back way."

"Wait," Lucy said. William dropped the neckerchief.

The jailer quickly blurted out the whereabouts of the secret stairs that led to a tunnel opening near the lake. They soon decided to send Aaron out to move the wagon while William tied the jailer up for his own safety and locked him in the cell.

Lucy turned back to the jailer. "We will never forget this, sir. You are a kind man."

His mouth gagged, the man nodded and Lucy hurried after her sons who now supported their father.

She held the lantern as high as she could but her short reach didn't light the three ahead. A few feet into the darkness they stopped to allow her to go first with the lantern, then followed on her heels. She stumbled and skirted rocks and boulders—the way was certainly not smooth—and prayed the jailer had told the truth as she walked farther and farther into the black. Water dripped more and more from the ceiling. Were they under the river now? Surely not. But at her feet water about an inch deep soon had her skirts sopping and her shoes drenched. To make matters worse, she couldn't see the rocks but stumbled along splashing herself with every step.

"Mama. Take my arm." Robert moved up beside her and she passed him the lantern.

She could hear William's labored breathing and John's huffing and puffing but couldn't look back. Her heavy skirts slowed her pace but she clung to Robert's arm and ignored the spidery webs clinging to her hair. The water deepened. Her legs were cold and stiff. Robert held tight. They staggered on together. Just when she was sure she could not take another step she glanced up. "Light." She tried to point ahead.

"Yes," Robert whispered. "Just a little farther."

The tunnel sloped upward and, as the light grew brighter, they left the water behind. First out of the hole, Lucy watched as Robert turned back to help William tug their father, blinking, up into the sunshine. Aaron pulled her to the waiting wagon, and parted the hay to reveal a hiding place. She crawled inside, John came after and then her sons. They were almost blind in the shadowy half-light, brown with the sun filtered through the layered hay.

A bright spot of light opened where they had crawled in and Aaron shoved a jug of water toward them. "Godspeed," he whispered and was gone. She prayed his part in this would never be known. The wagon lurched and they were off, the three escapees and her, now just as guilty in the eyes of the law as her men, and whoever was driving the wagon.

Chapter Six

JOHN DOZED BESIDE HER, his long legs reaching to Robert and William who sat hunched at their parents' feet. She had lain down beside John to try to cushion him from the bumpy road and hold his head on her shoulder. How could he sleep? She was acutely aware of each rut in the road and every stone the wheels scraped against as the wagon carried them to what she hoped was freedom. The horses snorted and panted up every hill and she found herself holding her breath hoping they'd make it.

They hardly stopped on the way out of the village, but each time they did everyone held their breath until the squeaky wheels started turning again. But the ride was uneventful. No one followed them; indeed, no one seemed to know they had escaped.

The wagon bed was covered with a thin tick meant to ease their journey and she thanked the planners for their effort even though it didn't help much. Nevertheless the clip-clop of the horses' hooves created a kind of rhythm and gradually her thoughts subsided into the sound as she released her fear and her excitement. Her body relaxed against John's. The last thing she remembered was putting a handkerchief over her nose to keep out the bits of fresh hay floating in the murky air.

• • •

WHISPERING WOKE HER. And a sudden burst of cool air, which wafted into the tight space, now dark. She pulled the cloth away and sat up. John groaned beside her and she felt his fevered forehead.

"Mama? Are you awake?" William's low voice caught and he cleared his throat. "We're stopping for the horses." He crawled through the opening and she followed after him feeling her way in the darkness.

"What about your father? He's burning with fever." Picking bits of hay from her clothing she looked around but could see very little. A few distant stars shone weakly and a slip of a moon hung over them like a curved sword. Two men switched the teams but in the dim light she couldn't see who they were. Only the occasional glint of harness bits and wide eyes—both horses' and humans'—bore witness to their task. Mr. Beasley had been as good as his word.

Robert went to help the men and Lucy turned to John. William opened up a larger hole in the straw so his father could breathe easier. Very soon the horses were hitched again, the spent team tied to a wheel for a moment, and its driver, spent also after six hours of driving, brought Lucy a package of food from under the wagon seat. They each found a brief moment in the bushes, William helping his father out of the wagon for the purpose, and soon stuffed themselves back into the tight space.

The plan was to drive all night, the new driver had said, but Lucy wondered how much more she and John could take. Her rheumatism pained her at the best of times but bumping along in the back of this wagon was pure agony although she uttered not a word to her family. William had kept the plug of hay out of its hole at the back of the wagon and she was glad of the air. She plunged her hand into the sack to find what their rescuers had packed for them.

Hours later the wagon stopped again. William woke and hastily plugged the hole against the dawn light but soon removed the hay and crawled out, Robert right behind him. John's eyes were on her and she took his hand.

"Where are we?" he asked.

"Another stop for horses, I expect." She touched his cheek. "Come. We'll have a stretch."

Robert helped his father from the wagon and took him into the bushes.

"Where are we, William?" Lucy asked. "Do you know?"

"We're going to Burlington Bay. That's all Aaron told me."

"Beasley kept his promise."

William squeezed her rough hand and she winced. "What is it, Mama?"

She forced a smile and took back her hand. "Look. The sun is just clearing the lake."

"That's the last we'll see of it today." Robert had returned from helping his father. "The driver says we're still many miles from Beasley's place."

"We'll be going through Stoney Creek. Best keep hidden." William took her arm to help her onto the wagon.

"I know," she replied, her thoughts on how they would all survive the heat today. "Clouds would help, wouldn't they?"

A DAY LATER, as darkness descended to hide them once again, the wagon wheels creaked to a shaky stop. Lucy woke with a start but could barely see the shadowy outline of John's head, which lay so close to her they almost touched. She could not hear him breathing. Her sudden shifting up onto her elbows woke him. With her worn fingers she traced his smile.

Voices loud and imperious but muffled by the hay stopped her. No one moved. William did turn to the opening. Robert shifted also and a soft shower of fine hay particles fell in her face. She willed her hands to stay still even though her cheeks itched and her closed eyes needed freeing. Her breathing stopped. She would not sneeze.

The voices moved off. She tipped her head forward and shook it ever so slightly. Her hand found its way to her face and slowly brushed off the bits but she still held back the sneeze… until it came crashing out of her. Her hands were wet, her nose was wet and she swiped at the mess with her sleeve. The dam broken, another sneeze followed the first. The third time she had time to think of their peril and sneezed into her sleeve to try to muffle the sound.

Like the stillness after a loud clap of thunder, their hideout was silent. No sound could be heard either from inside the wagon or from outside. Her hands held their place in mid-air although she couldn't see them in the pitch black of their hideout. John touched her leg but she daren't even smile. William and Robert hardly breathed but she knew they were both ready to fight if need be. The faintest rustling sound in the hay above came to her ears from over near William. She willed him to be quiet but the sound intensified.

It was the hay wedge.

Someone pulled it out but said nothing. A lantern lit the opening. Every other time their drivers had opened the hole to let them out, they had immediately spoken to the family. She didn't remember being frightened at all. Why was this time different? William's face, shadowed in the rectangle of lantern light, was taut and his fists stood, even if he couldn't, ready for anything.

The lantern inched back and a face moved beside the light. She and John were the only ones who could see. John grasped her arm as she started to shuffle toward the opening.

Robert spoke. "No, Mama!" and William reached to stop her.

"Mr. Beasley. Thank the Lord," she said.

THE EARLY MORNING MIST shuddered over the grey waters of Burlington Bay as the darkness receded and daylight came. She wasn't at all sure she could stand it. The wooden walls of the head-of-the-lake British camp where she and John had spent the last part of the war were now gone but she felt just as uneasy and every bit as trapped. Back then William had marched in with the rag-tag defeated militia and army. That day had been icy cold but her heart had thrummed with joy when she finally saw her missing son.

Today she was again seeking refuge but this time against the wicked crimes of their very own government. Maybe her family would all have been better off if the Americans had overrun the British and taken hold of this land. Her leg ached as she stepped closer to the steep cliff, her thoughts not on the landscape but on the scene back inside Mr. Beasley's rebuilt home.

John was sleeping again and her sons had not yet wakened. No one had stirred as she slipped the bar on the heavy oak door and let herself out to take a very early morning walk. A solitary rooster's cry startled her for just a second but its raucous call took her back to that lovely little farm so many years ago. Back in New York. Before two wars, and so many deaths, when she and John were sufficient unto each other.

A sob escaped her quivering lips. No. She would not feel sorry for herself. She sniffed the damp air, warming now with the first tepid rays of the sun, took a deep breath and turned back to the house. Two nights they had slept here since their terrible secret ride but she had not regained her energy. William and Robert were already helping Mr. Beasley with whatever they could around the farm but she could only tend to her husband and pray he would recover.

"Mrs. Garner." Mr. Beasley stood outside the open door, dressed only in his nightshirt. His bare legs caught her eye for a second but she looked away. "We need you," he said.

She followed him into John's bedroom, a makeshift affair just off the kitchen. Her hands were like ice even in the warming summer day. Her boys stood to one side of the bed where John lay, eyes closed, his chest rising ever so slightly with each breath. She took his hand and held it to her chest.

"Cold hands, Lucy." John fixed his eyes on her.

She held on as she forced a smile to her face for this man with whom she had shared everything.

"Mama," William said. "We've been talking."

"About the British and this infernal government of thieves they have here." Robert's voice drew her eyes away from John.

"What do you mean, Robert?" she asked.

"I think Robert is right. We fought for them, we lost our lands and our families in some cases and—"

"Of course! And you and I landed in jail for no bloody reason!" Robert's words filled the small room. "I can't even go home for fear I'll be caught!"

"Sh, boys." Lucy's eyes strayed back to John.

"We owe..." John strove to pull himself up in the bed. "...the British."

"Not from where I stand, Father. I agree with Robert about this."

Lucy looked at all three of her men in turn, fixing them with her steely gaze as she took a deep breath and then let loose a long sigh which gradually deflated her whole person.

"I must tell them, Lucy...and you, too."

"What, John?" She pulled her chair closer to the bed and took his hand.

"Why I chose the British." He sat up straight against the pine headboard. William pulled pillows from the pile on the other chair and stuffed them behind his father but John pushed him away. "Sit." His bony hand indicated the foot of the bed.

"What do you mean, 'chose the British'?" She thought she knew but was amazed that he was finally going to explain something she had never understood over all the years they'd been married. She didn't know whether to be angry or anxious. Her sons sat silent on the bed studying their father.

HE FELT THE COLD THROB OF HER PULSE on his once-hard hand, now grown soft with disuse. Such a lot of pain they had.... He tried to shake off his sadness. They must know his reasons.

"I was just a boy, back then." He paused, purposely looked away from his loved ones as though transporting himself back, back to England. "All of fourteen but just a boy. Should have known better. Did know better." His eyes closed.

Into the silent room crept a whiff of stale blood and offal; he held his breath against the smell that plagued him whenever he thought of that godforsaken time. The night was dark with no moon and no sound along the cobble-stoned streets of Pillerton Priors. A small English village, it had only a few buildings, which could hardly be called houses, they were so derelict. And every one had an extra lean-to attached where a creaking sign overhead or a smudged window drawing showed its possessor's occupation.

He crept close to the buildings, one bare foot after another, his ears a-tingle and his eyes peering at any shadow he saw. A scrawny cat landed in front of him and screeched, whether at him or at its painful landing from the nearby porch roof, he knew not. Scared out of his wits by the cat and the happenings of the night, he held his spot, strained his ears, and for the first time in his young life actually heard his heart beating like a drum calling him he knew not where. In a moment he moved ahead again. The cat watched him pass. Silently it padded into the blackness.

Suddenly a low-slung door beside him opened into his path. He stopped short and held his breath but the mountain of a man in front of him turned his way, slapped sideways with his sledgehammer fist, and sent John reeling into the stone wall where he barely registered immense pain to his head before losing consciousness.

He woke to a throbbing in his skull that grew each time he attempted to lift his head from the hard floor that transmitted icicles of cold through his thin rags into his every part. He blinked. Tried to see without moving his head. A dim flickering candle sputtered somewhere near him although he could only see its shadow on the ceiling. But the smell, now that he was fully awake, burst upon him like a dumped chamber pot out an upstairs window.

Fighting against the incessant throb of his head, he pulled himself up on his elbow. His other hand gingerly touched his head and came away wet. In the last light from the almost spent candle he saw blood on his fingers. He held his breath and sat up, wiped his hand on his filthy pants, and looked across the room where a small bed stood just a few inches off the floor. On it, looking right at him, but not moving a muscle, sat...

The candle died.

His pain forgotten he scrambled as best he could to his feet and edged to where he thought the door to the room might be. The noise would surely wake the man. But no, he'd seen the open eyes.

He was awake. Why didn't he say something? Just as John grabbed the knob on the door, it pushed open, and again he was knocked to the floor.

Light. Bright and painful. He shielded his eyes. A blaze of red burned into him but his eyes adjusted to see it was a soldier's uniform. The man set the candle beside the spent one on the table and turned back to him.

"Well, well, well. What...or who have we here?"

The man looked only at John who looked past the soldier to the bed where in the dim shadows sat the man who, John now realized, had smashed the outer door open into the street. He said nothing. The soldier studied John and didn't even glance at the stationary man on the cot.

"Answer me, boy. Who are you?"

Something in that demanding voice seemed a little off. John hesitated.

"Speak up!" He kicked his boot into John's shin.

"John."

"Why are you not home asleep, John?"

"I, I..." He didn't want to tell the man about the early part of the evening.

The soldier turned toward the bed and sat as far away as he could from its present occupant. "Now, John, I want you to tell me just what happened with the butcher. Why did you kill him?"

"Kill him?" John scrambled to his feet and peered at the fat butcher's vacant eyes. "Is he dead?" He backed as far away from the bed as he could. "I didn't, sir! I didn't!" His problems earlier in the evening were nothing beside this.

The soldier was silent a few minutes but his eyes never left John's face. While John fidgeted and fretted, more terrified than he had ever been by his father's beatings and his mother's scoldings, the man in red seemed to be judging both him and the situation.

"I think you murdered this man." He grabbed John's arm and held him with a vise-like grip. "And I'm taking you to the bailiff!"

So stunned he could not resist, John uttered not a word as the red-coated man shoved him to the floor and jammed his boot into his back. His hands were tied behind him before he even got his breath back. He was trapped. What's more, the other end of the rope was knotted around the frame of the bed in such a way that if John tried to move he'd bring the huge corpse down on top of him. For the rest of the night he lay on the filthy floor in the dark, inches away from the dead butcher, while the soldier searched for a bailiff.

He was gone a long time. A haze of light streamed through the high window into the whole room and warmed John's back where the sunbeam landed. He woke and rolled over. The bed shifted and just as he remembered the rope, he heard the soft plop of the corpse. He jerked around but the body had only fallen over on the bed.

In the full daylight he surveyed the room. Spider webs filled the spaces between the pounded dirt floor and the decrepit bed frame near him. A broken-backed chair and a huge thick-legged table both showed dark red streaks as though blood had dripped down over them. The wall opposite was splattered as well. Even the dirt was tinged dark red. This was the butcher's chopping room.

He could smell the blood and the dust and the cobwebs and even the stale sweat of the dead man lying so near him. His stomach retaliated and he retched up the remnants of last night's meager meal. His misery was complete.

Outside footsteps sounded faroff but getting closer with every step. He forgot the smells. Every muscle tensed. The outer door squeaked open and closed and more steps pounded closer. He sniffled. And immediately stopped himself. He would be a man.

He wrenched his head around. Two pair of boots met his gaze.

Chapter Seven

Nissouri Township
June, 1818

CATHERINE SAT ON THE PORCH, wee Solomon in her lap because once again he'd screamed in the night. She watched the paltry moonlight filter through the tall trees across the river and sparkle weakly on the black water below. She should be sleeping but her thoughts tumbled and jumbled under the cool night stars. The boy had long since dropped off again but she still held his warm body close.

At least she had the planting done. They would eat in the coming winter. And young Will's help with both the planting and the children showed how grown up he was even though he wouldn't be nine until next month. She shook her head. Where was his father? He'd promised to be back by now and not a word had she heard. As though right on cue a wail came from the cabin. She carried the sleeping boy inside, slipped him gently into bed and went to check Eva.

FAR TOO EARLY the raucous rooster's crowing jerked her awake to find all four children ranged round her bed, staring at her with wide frightened eyes.

"What is it?" She sat up and threw her legs to the side of the bed as both Eva and Solomon began to cry. "Tell me."

A loud pounding attacked the cabin door. And voices. She looked at Will. "What?" she whispered.

"I don't know, Mama. I can't see out."

She was too busy pulling on her shawl over her nightdress to question Will further. "Stay here." The pounding and shouting came again. She patted Eva's head and tried to smile at the children as she slipped by them and pulled the curtain to close off the bedroom.

Sunlight streamed across the pine floor but she barely noticed it as she grabbed her rifle from the wall. She always kept it loaded out here in this godforsaken wilderness, alone as she was with four children. At the window she tried to see just who was making the racket but Will was right. She couldn't see anything.

But she could hear. The door looked like it would spring its hinges with all the pounding. The very idea of strangers using her possessions so carelessly infuriated her. She banged on her side of the door. Silence. "Who is out there making such an infernal racket?" Her shawl slipped off her left shoulder. She set the gun beside the door and pulled it back in place, looping the ends in a loose knot in front of her. "Speak up! Who are you?"

"We need help, madam." A woman's voice spoke the words in a strange accent.

"Please open door, madam." This voice was deeper but in the same accent.

"Who are you?" Catherine was more curious than angry now and without waiting for an answer unbolted the door and stepped onto the porch holding her rifle ready.

The man and woman were dressed in Indian clothing, but when she looked at their faces she realized they were more afraid than she was. The man stood as tall as William and just as straight. His chin jutted out and his cheeks were smooth; in fact, she wasn't sure he'd ever held a knife to his face to shave. She blinked in the sunlight but saw the great need in his eyes and softened.

She turned to the woman. Her own height she was and with the same black eyes as the man. Black hair parted in the center and held tight to her head with a beaded band was pulled into a long braid that hung forward on the right side of her breast where little fingers clutched it. She said not a word but smiled and pulled back the blanket so Catherine could see her child.

A great sigh escaped as she peeked at the child but she held the gun tight. The mother kept smiling but Catherine could see her red eyes and the questioning tilt of her eyebrows.

"What is it? Why are you pounding on my door at such an early hour?" She took a step back from the couple.

"Need help." The man looked away.

"Are you hungry?" Catherine could easily give them food.

"Yes," the woman whispered.

"No." The man glared at his wife.

"Which is it?" Catherine was getting cool in her bare feet and her words were decidedly cooler.

The Indian woman jerked her head at the man and held the baby higher.

"Baby sick," he said in a strained voice.

Catherine brought them into the cabin and offered them chairs at the table. She noticed the long knife hanging at the Indian's side but hung her rifle on the hook anyhow and turned to look at the baby. The wee child, only days old by the look of it, just wasn't thriving. Catherine knew first hand what the problem was and at once called the children out of the bedroom.

Solomon's tears started up again but Eva, always the curious one, sat at the table beside the Indian and began to talk. Will took Solomon's hand and pulled him to the chair next to Eva. When Johnny sat, too, Catherine turned back into the bedroom and pulled the curtain. She put the Indian woman in the chair and settled close to her on the bed. The baby cried a soft whimpering cry, which stressed the mother as she tried her best to soothe it.

"A boy?" Catherine indicated the child and the mother nodded. "He wants to eat."

The woman's eyes brimmed with tears.

"I know. I'll help. He will be fine."

Together the two women held the child to his mother but he barely took hold. Catherine gently took a strong hold of the nipple and held a large bit of it between the baby's lips. At the same time she squeezed milk into the wee mouth. His eyes opened and he began to suck, weakly at first but gradually stronger.

"He just wasn't getting anything so lost interest," Catherine explained.

The mother gave her such a relieved grin, it almost brought tears to Catherine's eyes. "I'll leave you." She smiled as she left the room.

When Catherine left the bedroom she expected to see her kitchen full of boisterous children and a bewildered Indian. Instead only Johnny sat at the table gnawing on a piece of yesterday's loaf and completely immersed in its destruction.

A moment of doubt assailed her. "Where are the others?" She pulled Johnny's hand back from his mouth. "Johnny. Where did they all go?"

"Outside, Mama. Man pulled them out the door."

Still in her nightgown and shawl, she grabbed the rifle and ran out the door, her thoughts pounding along with her heart. Where had he taken them? The sun blinded her and she blinked furiously. Her head jerked from side to side to escape it. In bare feet she went down the steps and across the rough grass. She stopped. Listened. Eva's voice calling. "Mama! Mama!" She spun toward the sound.

Where the lush green corn rows started near the side of the house, Eva and Solomon sat in the dirt waving. Catherine stumbled toward them, looking for the others. Down the row she saw Will and the Indian hoeing side-by-side, the man obviously teaching her boy the finer points of getting the weeds out of the corn. None of the children were dressed but they were safe. She took Eva's hand and led her and Solomon back inside for breakfast.

Migisi and Kiwidinok set up their teepee in the trees to the south of Catherine's house. An open spot there let the sun in and gave them their own space yet they were near enough for Catherine's help if the baby needed it. As the days went on Migisi helped on the farm in any way he could, easing her load. He hoed the rest of the corn. He brushed down the horse and tethered the animals so they could feed on the grass to the north of the cornfield. He even worked on extending the fencing along the road allowance.

At times Catherine felt almost relaxed and happy but still her thoughts dwelt on her husband's absence and the knot in her stomach grew. In mid-July the pedlar's wagon appeared once again and on top of her box was a letter from William. She tore it open.

> *Dearest Catherine*
>
> *I trust by now you have learned of our predicament but I will explain it in my own words. We found my father in jail and soon learned my mother is working nearby trying to bring him, and now us, decent food. You may set your mind at ease. None of us has done anything wrong but Father has been unjustly locked up for trying to help his neighbors in their legal battles. The Governor's people do not countenance interference in their schemes. As for Robert and me, the jailer locked us up just for being our father's sons. Thankfully they have not learned Robert is an American.*
>
> *I trust you and our children are well and I hope to be with you very soon.*
>
> *Affectionately yours, William   May 2.*

"What is it, Mrs. Garner?" Old Tom stood next to her, his beard twitching as he stroked it. "Bad news?"

"Oh, no, Tom. Well, I suppose it is bad but it's good, too."

When he saw she wasn't forthcoming with explanations, Old Tom shifted from one foot to the other.

What was he waiting for? "Oh, goodness! Just wait here." Catherine ran around the house and inside. Back outside she paid Old Tom and with the children waved him off down the dusty road.

She led everyone inside and fed them with a lighter step and a broader smile than she'd had in months. William was alive. It wasn't until after the boisterous breakfast when Will had taken the other three for a walk in the shallows of the river that gloom settled on her once more.

Her husband had given her precious little information. She reread the letter for the fifth time looking for any details she might have missed. The words held no explanation as to why John was incarcerated. And what was Lucy doing while the three men were in jail? Finally she noticed on the bottom corner of the page the date. "May second!" She glanced at the marker on the wall. July twentieth. The letter was over two months old.

Solomon slipped in the door, sopping wet and dripping on her fresh-scrubbed floor. She ran to dry him and give him a reassuring squeeze. The others followed soon after and her thoughts were not her own for the rest of the afternoon. The Indian woman brought her child in for a quick visit while her husband carried on with hoeing the corn. Catherine was thankful for his work but the extra mouths to feed were a worry.

The last week of July saw the corn growing surely and steadily and the wheat holding its own as well. A long row of healthy green potato plants delighted Catherine and even young Will, who was beginning to take an interest in the farm. One cool day, the Indian took the four children for a walk in the woods across the road from her farm. No one had settled this crown land allotment nor cut any of the thick forest and she was grateful to Migisi for taking her brood to explore it.

In the afternoon, Kiwidinok knocked at the door, a great handful of daisies in her hand.

"Where...?" She started to ask about the baby but Kiwidinok pointed to the child sleeping on his board on the shady porch. "Come inside for some tea."

"Fresh air help him grow," Kiwidinok said as she settled at the table. "Where your husband?"

She is nothing if not direct, Catherine thought, but did not want to give the specifics about William and his family. "He's away on government business. In Niagara," she said as she stood to get more hot water for the pot.

"Long time."

The Loyalist Legacy

"Yes." She smiled at the woman. "He will come soon." She certainly hoped that was the case but had heard nothing more from him. Across from the Indian she spoke again. "What are your plans?" Kiwidinok's forehead creased. "I mean will you be moving on? For the winter?"

"We no go to winter home with tribe. We separate now." Her cup rattled in the saucer. "Stay here?" She looked directly at Catherine and smiled.

"As long as my husband is gone I am glad of the help." She stopped. "I can't speak for him, though. When he returns, I mean."

Catherine was just about to answer when a terrible cry broke their peace. She and Kiwidinok raced to the porch. A huge yellow cat of an animal crouched beside the wailing baby. It rested a giant paw on the tiny laced-in infant as though not at all sure what it had discovered. Kiwidinok howled and threw herself toward her wailing child but Catherine grabbed her and together they stared at the spiked ears with the telltale black tufts pointing straight up and the long mustard fur darkly spotted. The lynx looked toward the women but didn't move its paw.

She thought of her rifle, as the animal's eyes bore into her own in a staring contest the like of which she'd never before experienced. Her fingers tightened on Kiwidinok's arm, pulling her back ever so slowly. "Shh," she whispered, thinking to remove the threat and mollify the big cat.

But even though Kiwidinok retreated with her, the screaming went on, both hers and the child's. Catherine willed calm into those cream and black eyes and forced deep breaths up from her own churning insides. That cat could be on them in the blink of an eye and then how could they help the child? She forced a smile.

And slipped inside. She grabbed the rifle, jerked it down, and shoved Kiwidinok aside. As she sighted along the barrel, the lynx's eyes narrowed; it turned back to the whimpering baby. Her finger pulled the cold metal trigger but just as the shot fired a crushing blow smashed her left shoulder. She missed. Kiwidinok's hand rested in mid air. "I thought…the baby." The woman had destroyed her aim.

The lynx tore the child off its board and leaped off the end of the porch into the long grass around the corner of the cabin. Catherine grabbed up her rifle that had fallen and again pushed past Kiwidinok as she darted inside for bullets, knowing full well she couldn't stop the lynx now. Outside, she raced after Kiwidinok who was already staggering around the corner.

At the front of the house they stopped and listened. Silence. They crept to the roadway. Nothing. Across the dusty strip. Still listening. Still nothing. Kiwidinok straggled along beside her, quiet at last, as she edged into the woods across the road. An eerie feeling gnawed at her innards. Was someone watching her? Or something?

Kiwidinok caught up to her. Gone was the calm and composed person who had sat across from her sipping tea just moments ago. Her hair tumbled about her face, frowsy and frazzled, her arms criss-crossed her breast, and her hands beat a soft tattoo on her arms. The worst was her eyes. Always beautiful, black, and brimming with joy, they exuded terror. Catherine pushed ahead.

She could see where the animal had dragged its find in the long grass. She dropped to study the ground. Was that blood? She stepped over it quickly, blocking Kiwidinok's view. Not much farther along, she raised her arm and stopped. A soft crunching sound came from just up ahead in the trees. Her companion heard it, too, but this time kept quiet. They stepped closer, listening and looking.

Catherine checked the rifle but looked up when Kiwidinok strangled a sound. Ahead, partially hidden by the dead bottom branches of a tall pine, the lynx lay on the ground eating. She moved closer. The animal's wide jaws opened to reveal for a second its terrible bloodied teeth before red paws stuffed the gaping maw once more. Kiwidinok slumped against her and she eased her to the ground.

The gun on her shoulder, she sighted once more, forced concentration, thought of Lucy's instructive words, didn't even breathe. This time she'd kill the beast. The trigger moved with a deadly silence until the sound erupted and the head of the lynx split into red bits flying up and floating down to the ground to settle on the already bloodied blanket of the tiny baby.

Kiwidinok groaned. She knelt down and sat on the ground, cushioned by the coppery pine needles, and cradled the woman in her arms. She heard shouts from afar and knew that Migisi and the children had returned. She did not move.

Migisi crashed toward them through the woods, thankfully without the children, and when he reached them, she saw realization flood his features until he knelt over his wife and Catherine was no longer witness to his absolute despair. She pulled away, stood, walked a few steps closer to her kill. Her feet stopped, though, and she turned away. With the rifle lifeless in her hand, she limped home.

Chapter Eight

SOLOMON REACHED OUT HIS HAND to her. Young Will was on her other side with Eva and Johnny running alongside. She hardly noticed any of them, her head was so full of the blood smell and the feel of the trigger as it let go and the silence where such a short time before the child's cries had filled the air.

They led her inside, all of them so quiet that eventually her thoughts came back to them and she wondered what they had seen. Will pulled out her chair for her. She sat. He put the kettle on to boil and motioned the young ones to the table. Their eyes were all on her but not a word did they utter. The kettle sputtered on the stove and Will filled the teapot and covered it with her favorite tea cosy, the blue one the color of little Eva's eyes.

She did not want to get up from the table ever, nor to do any of the chores awaiting her touch. She just wanted to go on sitting and sipping and shutting out the awful pictures in her head. Will sat across the table, watching her. She couldn't let him down. Or the other three either.

The door squeaked open. They all turned. Kiwidinok slipped through the narrow space, Migisi right behind her. Catherine's eyes, however, went immediately to the drab bundle the Indian woman held tight. She pushed back from the table but the children did not move.

"Come." She motioned Kiwidinok to take the large rocking chair, helped her to sit in it with her burden and pulled her own chair close. "I am..." She couldn't find words. Migisi stood like a sentinel by his wife, his arms crossed, and held his head stiff but high, saying not a word. "We can put him over across the river. There's a lovely spot on the edge of the ravine." Neither parent spoke or indeed showed any sign of having heard her. "Unless..." She stopped. Perhaps the parents wanted to return to their tribe but no mention had ever been made of any relatives or family. It was as if they were alone in the world until they came to her farm.

Migisi didn't move a muscle but stood with his eyes on some immovable spot across the room that seemed to give him what little strength he had. The young mother, however, slowly lowered the blanketed baby to her lap, patting him ever so softly as though he might wake. She raised her head to Catherine. The beauty of her dark eyes shone through bright tears which dripped at first slowly and then faster and faster down her cheeks. Not a sound did she make.

Her eyes drifted to her husband. "Must look after child." When her husband showed no sign he'd heard, she added, "Now. Send him on his way." She choked on the last words and Migisi at last turned to her.

"Yes." He turned to the door and slipped outside. In a moment he was back and strode to Catherine. "Bury as you say. Across water."

"Of course," she answered and went for the shovel.

SOMEHOW THEY GOT THROUGH the rest of that day of whimpering and wishing and wondering why the lynx had ever come so close to the cabin. On the far side of the river, low enough to cross easily just now, the parents stayed by themselves, Migisi shoveling earth over the mangled body, facing west in a sitting position as was their way, while Kiwidinok watched, mostly in silence. Every so often from inside the cabin, Catherine heard a forlorn cry upraised to the Great Spirit. Her fingernails cut into her hardened hands.

Will sat at the table with his slate. The other three played on her bed, but softly, oh, so softly, as though this threatened their own young lives in a new and unthought of way. Being on her bed gave them comfort. She called them to eat; they came, they nibbled, and went back to their vigil. Will joined them and soon she did, too. They lay on the bed in a tangled but close mass as she told them stories of her parents and their father's parents and together they filled the hours until the sun went down.

In the night she woke more than once to the mourning cries across the river. By daylight, when she rose with the sun and tip-toed over to look out the door, she heard nothing. She stepped onto the porch, saw a white column of smoke just to the south, and caught a whiff of cornbread.

THE SUN GREW HOTTER DAY BY DAY and each night Catherine was sure the corn had grown an inch or more during the day. Kiwi and Migi—little Eva had shortened both their names—did their best to help with the work both inside and out, but often in the evening they slipped across the river and the sweet smell of hickory smoke came back to where Catherine sat on the porch for a quiet time before bed.

New neighbors claimed the lot just to the south of them and Catherine walked over with Eva and Solomon. She took bread fresh from the oven and Solomon carried a small pail of berries the children had picked along the river. Their gifts brought broad smiles from the two little girls whose mother had a time restraining them. As she thanked Catherine, her husband approached with a smile and before long they were all talking while Eva sat in the grass giggling with the little girls; Solomon stood to one side a few moments before he, too, joined in.

The adults sat nearby on a huge log shaded from the searing sun by a flowing maple, the one tree left standing in the small clearing where stumps and branches showed Mr. Dickson's preparations for a cabin.

"Are you having a bee?" Catherine asked.

Mr. Dickson looked to his wife and back at Catherine. "I don't understand." His brow was furrowed.

"The neighbors will come and help build your cabin." She stopped at the blank looks on both their faces. "A work bee.

Everyone comes and helps. We just pass the word along and those who can will come to help."

"But I have no money to pay..."

"Not needed. You just help when other new people come."

Mr. and Mrs. Dickson were delighted with the idea and before Catherine left had set the date for two days hence just before harvest. Catherine promised to start spreading the word and instructed the Dicksons to do the same. Meanwhile her children had found new friends. They left with promises from Mrs. Dickson to bring her girls for a visit.

Two days later while the morning sun started its climb up through the trees all around them, Catherine and the children ate early and walked to the Dickson's section. Everyone carried something, Catherine two baskets of bread and preserves she'd made from wild strawberries the children had picked a few weeks earlier, William a pot of rabbit stew, the little ones each with a gift they'd made for the two Dickson girls. Johnny had at first balked at taking a gift to girls but agreed soon enough to her suggestion of making a slingshot and finding smooth pebbles for it.

Migi, with a huge saw and a thong-bound stone mallet, and Kiwi, carrying her own pot of something that smelled delicious, walked along with them. As the Dickson's clearing came into view, Catherine stepped ahead, anxious to set down her burden and to get the day started.

The Dicksons were ready, too. A huge fire had been burning for quite some time and over it hung a large pot, steam escaping its lid. The smell made Catherine hungry even though she'd only just finished her oatmeal not an hour earlier. Surrounded by people they'd never met, Mr. and Mrs. Dickson shone with gratitude and right off Peter Logan took charge. People kept arriving, laden with tools and baskets of food but Mr. Logan organized them all.

Women settled their children either playing or stripping bark and saw to the food requirements for the large army of workers. Some of them stepped up to the saws with their husbands and

Catherine had a fleeting thought of her morning across the river sawing with Peter Logan and the rest of the men. These women held a saw every bit as well as a kitchen ladle. Catherine worked close to Mrs. Dickson—Emma, she said—stirring the fire, organizing the food on the huge slab table that seemed to come out of nowhere, and keeping a watchful eye on the children.

"Nigger!" The angry word carried across the workplace even to the men hauling on saws and certainly to the women preparing the food. Catherine dropped her knife and the half-peeled potato on the table. Solomon was in trouble and she rushed to him. Will was already there, his arm around the little boy, and she silently blessed her son.

Anger rose from her depths but standing there in the heat of the day, the sun beating down and the frightened children staring, she forced a smile to her face. What should she say? Immediately she saw the culprit. A boy about Will's age wore defiance like a badge on his dirty face, his chin jutting out as he dared her to speak.

She did not know this boy, nor his parents, nor where they lived. Perhaps they, too, were new to the area but that did not excuse his rudeness. Solomon was one of her own now and she would fight for him. "What's your name?" she asked in as soft and controlled a voice as she could manage. The boy said nothing but looked away for a second and the hint of a gloating smile covered his dark features. She glanced around to see a man had left off sawing and was walking their way.

Will led Solomon over to the fire. Several of the other children followed including Johnny and Eva. Others looked curiously from the defiant boy to her and stayed where they sat on the ground. The man strode into the circle and straight to the boy. She didn't know him either but his look told her he was no ally.

She choked the dust from her throat. "Your boy has insulted my child—"

"Your child! He's not yours. Anyone can see that!"

"He's just a little boy and needed a home."

"I can tell you he would have no home with me." He waved his arm around. "Or with most of the folks here. Send him back where he came from."

"That's just it. He has nowhere to go and I have given him a home. Surely that is a good thing?" She meant to shame him into accepting the boy and appeal to whatever good was in his heart but he took his son and brushed past her to pick up his saw and start working again. His son shifted from one foot to the other watching his father and ignoring the children who were now all at the fire.

"Lunchtime!" Mrs. Dickson called into the tense air and the children moved to form a line before the makeshift table heaped with cold meats, freshly baked bread, lard and butter to spread on it, and a variety of other vegetable dishes from gardens all over the township.

The adults followed and made short shrift of the platters of food while talking amongst themselves during this work break. Laughter reigned as the isolated settlers had few opportunities to meet their neighbors. Soon, though, the talk turned serious and quiet. Catherine wandered closer. One man, the father of the angry boy from this morning raised his voice. "Governor Gore is an out and out crook. Gathers his cronies and henchmen, gives them all the powerful jobs, and even opens all the mail he can get his hands on."

"Surely not." A softer voice interjected and she saw it was Mr. O'Brien who had been so kind to her on the tree-cutting day months ago.

Others chimed in but the loud man stood up and harangued them all with such passion and facts, Catherine tended to believe him.

"And we have no say! The Governor and people like Strachan are ruining this country."

"Who's Strachan?" Several men nodded at Mr. Logan's question. They all wanted to know.

"Some priest who runs a school and takes his pick of the boys to take all the government jobs they can get their hands on. Nice little setup!" He stood shaking his head as he looked from one man to another. "You'll see. Why do you think our roads are so bad?"

....

The men nodded at each other.

"We all had to build our section and fence our front but the clergy reserves"—he spat on the ground beside him— "those reserves don't have to. So legally our road is only built and maintained by us." He stopped a moment.

"We only have a good road where someone has occupied the land," Mr. O'Brien said.

"But we'll have churches soon and they'll look after it." Mr. Logan stroked his stubbly chin.

"That's just the thing. Strachan's managed to restrict it to only Church of England. How many of us are Church of England?" He looked at them all one by one. No one spoke or raised a hand. Catherine knew almost everyone was a Methodist, lapsed these last couple of years because no preacher visited and they had no church.

Soon enough the break was over and the men muttering in twos and threes went back to building the cabin whose walls were already two feet high, almost three on one side.

It was back breaking work, especially in the hot sun. The women and older children stripped bark and some used the adze to square off the sides of each log, a tedious yet important job that would make chinking the spaces much easier and keep the home warmer in the winter. The very young children slept in the shade on the far side of the opening in the forest and two of the mothers sat nearby knitting even in the heat of summer. Their conversation buzzed low over the children and Catherine thought how soothing it was as it drifted to where she stood washing plates with Emma Dickson.

By evening the walls stood high and solid and rough sawed boards for the roof arched over the whole. The men didn't want to stop before nightfall so the women fed the children and ate themselves as they watched the home take shape. They had made a door opening, of course, and two window openings, one on the front facing the road and the other beside the door to the north. Catherine wondered about the wisdom of having the door on the north side but that was Mr. Dickson's plan and he wasn't to be swayed. Perhaps the cold winds of winter and snow banked up over his lintel would change his mind.

Once the supper was cleared and the chores done as well as they could be what with hauling water from the river and washing up on a long pine table that had seen quite a lot of life, Catherine took her family home. They had all done what they could; even little Eva and Solomon collected the shavings from the logs and piled them together for Mr. Dickson to use in his garden or on the path to his new front door. Young Will looked after Solomon with a kindness and determination that thrilled Catherine.

Her legs pained on the walk home but she still took up Eva into her arms when the little girl flagged and Will managed to set tiny Solomon on his shoulders. Johnny carried the empty pot, proud that he could help and walk on his own. He was a big boy now.

They were all ready for bed, even Will who often wanted to stay up later. Catherine went into the boys' bedroom, where she had persuaded Solomon to sleep on a trundle bed wedged into the corner, and Eva came for their story time. Her mother rushed through the tale of the fox and the grapes that her own mother had told her so many years before. She carried Eva back to her little bed.

On the porch she sat in the one chair she'd dragged out at the beginning of the summer and watched the stars blink to life in the clear night sky. Azure to royal to dark blue the hues spread across the sky like an ever-changing quilt of many colors and it gave her peace. But also loneliness. As she rose to go in she thought she heard noises on the road. She grabbed the rifle, checked it was loaded, and ran to the edge of the porch to peer around the house.

She was in the dark, the better to see what or who was coming, but that didn't help. The chickens started to squawk in the hen house and a horse neighed. The sky was quite black now but bright with stars; she wished they'd light up the road. She tightened her hands on the rifle, across her chest now, ready to use. A night breeze rippled the hairs on her bare arms; she paid it no mind. Horses neighed again on the road not far away, coming slowly. Pulling a wagon, she thought, by the squeaks and bumps. Who would be so foolish as to try to navigate this godforsaken road in the dark?

Perhaps they would go on by. She hoped so, and yet…she made out the form of a man hauling on the lines to stop the horses and she heard his words. "Whoa, hold up, Maudie."

She dropped the rifle beside her and flew off the end of the porch. Her bare feet clambered over the uneven grass. She stumbled and ran again. "William," she called. "Oh, William." And then she was in his arms, sobbing and smiling as she held his face in her hands and smelled the sweet sweat and grime of him. "I thought you were dead." She stepped back to look at his face and rubbed her hands over his beard grown long and wild over these last five months and more.

"No, not dead, but I've quite a story to tell." He stepped to the side and she saw a figure on the wagon. William took the woman's hand and helped her step down ever so carefully. She turned and Catherine recognized the wonderful lady who had been so insistent she learn to use the rifle. From head to toe Lucinda wore black.

Chapter Nine

Richard Beasley's house on Burlington Heights
June, 1818

JOHN SETTLED BACK against the pillows and closed his eyes against the concerned looks all around the bed. If he did not get the story out now, he feared he never would.

He saw again those red stockings and shiny black shoes with silver buckles. The britches were black and clean, as though they'd never been worn before. So was the waistcoat which covered the man's ample stomach with little stemmed flowers and leaves trailing willy nilly under a navy greatcoat with garish gold buttons and massive cuffs at the end of the sleeves. John sat up and the rope tightened but the corpse only shifted on the creaky bed. He kept his eyes on the new man, a bailiff. A neck cloth tied tightly beneath the stubbled chin was stained, as though the man had rushed his breakfast.

"Stand up," the man roared and his cavernous mouth showed almost no teeth; bits of his hurried breakfast flew out with his spittle.

John ducked. He could not stand because of his tether.

"Up, I say!"

The British uniform leaned over to untie the tether, jerking the line away from John who scrambled to his feet. Before he could get a word out, the bailiff, not even taking a moment to ask about the dead man on the bed, grabbed his arm and pushed him out the door. He had hold of John's shirt and practically tore it over his head as they hustled down the street.

John flew into a dingy room, barred and barren, and crashed against the stone wall. The cell door clanged, the outer door closed and, once more, his eyes became accustomed to the dark. Morning had come but no windows attested to that where John sat against the wall nursing his bruises and worrying himself into a frenzy. Just what had he stumbled upon? His father's beatings seemed inconsequential now. At least he knew he could go home after those drunken rages subsided but now he had no idea what to do.

The day passed and no one came. He had nothing to eat, no company, and the rough planked floor tortured his skinny backside. He stood and rattled the bars numerous times and shouted as loud as he could to no avail. The room darkened even more and he realized he'd been locked up the whole day. Pissing in the corner of his small space relieved one ache but not the greater ones. When he had to squat to shat about two feet from where he'd sat all day his humiliation was complete.

The door crashed open. A clanging key slammed into the lock and rough hands grabbed him from the floor as he tried to tie his breeches. A black sack scraped over his head; he could see nothing. Hard hands gripped his arms. His feet could barely keep up to the pace set by the men on either side of him. "Help!" he called, and a fist slammed into the side of his head.

He woke to the steady clattering of a railway car; the swinging and swaying reminded him of his empty stomach and he stretched out his hands around him. Maybe he could find food.

"Aah!" roared a voice out of the dark and a heavy fist hit his head again.

When he woke once more, light came through the cracks of the boxcar; the train slowed and stopped. The door slid open and John blinked in the brightness but no one was there. He moved to escape but as soon as he crawled down, landing on his injured foot, rough hands grabbed him again and he recognized the bailiff from the night before. He was still dressed up like a dandy and looked like he'd slept in a much better car than John's.

"I didn't do anything," John said as they rode in a buggy.

"You'll be quiet, you murderer, or I'll beat you senseless again."

He watched the buildings go by and realized they were in London. In a few moments the buggy stopped and they got out. Old Bailey. He'd heard of the place. No one ever got out of there and he feared he was headed for the gallows. How he wished he were back in Pillerton Priors with nothing to worry about but his father's next punch and his mother's beer breath.

They manacled his hands in front of him and hauled him right into the massive courtroom to a box seat full of others just like him—two men and even a woman whose eyes when they lit on him burned into his flesh. She leered. He looked away. The man next to him smacked his bound hands down on John's thigh. He squashed himself against the side of the box seat.

A name sounded in the smoky air of the huge room and the man next to John shuffled out of the box stepping on John's feet as he passed. In no time his case was over and the man filed out a side door with the other prisoners. He studied the wigged and robed keeper of that door and thought he'd seen him before in a childhood nightmare that came still on the nights when his real terrors got the better of him.

"John Garner!"

He bolted out of the seat and was suddenly glad he'd shat in the jail cell back in Pillerton Priors. Hands shoved him into the prisoner's dock, voices roared over his head—those of the packed crowd leaning far out of their wooden boxes and those of the wigged and robed specters speaking interminably in front of him. He didn't understand a word. Soon, though, one word pierced his eardrums and he staggered against its force.

"Guilty!"

He paid close attention to the red-faced judge, then. The man's eyes protruded from his head so that the terrible whites encircled tiny cruel dots boring into John. "Sentenced to life as a prisoner in His Majesty's Penal Colony in Australia, for the rest of his natural-born life!" He slammed the gavel on his desk and John felt it as a fist in his gut.

He barely noticed the door as he stumbled through it but hands reached out to touch him and he stopped. Strong hands. He jerked to look. A British soldier, his red uniform magnificent in the dull confines of the room. The man's blue eyes bore into him and John's own opened wide in appeal. A freshness in the dank air crackled between them before others shoved him along with the rest of the rabble.

IN HIS OWN TINY CORNER of the holding cell, John cringed away from the harlots and thieves, pick-pockets and murderers, all waiting, like him, for the next step in this hideous process. Perhaps others were as innocent as he was but he had no way of knowing. He retreated. Who was that soldier? He hardly dared credit it but somehow in that short exchange a wisp of hope had stirred within him. The man's features burned into his thoughts and he turned the whole incident over and over in his mind; it was much clearer than the so-called trial and all its proceedings.

HE FELL BACK IN THE BED, his eyes shut, perspiration shining bright on his lined brow. He looked again and saw Lucy and eased his thoughts away from the past. She wiped his face and their sons stepped in closer.

"John," she whispered close to his face, but he barely breathed and his features contorted with some great pain, but whether it was real or from the past she could not tell.

William reached for his father's huge hand and held it but said not a word.

Robert, however, raised his voice. "Father! Come back to us. You have to finish your story." He shook the bed and John's eyes fluttered. He reached for his father's foot under the coverlet and wiggled the big toe.

"You don't need to annoy me." With an obvious effort John struggled up in the bed. Lucy and William shoved his pillows in tighter behind him.

"Get to the story, Father."

William's gentle voice soothed him back to the stench of fear in the holding cell; he must go on. "He came back."

"Who, Father?" Robert asked.

He looked into Lucy's eyes and marveled they were still the same astonishing blue she'd inherited from her father. "The British soldier, from the courtroom door."

No one spoke. John struggled to his elbows but Lucy stroked his hand and he lay back, remembering and seeing and smelling the dark and dirty cell where every breath carried with it the double-edged sword of tortured life and pestilential death.

Into all that the clean and shiny red coat pushed and sat on the hard bench next to John. He asked questions; John answered. His words washed over the boy in a cleansing bath of trust and honesty. Before long he had John's whole life story, including his upbringing.

"I thought as much." He leaned back against the wall. "And this murder?" The man didn't look his way but John knew his answer was everything. He told all he knew including how the man had saddled him with the dead body for that whole night while he went to get the law.

"I know this so-called soldier. He preys on the weak. You were a god-send for him."

John asked about the murder but his new friend had no answer. "I can't solve that, John, but I can work to get you free." With that he stood up and John stood, too. The other prisoners shifted away from the man's powerful aura and he banged on the door to be released. Would that he could go, too, John thought.

Somehow he slept, ate slop, and used the stink-pot in the corner under the leering eyes of the harlot until morning came with a banging and clanging of the opening door. For a brief second he hoped it was his newfound friend. His eyes stung from the sudden brightness but guards shoved them out of the cell and along the stone floor of the hall towards an open doorway. Into a waiting wagon they climbed, cudgels clubbing the slow; John's hands were tightly chained behind his back. He could not move without tugging on the harlot on his one side or the slimy black-faced man on his other.

There was sun, he remembered, and noise. People on the cobble-stoned streets hawked their pork pies and gawked his way with a thousand burning eyes but he only looked for one. He saw red coats. He did not see his friend. And with each knock and bump along the uneven street he sank deeper into his seat. Even the harlot paid him no mind.

At the low-tide docks on the Thames, dozens of ships elbowed for space. In spite of his fear, John felt the freshening breeze above the harbor stench and watched sails slipping up the rigging and jerking their lines. He slipped along the slop-laden stones in his tortured bare feet watching for help. No one paid him any mind; in fact, everyone seemed preoccupied with a decorated barge lurching under the famed bridge with its fast tides and perilous path to safety.

He followed a long line of prisoners up the gangplank and along the deck where he could see heads bobbing down into the hold; if they didn't move smartly a sailor smacked them with a club.

"Stay by me, boy," the harlot twisted around to whisper. "I'll see no harm comes to ye."

He didn't answer. The harlot stepped into the hatch. Just as his bare foot slipped on the treacherous decking, a hand clapped onto his shoulder and stopped him. The harlot jerked to a stop also as they were still chained together. She wheeled around. "What trick is that, boy?" She gnashed her blackened teeth at him.

"Hush, woman." A soft voice from behind John silenced her. He righted himself on the slippery decking. "Come. All of you." He indicated the two behind still connected to their snaking line.

"Hold!" Three muskets jabbed toward the prisoners who stopped like the pawns they were in this elaborate game that had been playing forever. "Release 'em!" Beside John the musket jabbed into his friend's British red chest.

"I want the boy!"

"You'll not get 'im." The guard pushed John toward the gaping hole and into the harlot who had stepped back up to the deck. The weight of the chain on the other two kept them both from careening down into the depths of the ship. This was hopeless, John thought, but just as he resigned himself to entering that foul hold his friend spoke again.

"Cut the chains." He dangled a cloth purse bulging and clinking in front of the man's eyes, suddenly glinting from more than the morning sun.

"I can't cut 'em. Take all four or none. Yer pick." From behind, shouts and shoving added urgency to the situation. John had a time keeping his footing but he wasn't going below.

With a quick glance at the angry mob the redcoat thrust the purse into the guard's eager hand and pulled his charges out of line. No one noticed the uniformed soldier who marched the four prisoners off the ship again and along a tightly packed alley surely full of pickpockets and all manner of the underbelly life of the great city of London. Suddenly John's feet no longer hurt, the chains didn't chafe, and the chamber pots being emptied up and down the alley couldn't touch him.

At a hole-in-the-wall shop with its sign—Shoemaker—barely hanging on one rusted bolt his friend stopped and dragged them all inside. "Cut these chains off," his soldier said.

The weight of the shackles gone, John dared to hope again.

The man sent the other prisoners on their way and hauled John out the door after them but not before grabbing a pair of shoes for him to wear. He threw coins on the counter in front of the astonished shoemaker and did not wait for anything else in return.

"Put those on." He stopped for just a moment. "Come." He pulled John to another ship and suddenly his newly shod feet halted on the slippery cobblestones. What was this? Was he saved only to go on a different ship?

The soldier stopped with him. "We have to get you away, John. They'll be coming for you and perhaps me, too. Come." He pulled and John followed him up the gangplank where money and words passed, the soldier watching the docks the whole time. Suddenly a kerfuffle broke out in the milling crowds and John saw more red coats coming their way. His friend grabbed him and ran toward the ship's wheelhouse which they slipped behind.

"I DIDN'T EVEN HEAR IT." He looked into Lucy's eyes and stopped his story.

"What, John?"

He blinked away the tears that still came after all these years at the thought of his friend's kindness, and, yes, sacrifice. For the man had been shot. Over top of all the crowds and lines and rigging, the soldiers on the dock had taken him down with one shot. "Run, boy," he'd whispered to John at his side on the deck. "They'll never find you." And he did run and hide deep in the hold with the others taking this hopeful trip to the new world.

His voice still shook with the wonder of it all as he filled in the halting details for his family. The man had sworn him to secrecy; John had spent his life trying to understand the man's kindness but he never had.

"And you do not even know his name, Father," William said, shaking his head.

"I can hardly believe..." Robert, too, was shocked into silence.

He smiled at them all. They were his family. Helen, across the Niagara, Thomas, killed in Queenston, and even wee Harper John, who'd died in a terrible childhood accident during that first war. Lucy's hand was in his own and he raised it to his feeble lips. A weight lifted. He would never know the story of the dead butcher or the tainted soldier who'd framed him, nor his hero's reason for saving him.

"It doesn't matter, John. You came here. We met and we have a life."

Beside him her voice softened and broke. His head sank back into the pillow and he closed his eyes. The smile stayed on his face as he rested, glad of her touch on his hardened hand. He slept then and later barely woke to sip some broth but his lips wouldn't quite move and it dribbled warm on his chin. A cloth swiped at his beard. The spoon didn't come again but she did, her lips warming his cold forehead. She sobbed ever so low but he heard and tried to open his eyes for one more glimpse. Her eyes, like her father's. Brilliant blue...

THE BEREFT FAMILY SAT SILENT around the kitchen table but the story still floated in the flickering candlelight spreading over them all. William, across from his mother, reached over and covered her worn fingers with his massive hand. Lucy's tears slipped down the deep fissures carved over hard years but she made not a sound. Telling the story of John again had brought it all back and she struggled to package it away once more.

Young Will had come from his bed with the noise and listened to the story, shy at first with his father, but ultimately standing near while William wrapped his arm around the boy who so resembled him. Catherine pushed her chair back. "You can sleep in Eva's bed, Mother," she said.

In the morning they sat again but this time on chairs dragged to the porch where the hazy August sun washed over them as they clutched their teacups and sipped. The river was low with barely a sound of water and the corn to the north obscured the view.

"You planted all of this, Catherine." William stood to see better. "Corn and wheat and potatoes, what a marvel."

"Your son helped me."

"And trees across the river. How did you do that?" He turned to her and she felt his eyes burn into her as her skin warmed even more than the sun warranted.

She told the tales of her and the children, of the tree cutting, of Mr. Logan and Mr. O'Brien and the others, of wee Solomon—his eyes widened at that—and of the new neighbors to the south, and the cabin building. Just as she started to mention Migisi and Kiwidinok, the two of them rounded the corner of the cabin. William stepped forward and Lucy almost dropped her cup but Catherine spoke.

"Good morning, my friends. See what last night brought me?"

AS THE DAYS SHORTENED and the wheat turned golden everyone worked to bring in the promising harvest. Migisi and William manned the scythes, cutting and stooking the sheaves of grain, while Lucy and Catherine cooked food for days and days. On many an afternoon, Lucy took to sitting on the porch with little Eva on her lap and rocking back and forth as she sang songs and told stories. Johnny perched nearby always but refused to actually climb into his grandmother's lap, a good thing probably as he had fleshed out into quite a solid boy this summer.

Little by little the remaining story of Burlington Heights and Mr. Beasley's sanctuary came out. John's body lay in a grave on their benefactor's land overlooking the bay. He would have liked that, Lucy told them, but she wished he were here. William spoke of the lawmen coming on the day they buried his father and of his and Robert's hasty hightailing it down the mountain path along the ridge and into the thick woods below. They were still fugitives even though they had been jailed on no charge. William just shrugged his shoulders when Catherine questioned the legality of this. Such were the vagaries of the law of the land.

"So they are still looking for you?" Catherine asked. "You're a fugitive?"

"Yes, I suppose I am but Father's dead and he was the one they'd charged, albeit for nothing illegal." He sighed. "This whole thing arose because Father had the audacity to question them and fight for our rights. He spoke against the Governor and Strachan. Opened a real hornet's nest. Big ones, with sharp stings!" He practically shouted this last and Catherine reached across the table to stroke his brown hairy arm below his rolled up sleeve.

When the last grain had been threshed and stored they dug the potatoes. The corn would be next. William ran his hand over the cobs and knew he wouldn't have to wait long; the kernels were filling out nicely, such a relief after the harvests of the last couple of years. Perhaps way out here in Nissouri they could just ignore their worries about the crown lands and the church lots and the rotten roads and, above all, his sense that, in spite of the reassurances he gave Catherine and his mother, someone or something was coming for him.

Chapter Ten

Nissouri Township
Fall, 1818

SOLOMON STAYED CLEAR of the man who slept with the kind woman and smiled at her but glared whenever he looked Solomon's way. He wished she would sit with him as she did before the man came back. He kept quiet most of the time but his tummy ached more. She could always make it better. He often ran along beside Will as he rubbed down the horses and pulled milk from the cow, and he even liked helping to spread the bits of dung on the now-clean wheat field.

Still, Will's father didn't like him. He was glad when the man and Migisi loaded sacks of wheat on the two horses and disappeared into the trees. She said they would be gone a few days and a tiny grin found its way to his face.

"They're taking the grain to the mill, Solomon." She smoothed her hand over his hair and smiled at him. "They'll come back with flour, but not for a few days."

He reached up and hugged her.

"Aren't you the happy boy this morning?" She took a basket and headed for the door. "Would you like to help?" He ran after her.

They spent the morning tipping onions out of the ground, shaking them clean and leaving them on the ground to dry. Lucy also dug a basket of carrots but left most of them in the ground, heaping leaves over them and marking their row with tall branches in order to see them in the deep drifts of winter. Solomon divided the carrots by color, laying them out on the ground where Lucy helped him count them. The dark purple ones were the rarest; he put them in the basket last.

That night he snuggled with her in the bed and was glad the man was gone. He woke in the dark twitching and tossing, his head on fire and his tummy sick. He moaned and she was instantly awake but he sat up and retched all over the two of them. She didn't yell. He was afraid she might. She cleaned him and the bed and settled him to sleep once more with a cool cloth over his forehead and her warm arm across his tummy.

"You've got spots, Solomon!" Johnny stood beside the bed in the morning-bright room. "Red ones." He reached out and touched the boy's arm.

"Johnny, no!" Catherine shouted. She jumped out of bed and drew her son away but not before Solomon sneezed all over them both. Little Eva ran into the room and Catherine shooed her out, too. Solomon's forehead was hot and his eyes bleary with tears as she sat beside him and checked his tiny body for spots. "Don't worry, little one. I'll take care of you." She pressed a kiss to her fingertips and lightly placed it on his forehead. "Stay in bed. I'll bring you something."

Lucy kept the children away, entertaining them with stories and taking them outside, but by that night Eva was coughing and Johnny seemed completely listless. Neither had spots yet. Will insisted on washing down Solomon and she let him, hoping he would not succumb again as he had when he was four. Measles.

She made up a sign and nailed it on the door outside but didn't know if Kiwidinok or any others who might come could read it or not. By morning three children were spotted and she put them all in her bed where they languished and slept as the day went on. She would sleep in Eva's bed and William, when he returned, could have Johnny's although his long legs would hang over. Her mother-in-law was still on the long settee in their main room.

On the third day all three of the children were really cranky; Will lost patience with his brother and stormed out of the room. She and Lucy calmed him down but she felt the same way. Nursing three children night and day was wearing. Just as she took a moment to sit at the table with Will, a soft knock came to the door. "Go away," she said. "We have measles here." Lucy came out of the sick room. The knocking continued, louder now. Finally she dragged herself over and threw open the door. "We have—" She stopped.

"Ma'am?"

"Who are you?" She managed to get out the words but, inside, her confusion pushed out all rational thought. "What do you want?" She made this sound a little more polite.

The man removed his hat; his hair stuck to his forehead as though he'd been riding hard. His horse was tied to her porch post. How did he manage to ride fast on that awful road?

"Mrs. Garner?" He stepped back a little. "I see your sign. Is everyone alright?"

She relaxed into a bit of a smile. "We have measles here. Well, the children do," she said. "Not all of them. Just three." She glanced back into the cabin.

"I'm sorry to hear that, ma'am. Is your husband here?"

"No. He isn't." A doubt niggled in her brain. "What do you want?"

The man, pleasant as he seemed, would not tell her what he wanted with William. She did not tell him where her husband was or what he was doing. Nor would she answer any of his questions which seemed to relate to John and Lucy. The more he talked the more she kept quiet. William had told her the whole story of the jail, the escape, and their brief stay at Burlington Heights before he brought Lucy back to live with them. Stay inside, Lucy, she thought to herself.

"I need your husband, ma'am." He stepped closer. "And I will have him answer the charges against him."

"Are you the law, then?"

"You could say that." He turned away. "I'm certainly after your husband and all like him who think they can flout the Governor and Mr. Strachan!" He stomped off the porch, grabbed his horse and rode off around the corner of the cabin back to the road.

Will came to stand beside her and they moved to the end of the porch where they watched the man ride north through the autumn trees lining the road.

She had little time to wonder where the man went or if he was coming back, she and Lucy were so busy with the three sick children. Their fevers soared, especially Solomon's, and the women took turns wiping down the hot bodies night and day in a desperate effort to save all three children. Little sleep was had by any of them, even Will whose tender nature stayed tuned to the fear and desperation in the cabin.

Catherine knew many who had lost children to measles; she fought to save her own. And Solomon was definitely one of her own now. She gave him as much care as Eva and Johnny, tears coming to her eyes as she watched him cough yet again with no way to help him. She pressed the water glass to his burning lips.

Lucy came into the room where the window was open even though the fall breezes were cool. "How are they?"

"So hot. Especially Solomon."

"I once heard of someone putting them into a cold bath to break the fever." She stroked Eva's arm.

A soft knock came at the door. She glanced that way but could hardly feel anything. Maybe William was back? She'd locked the door and kept it locked after their other visitor and then promptly forgot about him for the next two days while she and Lucy worked to save the children. Another knock, insistent but not loud.

"I suppose we'll have to go," Lucy said.

Catherine handed the cloth to her and wiped her hands on her apron. "I will."

She peeked out the window but could see nothing. She picked the rifle off its hook and ran her hand along its cold barrel. "Who's there?" she called.

"Open the door, ma'am."

She recognized that voice. Thank goodness William had not returned. "What do you want?" Should she talk to him, open the door and point the rifle in his face, or just ignore him and hope he went away? Her sleep-deprived brain just wouldn't sort her thoughts in any meaningful way. She held back a sob, squared her shoulders, and unlocked the door, expecting she knew not what.

Of its own accord the rifle seemed to leap into the face of the man from two days earlier. She saw nothing but his surprise as he stumbled back and his empty hands flew up in the air. She squinted in the bright sunlight, really the first she'd seen in two days. "Why are you here again?" She spit the words at him wondering where on earth the energy to do that had come. "We have sick children here. I can't help you." Her voice became a plaintive whisper. "Please...go away."

He dropped his arms but didn't move. She could see his eyes, though, and thought she saw pity. Perhaps he wasn't so heartless as she'd thought.

"Let me help, ma'am," he said. "I have children, too."

Should she? Or should she just lock him out and go back to her crying babies?

"Let him in, daughter." Lucy said from behind her.

She looked from one to the other and lowered her rifle. "Come," she whispered and led the way into their home.

The man's name was Mr. Matheson, a detail he readily shared with them but more he would not say. He went right to the bedroom where the three sick children lay, though, and ran his hand over their brows. "I have a little training from the war," he told the women and went right to work. He approved of the idea of putting Solomon in a cold bath and set it up in the kitchen with Catherine's largest kettle. He stepped in front of Catherine and scooped Solomon, unprotesting, into his bared arms and carried him to the cold bath. So gently did he handle the boy and talk to him that there was barely a whimper when he felt the cold water.

Soon all three had been bathed. Their fevers seemed less but Catherine worried the effect would soon wear off. They had no ice this late in the fall but the man carried cold water from the rising river below and used it for cold compresses all over the little bodies. He was tireless and Catherine and Lucy marveled to see him work so hard to save children he didn't even know.

Sometime in the afternoon when the children were finally sleeping peacefully for the moment, a horse neighed in the yard. Lucy looked out the door. "William," she called.

Catherine rushed to greet him, her sleeves still rolled high and her hair none too tidy. Young Will left his tending of the oxen and ran for his father. Even Lucy hurried off the porch and joined William's embrace of all three of them. All talking at once, they led him onto the porch and into his home. He stopped. Catherine glanced at him.

"Who is this?" he said.

Mr. Matheson didn't reply. He carefully rolled his sleeves down, his eyes on William the whole time. The pot on the stove bubbled into the stillness, suddenly tense and terrible. William gently disengaged himself from her and looked across the room. He flexed his fingers. Mr. Matheson, too, seemed at a loss. Gone was the cocky confidence of the pseudo lawman.

"I've been looking for you, Mr. Garner."

Catherine gasped. Through all of the man's help with the sick children she'd actually forgotten why he was here. She laid her hand on William's arm and felt its throbbing heat. "He helped us, William." He frowned. She had forgotten to tell him. "The children. They're all sick!"

Lucy and Will and Catherine then spoke all at once trying to tell William what had happened but he never took his eyes off Mr. Matheson. Catherine spoke again. "This is Mr. Matheson. Mr. Matheson, my husband, William Garner." Her voice rose as she mentioned William, ending on a note of pride as she turned to their guest with a smile.

After a brief nodding of heads the two men sat at the kitchen table. Young Will tried to unload his father's horse but the flour bags were too heavy. Migisi stepped in to help but Catherine would only let him carry them to the porch for fear of the measles. She and Will together hauled the precious sacks into the cabin and dropped them heavily on the table where the two men seemed to have nothing to say to each other.

"William," Catherine began, but a cry from the sick room stopped her. Mr. Matheson was out of his chair and into the bedroom before any of them. He grabbed the cloth out of the basin and swabbed the three children down as though he'd done this forever. William stood on the opposite side of the bed watching as Eva's whimpering stopped and she drifted back into a fitful sleep. He stooped to kiss her forehead, patted Johnny and went back to the kitchen.

Catherine ran her hand over his shoulders and sat beside him. In a moment Mr. Matheson joined them and William nodded as he sat.

"Who are you, Mr. Matheson?" he asked. "Why are you here?"

"It does not matter now." The man's voice was low as he stared at the table.

"What do you mean?" asked Catherine. "You were most insistent that you see my husband."

"I know. And I was wrong." He looked from one to the other. "Let us leave it at that, shall we?"

He was a bit of a puzzle, Catherine thought. Why did he come? And who sent him? He obviously loved children, had experience with them even, but she needed to know what he wanted from William.

That night the fevers ran their wildest but somewhere toward morning when Catherine checked the children yet again they were cooler, especially Solomon. Mr. Matheson wiped them down, just in case, rising from the chair in the corner of the room, which he insisted on occupying all night. She and William had crowded into Eva and Johnny's beds glad of some rest.

"I came from Mr. Strachan in York," he said. "He was my teacher, a good one, and I wanted—still want—to please him. It's how I'll get on in this land." He looked from one to the other as they sat eating breakfast, the sun slanting in the one window above the dry sink and lighting the knots in the table.

William nodded but said nothing.

"Did you go far in school?" Lucy had joined them at the end of the table.

"Yes."

"And were you good at it, Mr. Matheson?" Catherine piped in, thinking it could not be long since he had left school.

"I was good enough," he answered. "Good enough for Mr. Strachan to notice me when I won a gold star for my spelling and another for my arithmetic." He chuckled. "Much good it did me. He sent me to this godforsaken wilderness on a fool's errand—." He stopped himself and glanced around the table, his face turning red as he dropped his gaze.

Suddenly William began to laugh and Will beside him joined in. With sheepish grins all around the whole table finally erupted until the noise woke the sick children. This time Lucy went and the others relaxed enough to eat their biscuits and beans.

"What will you tell him?" William asked later in the morning as Mr. Matheson loaded up his gear to head out.

"I...I...don't know, but I will spend the hours between here and York thinking up something.

"You might be faster to cross the river and pick up the old Indian trail rather than struggle across these roads; in fact, when you see Strachan try to get him to do something about the road situation. That old Indian trail runs right across my property and people would rather use it than risk themselves and their livestock on the treacherous holes in the legal road." He stepped back from the horse.

"I will try, Garner." He smiled down at William. "I cannot promise anything, you understand. Mr. Strachan and the Governor want their own way." He kneed the horse and headed up the road, waving once to the group watching.

....

Before the snow fell the pedlar made one last trip down the road with supplies and baubles to tempt them and also a letter for William from Mr. Matheson. The man had tried to erase William's name as a criminal, which indeed he was not, but Strachan was vindictive and couldn't forget William's part in the jailbreak in Niagara. Mr. Matheson apologized for his inability to help and in very strong words warned William to be careful.

Part Two
Across the Niagara River

Chapter Eleven

Buffalo
Fall, 1818

ACROSS THE NIAGARA RIVER from the forlorn mill still pointing black into the blue skies, the little border town inched its way forward with new frame houses built out of sawed lumber instead of logs and all organized along pleasant streets radiating out from a hub. The design was like a giant wagon wheel. No traces remained of the fire that had devastated the town five years before; the war with the British was all but forgotten. Near the popular cold spring the first brick house in the area promised to withstand the winter winds and the threat of fire much better than the one-room log cabins surrounding it.

Robert paused a moment from his chopping and gazed again across the river. Mary Anne, who had refused to let him out of her sight once she got him home again, stopped midway on her walk from the woodpile to the neat stack she was building near their cabin. She stood beside him, short but substantial now, and he put his arm around her.

"You're always looking across there. Do you want to go?" Her voice was quiet and her words hesitant.

"I barely made it back last time." He thought of his harried journey from Burlington Heights to the border, the fear of being caught hounding him the whole time, and the sound of the horses neighing in the night and men shouting as he grabbed a broken-down canoe abandoned at the river's edge and tried to drift across. He had had no paddles. The strong current had carried him along toward the great falls and he was helpless to stop it. Finally, he saw in the light of the moon something floating on the water. It was a freshly sawn board. He had reached far out of the canoe, grabbed it, and paddled across the surging river.

"But you did and we're glad." She touched her distended belly.

He set the axe against his chopping block and turned to her. A slight thing she was with pale skin and dark hair tied tight to her head and shining in the sunlight. He had almost lost her and they had lost their wee girl in the British burning of Buffalo but once he was there to tend her and nurse her she came back from her brain sickness. And now another child was coming. Soon. She smiled up at him. He brushed away his fears and held her to him, her scent like lemon balm filling his nostrils.

"You should rest, Mary Anne."

"In good time. Tell me about your mother, Robert."

"Tonight." He squeezed her and released her. "Once I've got this wood chopped. Go inside now and rest." He pointed toward the cabin and she went.

That night he did tell her about his parents, especially his mother as Mary Anne seemed so taken with stories of her. Robert lay in the bed with her and together they talked and laughed and every once in a while he ran his hand over her nightgown-clad belly pausing when the baby moved. He was ever so glad to be back with her and to have her well. He pushed his dark thoughts to the shadowed part of his mind.

She glowed with health, and she'd already birthed one child successfully. That wee Mary Anne died was an accident. She was a casualty of war just as much as his brother, Thomas, who'd been fighting on the British side when Robert's American troops attacked up Queenstown Heights. William had found him in the stockade and given him food and blankets

The Loyalist Legacy

while he went off to their parents with Thomas' body. He shook his head.

Mary Anne ran her hand over his face, her touch like snowflakes landing on his hot brow. "Tomorrow you start the job." Her hand settled on the back of his neck pulling him to her. "Are you sure?"

He would be working at the big tannery near the wharves that a shoemaker had started and now was owned by a group of businessmen. Tanning the furs right where they arrived in the town provided work for local men and saved the businessmen shipping raw pelts to the waiting markets in New York, Boston, and across the sea. They could demand a much higher price for tanned leather. Robert, however, would reek of tannin and guts and mold when he came home, not to mention breathing it in all day long. There were other jobs but none that paid so well. He so wanted to build a good life for them here.

ACROSS THE RIVER and down toward the great falls, the chimneys of Chippawa belched into the sky heralding the growth that was happening in the area. Bigger than Niagara and certainly moving faster with reconstruction and new buildings, Chippawa was full of merchants and money men who saw the value of doing business right where the Portage Road around the Falls met ships waiting to navigate up the lakes to new and growing markets. And the reverse was true, as well. The goods from inland would find their way to waiting markets in Europe and the world. Beaver hats, mink coats, otter muffs, and even the odd jug of sweet maple syrup made by the Indians traveled up and down the waterways.

He wished he could be part of that. The distilleries hired men by the dozens but he had no way to get across the river every day and, even if he could, the law might be waiting for him. No, he'd have to stay here and brave the stink and stench of the tannery. He disengaged his arm from around Mary Anne, sleeping now, and rolled over.

NOVEMBER CAME and with it the new baby, born on the seventh of the month. Thomas, they named him, after Robert's twin, and the proud father immediately sent off a letter to his mother, Lucy. When she would receive it he didn't know, but he started it on its long way as soon as he could. Now when he walked to the tannery along the cold shore of the river he noticed on the distant shore smoke curling up from the mill where once his father had been the miller and he had been a young boy, running free in the woods with nary a care. Too soon he reached the reeking tannery and stooped low under the lintel to step inside.

With this child, Mary Anne shook off her lingering sadness and Robert saw the joy that colored all she did, from sweeping the snow off the front stoop to cleaning the child's soiled diapers. She carted water to the stove and heated the heavy pot with a satisfaction he'd never seen in her before. Of course he'd been fighting a war when young Mary Anne was born and had barely seen either of them. He saw and held Thomas every single day.

As Christmas approached that year he knew he should be happy with his life and his family and, for the most part, he was. Something, however, swept over him whenever he saw the thin spiral of smoke across the river. It was not visible in the dark of the early morning or late evening when he walked to and from work but on his one day off he'd bundle up his son and carry him to the edge of the frozen river. Though he knew that white column floating into the sky above was not from a fire built by his parents, still it tugged at him and he'd stand motionless holding his son. Suddenly the wee boy would cry out or kick him into action and he'd bounce the child along in his arms once more.

Back to their cabin along Beaver Street this day he carried the wee boy, his step light in the frosty air. Snow was in the wind and he snuggled the child to him. A strange horse and wagon was tied to his hitching rail. He hurried to the front door, painted a soft tan color to please his Mary Anne. As he reached for the latch the door opened.

"Where have you been, you snow-covered wastrel?"

Helen. His only sister. He passed the child off to Mary Anne and folded Helen in a monstrous hug. Timothy was there, too, and their three boys, now big enough to take part in the adult conversation but small enough to love the marzipan Mary Anne had made. Helen's hair reminded him so much of his mother's—dark red, curly and wild. And her freckles. He had teased her endlessly about those but now they were the most beautiful things he had ever seen.

He watched her across the room ordering her family about just as their mother had, with a little authority and a lot of love. Finally, they all sat, the hubbub stopped, and one at a time they caught up on the two years since they'd seen each other. Helen and Timothy owned a farm ten miles southeast of the fledgling city of Buffalo and they'd just decided to spend Christmas with her brother. Neighbors agreed to tend their animals and they closed up their cabin, loaded the children and their belongings and packages on the wagon and headed for Robert's in Buffalo.

"How did you know we'd be here?" Mary Anne asked.

"We didn't!" Helen's voice exploded into the room. "But where would you go?"

"Robert just got home in the summer after months away. I wondered if he'd make it in time."

Helen's face crumpled and her eyebrows twisted up in that questioning look he remembered so well. "Where was he?"

Robert hesitated. The room went quiet and even the baby stopped his gurgling in Mary Anne's arms. She looked at her husband and nodded. "I was in jail," he said.

The room exploded with Helen and Timothy demanding the rest of the story and their three boys suddenly much more interested in the conversation. Mary Anne looked up from the baby. "You'd best tell them."

So tell them he did, ending with his flight across the river, which he embellished just a little for his nephews who moved to sit on the floor near him and made not a sound. He told them of the empty mill, his flight to Nissouri to find William, the McKie's story about their mother, and their misfortunes in Niagara. He told Helen of their father wasting away in jail for no reason other than he was inconvenient to those in power whose decisions were all made to line their pockets.

Helen could not understand why any of them were in jail; he did his best to explain but, truthfully, they had done nothing illegal. Finally, he described their escape while Mary Anne put the child to bed and ended with his father's death and their flight just ahead of the law, he to make his way home to his family, and William and Lucy to Nissouri.

Helen sat weeping in the corner, all the puff and sputter gone out of her, while Timothy held her to him. "I didn't know," she wailed and looked at Robert. "This has been terrible for you. I'm so sorry."

Robert regretted having to tell them the bad news and left off the part about his being chased to the border and almost drifting down river to the falls in his desperate escape. He'd tell the boys later. For now, he helped Mary Anne set out food for the subdued crowd. How happy he was that he'd fashioned a huge table out of pine boards, sawn at the sawmill nearby and sanded relentlessly before and after he glued them all together. Everyone had a chair and though they were no longer so merry they ate in harmony, thankful to be together. Robert said his father's grace before the meal.

The little house was full to bursting with five extra people in it but Helen had brought bedding and mattresses that they put on the floor at night and stored away in the extra bedroom during the day. She'd also loaded pots and boxes with food to add to Mary Anne's supply. It was a joyful time, even with the sad news Robert had shared. On Christmas day he and Mary Anne were delighted to watch their nephews' bright eyes as they all opened gifts.

All too soon the holiday time ended and on a clear frosty day the Greenstone family packed up their wagon and their boys and waved goodbye. Mary Anne put her house back in order in between caring for Thomas and by nightfall everything was in its rightful place. Tomorrow she'd start on the huge pile of washing stuffed under their beds.

....

The Loyalist Legacy

Robert cared for the animals first thing in the morning but then moped around the house. He didn't even want to take wee Thomas for a walk to the lakeshore but rather, looked in on him now and then and shook his head before closing the door. The next day he'd be back in the tannery breathing in wood ash fumes. Helen's family visit had been a godsend yet he still longed to see his mother and William's brood. He shook his head and his hand struck the table so loudly Mary Anne called out and the baby began to wail.

"What are you doing, Robert?" she called across the room.

"I...I just can't see a way forward."

"What do you mean?" She settled the feeding baby once more and looked his way.

"We should have land," he answered. "And raise crops and animals." He moved over to sit on the other end of the settee near her. "I want my son to be proud of me." His hands covered his face for a moment.

"But, Robert, I thought you were happy." She kept her voice low; the babe had dropped off to sleep.

"I need to provide for my family and this job at the stinking tannery is getting us nowhere."

"I am sure it is not as bad as you say." She slid off the settee and tiptoed into the bedroom. In a moment she returned. "He should sleep, now."

"Don't you see, Mary Anne? We need to do better than just eke out a pittance at the tannery."

"Sh," she whispered. "I thought you liked the wage."

"Just now we only have one extra mouth to feed. What happens when more come along? It won't be enough." And he was at their mercy. He didn't tell her that.

"And you hate the work." She sat beside him and laid her soft hand over his leather-colored one. "Is this all that's worrying you?"

Finally he admitted his frustration at not being able to visit the rest of his family. Helen's visit had only grown that ache into a gnawing hunger and he could see no way past the fact that he'd broken out of jail with his father and brother. "I know I should forget about them. They will all survive. But in here," —he touched his chest— "I can't forget. They're my...family." He choked.

"We will find a way, my dear," she said and stroked his bent head.

A few days later Mary Anne took the wagon to the general store across the bridge over the canal that set off their particular part of town. The horses clip-clopped along the snowy streets lined with huge banks of snow shoveled out of the way of walkers and wagons alike. Wee Thomas was at her feet in a wicker basket and wrapped so tightly against the cold she could not even see his face as she drove the horse to her destination.

Robert was working. She had hitched the wagon herself so as to have a way to carry home the supplies she intended to buy. Also she had a bundle of odds and ends Robert had made in the winter evenings to try to sell for some extra money. He carved dolls and fashioned wagons with wheels that turned. Helen's children had played so happily with them she got the idea to trade them for what she needed.

When she hitched the horse to the rail outside his shop, the shopkeeper rushed out to help her and soon she and the baby were inside. The man's eyes lit up when she unwrapped each piece of her husband's handiwork and they reached an understanding in no time. He would take more once Robert made them. The man's wife cuddled wee Thomas while Mary Anne browsed the shelves and indicated to the man just what she needed. Very soon she had to take her child and brave the cold again but this time with a light step and a lighter heart.

Robert would be pleased. She smiled all the way back to Beaver Street where she carried the baby inside, unwrapped him and put him in his crib while she tended to the horse and wagon. She carried the boxes in and like her nephews at Christmas unwrapped the packages. When Robert returned long after dark, tired and hungry, she brought a smile to his face with the tale of her adventure. To keep away the cold, they went to bed early, where they lay a few feet away from their sleeping child's cot and talked of her discovery. She sat up in bed.

....

"I hear something."

"Only the wind, my dear," Robert whispered.

"No. Don't you hear it?"

"Hear what?"

"It's like a child," she said. "Crying." She slipped her legs over the side of the bed.

"Come back into the warmth."

"No, Robert. There's someone out there." She wrapped her shawl around her thin shoulders.

By now he heard the noise, too. "It's just the wind. I'm sure of it." But he slipped out into the cold, too. Together they tiptoed across the icy pine floors toward the window but thick hoarfrost covered it.

"There," she whispered. "Sounds like it's just outside."

"Who would be out there in this storm?" He shook his head but crept over to the door and listened against it.

"You'll have to open it," she whispered.

He lifted his musket from above the door and checked it in the candlelight Mary Anne provided. "Go back into the bedroom with the baby."

She backed away with the candle as he lifted the bar and pulled the door open. The full fury of the storm met him in the face but he stepped right into it, his hair blowing straight up, his hands gripping the weapon. He tripped over something and fell. She ran forward and saw him sprawl full out, his face at the bottom of the steps, the musket flying through the air to land in a snowbank and the snow swirling everywhere.

In the dim candlelight she saw, just before it blew out in the wind, a bundle across the doorway. She bent and touched the snow-covered mound.

"Ahhhhh." A tiny voice wailed in such a thin sound she wasn't sure she'd even heard it. She pulled at the cloth, dark against the new-fallen snow. Robert leaned down on the other side and together they heard the sound again.

"My heavens, it's a child!" Robert passed her the musket and picked up the bundle. She closed and barred the door, shutting out the ferocious storm. When she had the candle lit again they unwrapped the child and wrapped him again in dry clothing and her favorite quilt folded twice.

"He's so cold," she said and rubbed his hands, first one then the other, but they were like ice. She gave him to her husband to hold against his body while she heated milk on the stove that still had enough fire in it. Together they forced his lips apart and the child sipped ever so weakly at the liquid.

When they realized he needed more warming still, Robert carried the boy into their bed and they climbed in on either side of him. The candle out and the fire banked once more their arms met across the body of the young child. Robert's mind was a-jumble but Mary Anne soon lapsed into steady, soft breathing. She's glad to have another one to help, Robert thought, and he smiled in the dark.

The child looked to be about ten years old although knowing for sure was difficult, his little arms were so thin. Not much meat on the rest of him, either. Tomorrow they'd get more food into him. He still hadn't let his mind wander to the biggest question of all. Mary Anne didn't even mention it. Perhaps she didn't notice. He stroked the boy's head. Yes, he was right. Where did the child come from? In the dead of winter? He shifted as a now-warm hand grazed his neck and he smiled again. The boy was a nigger.

Chapter Twelve

Buffalo
Winter, 1818-1819

A LOT OF THOSE LIVING IN TOWN housed their horses in community barns and a large one stood two blocks away from Robert's house, but he had built his own just behind the cabin. Mucking out the stall and curry combing his horse gave him time to think and plan. This morning was no different. He left Mary Anne with the baby and their late-night visitor and trudged through the snow to his sanctuary, glad the tannery didn't need him this day.

He had to clear away the snow before opening the swinging door and going inside. He hung the lantern on one of the hooks he'd installed for the purpose and grabbed the shovel. The muck under the horse's feet was deep; he pulled his homemade bin over close to the stall and started pitching shovelfuls over the rail and into the bin. The horse stayed out of his way. He soon had a rhythm going and stopped only a moment to remove his outer clothing and hang the items on the hooks outside the stall.

On one such break he thought he heard a rustling sound on the far side of the small barn; he paused. All was quiet. Back to work he went, rushing to finish and get back into the cabin to find out more about the young boy who'd spent the night in their bed.

There it was again—a rustling sound, loud enough to be heard over his work. As he paused, a cry pierced the stillness. He had not brought his musket with him this morning. Again a baby's wail sounded, this time much louder. He crept out of the stall, carefully closed the gate, and, with the shovel in both hands, moved across the barn to the far side where he'd stacked hay for the horse up out of the damp so that it would stay sweet and dry the whole winter.

The baby was crying full out now; other sounds, sobs maybe, came intermittently. He felt a little silly holding his shovel like a weapon. On the back side of the haystack at first he didn't see the man, so dark was his skin and all his clothing, but suddenly his eyes betrayed him. Robert stopped. As Robert's own eyes adjusted, he realized the man was protecting someone sitting behind him. The man's arms stretched wide and he held a large club in one hand. Time seemed to hover above them as they pointed shovel and club at each other. He said nothing.

"What are you doing here?" Robert asked.

The man took a half step forward but still held the club high. The child was wailing now and the woman stood up, rocking the child in her arms in a vain effort to soothe. Both of them were black-skinned just like the boy in the cabin. Robert lowered his shovel. "Have you lost a child?"

The woman's head jerked his way and she stepped closer to the man, pushing him forward. He lowered his arms.

Finally the man spoke. "Yes, master." He didn't seem to want to go farther but the woman nudged him again. "In storm. Last night."

The woman could wait no longer. "You have him?" She was so close to Robert he could smell her unwashed body and clothes. "Tell me, master," she said. "Please, sir."

"Yes. We have him. My wife and I found him on our doorstep half frozen to death. He slept between us all night."

Tears glistened on her sunken cheeks. The man's shoulders lifted and fell as though he had just dropped a huge load.

"Come in and get warm." Robert turned his back on them, put on his warm clothing, and led them to the house. Their fear at crossing the open yard in the daylight did not escape his notice; he hurried them inside to an astonished Mary Anne and bolted the door behind them.

The child was up now and sitting at the table, a bowl of oatmeal before him. Such a joyous reunion took place that Mary Anne and Robert simply stood back and watched. Even their baby seemed to sense the upturn in their family fortunes and was silent, a happening for which Robert was grateful. Finally, Mary Anne was able to get them all back at the table where she fed them with a speed that amazed Robert as he sat holding their own baby, now awake and ready to howl himself.

They were slaves. Escaped from some place in Virginia where the man's striped back, when he stripped off his tattered shirt for Mary Anne to wash, attested to the cruelty of at least one master. They ran when the master threatened to sell off her husband and children if she didn't please him. He gave her a night to think it over. That night they ran as far and as fast as they could with their two young children and a small satchel of food stolen from the kitchen where she worked.

The two told their story haltingly in low voices and glanced often at the door during the telling. Mary Anne had convinced the mother to release the baby into her arms and sat rocking back and forth, back and forth. Her own child was happily sleeping again. The woman's hands opened and closed over and over and the man, sitting beside her at the table, reached over to lay his own hand over hers.

"Where are you going from here?" Robert asked.

"Yes," Mary Anne piped in from her chair. "What will you do?"

They looked at each other. "We cross the river," they answered in unison.

Such a flow of water rushed toward the Falls that the river cut through the ice well into winter and sometimes never completely froze over. Robert had walked out many times, taking his life in his hands, and his stomach clenched at risking the parents let alone their two children on the treacherous ice. He shared his experiences with the couple and their faces fell. The light went out of the woman's eyes as she watched her son playing marbles at her feet but the man sat for a long time without speaking, his head nodding slightly every so often as he, too, watched his son.

"We must wait," he said.

Robert wondered for an instant if he and Mary Anne should dare to keep the fugitives but he put that thought aside. Many had risked for his father and William and even himself. He looked at Mary Anne who was watching him, a question in her eyes. He nodded. The family could stay. The solution might be to carry a small boat across the ice and row it across the open water to the ice on the other side. So many problems came into his mind with that solution that he didn't even voice it out loud. If one of them fell in....

That night clouds obscured the moon as the men carried loose hay inside and the women filled sacking to make a rough mattress for the couple. The baby slept in Mary Anne's drawer on a soft quilt next to his parents. Mary Anne had moved her own child to her room. The boy she put on the settee with her last quilt. They'd have to keep the fire burning or everyone would freeze. Robert watched her fuss with the boy's coverlet before he took her arm and urged her to bed. In the morning, he went to work, leaving her to manage four extra people in the house. Fugitives, at that.

But manage she did. They all rose early with Robert who rushed out to his work. Sally, for that was the woman's name, sang softly to her children as she washed them from head to toe with a scrap of cloth and a lump of soap Mary Anne had given her. With Robert at work the woman next stepped out of her own ragged clothes and right there in the kitchen with the fire raging and their midday meal bubbling on the stove she washed herself from head to toe, all the while singing with such a voice as Mary Anne had never heard. She didn't want to intrude but sat on the bed in her room and just listened. How could Sally sing with such joy with all she'd been through?

....

When Sally was finished she put on the gown Mary Anne lent her, filled the pot again with clean water from the pan on the stove and took it into the bedroom for her husband. Robert's pants were too long for Sam but the man soon appeared, scrubbed and smiling, with the dirty water that Mary Anne took outside. The house smelled fresh again. Tomorrow she and Sally would wash clothes. Mary Anne busied herself preparing food, glad she'd bought so much at the store and that their own larder held the fruits of their huge garden last summer.

In mid January on his day off, Robert left his son at home when he went for his walk by the shore and this time he couldn't see any bit of blue or gray out across the ice. The river looked frozen but he was fearful the ice would be too thin to hold the family of four. He wished they would wait and cross in the spring but the talk at work often meandered into escaped slaves and what the punishments might be for harboring them. The worst thing was the slave owners themselves, some of whom chased their runaways with vengeance and swift retribution for the slaves and any who helped them uppermost in their minds. He kept quiet about his houseguests but feared the danger to his family.

He stepped out onto the ice, walked a short distance and bent down to brush away the snow. He could see through the ice. He walked on. The wind blew the snow banks in his face but he kept going, pushing his chin into his coat and wriggling his mittened fingers in his pockets. It was beastly cold. Perhaps this was not such a good idea. He did want to check for himself whether sending the small family to walk across was feasible.

In the silence broken only by the gusting wind a cracking sound froze him in his tracks. He looked down. Beneath his feet a small fissure opened. He inched back. Nothing happened. He took another step. Still nothing. Standing still he looked out across the broad expanse of ice which did indeed stretch to the far shore, the shore he watched so often on his walks. Smoke puffed out of the mill as always and he relaxed to see the signs of life in his old home.

How he longed to keep going.

But he did not dare. The ice was shifting and moving with the strong currents underneath and he knew it wasn't yet thick enough to trust. He turned and made his way back. Maybe in another week if the cold held.

Back in the cabin anxious faces met him; he knew they wanted to hear about the ice on the river. He shivered out of his coat and stretched his hands over the stove wondering just what to tell them.

Mary Anne moved beside him. "We've had a visitor."

He turned to her and grabbed her shoulders. "Who? Did they see? Is everyone alright?" He looked across the room where Sam and Sally sat alone on the settee. "Where are the children?" He didn't even wait for Mary Anne to answer but ran into their bedroom. "Where are they?" he shouted, as he ran back to her.

She grabbed his arm. "Thomas is right here," she pointed to the cradle near the stove, "and the others are sleeping. Be quiet, Robert."

"But...but who was here?"

"Mr. Gladstone from next door."

"Well, what did he want?"

"Sh, Robert. The children."

He made a great effort to lower his voice. "Tell me, Mary Anne. Why was he here?"

"Only to invite us to his home for a small party." She smiled at him. The Gladstones were having a party to celebrate Epiphany, although neither Mary Anne nor Robert knew exactly what that was. On January sixth they were to gather for the evening meal. There might even be dancing as Mr. Gladstone had asked her to bring her dancing shoes.

Robert was still fidgeting for fear the man might have seen their guests but Mary Anne assured him they had hidden in the bedroom and not made a sound. He looked toward the couple who nodded agreement. "But that's just two days away."

"Yes, I know, but we'll enjoy it and our guests can simply stay here." Her eyes shone and he couldn't think of any other reason to object. They would go to the party.

"I almost forgot." Mary Anne spoke up again. "What about the river ice?"

He sat at the table, motioned them all to join him, and told them of the shifting ice and the terrible danger he saw there. Anxious as he was to have the black-skinned family move on, he could not send them out on that ice with their two children. It was suicide.

Two days later they wrapped up young Thomas and carried him through the snow to the party next door where already music drifted outside and triple candle-holders in the window lighted both inside and outside, melting the window frost and showing the house full of people. Mrs. Gladstone insisted on taking Thomas while they removed their outer clothing and passed him around the admiring ladies in the parlor.

"At least he's made friends," said Robert as he took her arm and led her into the stuffed room. There were no empty seats and those that were there held an assortment of ladies complete with lacy fans and up-swept hair pinned with feathers of green and blue and even red. Mary Anne supposed that must be all the rage in Boston but she really didn't know. Nor care. She turned to the woman holding Thomas out to her.

Soon the call for supper came from the direction of the kitchen—they even had a separate room for a kitchen—and Robert took the baby and laid him in his basket. Surprisingly enough chairs for all the guests were pulled up to the huge table. He must have made it himself, Robert thought, and immediately leaned over to say as much to Mary Anne.

The food was exquisite, the company happy, and the hostess completely in control. Her husband at one end of the long table and Mrs. Gladstone at the other, they smiled often at their guests and just as often at each other. Were it not for the secret Robert and Mary Anne were keeping in their own house not two hundred feet away, they might have relaxed and really enjoyed the party.

When the meal was over the gentlemen stayed at the table and the ladies retired to the small sitting room. They were not completely separated but the men could smoke without annoying the ladies and the ladies could direct their own conversation to exchanging favorite receipts and rearing children. Mary Anne was happy to sit beside Thomas and listen to her neighbors. The men's conversation in the background provided a bass line, deep and solid against the tripping notes of the ladies.

She listened for Robert's voice, an urgent and forceful note against the stolid sound of the others. He always did like to charge in, she thought, and smiled. Suddenly the voices rose. Not Robert's voice, but others. The ladies all stopped talking.

"Oh, they're on about the niggers," Mrs. Gladstone said. "We must not let their silliness bother us. Please, Mrs. Garner, tell us about your lovely little boy."

Mary Anne gulped and tried to let go of her shock. "He...he was born almost two months ago. In November," she said and put on her broadest smile for her hostess.

"And he's your first?" another woman asked.

"No, I, no." She fought the urge to cry.

"I only ask because you're not so very young, my dear." The woman gave a little laugh.

The urge to flee, to grab Thomas and run, to escape the pain came upon her and she willed herself to stay in the high-backed chair. She twisted her handkerchief in her fingers and tried to hold her tears at bay. The men's voices filled the awkward silence which seemed to go on for hours.

"We must plan a card party." Mrs. Gladstone's voice was pitched just a little higher than normal but Mary Anne silently thanked her for changing the subject. A short time later the men rose from their chairs and came into the sitting room. Mr. Gladstone took out his fiddle and began to play softly and slowly at first, but he soon had their toes tapping to a jig. The furniture back against the wall, couples paired up and the floorboards vibrated with the dancing. Robert led Mary Anne to the floor and held her close on one of the slower tunes but she murmured her wish to take the baby home.

Soon they were back inside their own cabin where Sam's snores assured them all was well with their secret guests. Mary Anne tucked Thomas into his crib and crawled in beside her husband who wrapped his arms around her.

"What is it?" he asked.

She told him of the question that took her by such surprise and he held her close. Losing baby Mary Anne would never be far from their hearts. He told her of the men's conversation. One of the men there was leading a search on behalf of his brother. He asked every man around the table if they would help him. His brother lived in Virginia and a slave couple he owned had escaped.

"Did they have children?" Mary Anne asked.

"Yes. Two." He held her shaking body next to him and together they tried to forget their predicament and the frightful danger Sam and Sally faced. In the wee hours, Robert rose and checked the locks on every window and door before crawling back in with his wife.

Chapter Thirteen

Winter, 1819

SURELY THIS WOULD BE THE DAY. A further three weeks of the coldest January into February Robert could remember had brought, each day, more fear and more stress into their tiny home. As patient as Mary Anne was, even she was cracking and yesterday had walked with baby Thomas over the canal and as far as the store. She took a sack but bought only a few items both for her slim pocketbook and the fact that her arms were already full. When he'd questioned her in the privacy of their bedroom she'd let her tears fall and even though she said nothing he knew she made the trip just to get away.

Last night the moon was a sliver; he daren't hold them back any longer. The moon would become brighter every night now. Today Robert would test the ice again and, the Lord willing, Sam and his family would strike out tonight before the ice began to break up. He would walk as far as he could with them and send his good wishes along with a sack of food and extra clothes for the children. The family could not carry much as they headed for the mill on the other side.

They should not knock on the door there, but Robert had told them about his Scottish friends down the road. Mrs. McKie would be sure to help a family in need.

The day was clear with a cold sun sparkling on the ice as he hurried along. Snow blustered around him in the brisk wind. He hoped it would die down by evening. As far as he could see, though, the ice was solid. When he'd gone at least halfway two men came to stand on the distant shore, rifles in their hands as they watched him.

He gave a friendly wave before turning away. No one answered his gesture. He looked back once or twice but the men remained and when he reached his own shores, they were still tiny specks across the ice. Part of him rejoiced at this night's adventure for Sam's family but he also feared for them. A tiny sliver of his thoughts went to relief at having his home his own again.

All three children were sleeping like angels when Sally went to wake her two. She clothed them with heavy mittens and long scarves which she wrapped round and round her ten-year-old's neck giving him lots of room to cocoon down inside against the wind. She wrapped the baby in the same way. His arms she tucked inside the small quilt Mary Anne had given her, a new one they had worked on together over their weeks crowded together in the cabin.

The boy was full of questions that Sam answered with as little information as he could; thankfully he seemed to accept his father's short replies and soon started to complain about how hot he was with all of this clothing covering him. Sally stood before Mary Ann, tears streaming down her dark cheeks whether for her thanks or her fear Robert did not know. He edged the boy toward the door, and Sam pulled his wife's arm. The women embraced and Robert quieted them before blowing out the candle and leading them out the darkened door into the black night.

They soon reached the water's icy edge. In the darkness pierced by intermittent stars and a slip of a moon, the vaguest outline of the distant banks was topped by the mill of Robert's childhood. He led the way, the boy following close behind him and Sally and Sam walking together, taking turns carrying the baby. They could hardly see the night was so dark but Robert didn't mind stumbling

The Loyalist Legacy

and tripping over the snow and the icy outcroppings underfoot. The black night made them all but invisible.

Occasionally the ice cracked and everyone stopped in terror but Robert assured them the ice was thick enough to hold them; he hoped he was right. About half way across he turned to face the family he'd come to know so well. He gave the boy a pat on his well-padded head. He could only see Sam's wide eyes as they shook mittened hands and Sam stepped away to allow Sally to give Robert a quick hug.

"Thanks to you and to God," she said and he nodded but said nothing. Sam stepped out to lead his family the rest of the way across the creaking and cracking ice. He took his son's hand and Sally followed with the baby. Robert watched a moment, swiped at his eyes, and turned homeward. He still had to avoid the night watch and he could already see the threads of dawn streaking along the horizon. He willed Sam and Sally to hurry.

Though he had told Mary Anne to go back to bed she was awake and full of questions when he rattled the door latch and slipped inside. He undressed again and crawled in beside her where he watched the light filter in under the curtains as he answered her. Soon she slept again but his night's adventures replayed over and over in his mind. Tears threatened, just for a moment, as he fervently prayed for a safe journey for the family.

THEY NEVER REALLY KNEW FOR SURE if Sally and Sam had arrived safely on the far shore. A couple of years later, however, another couple came in the middle of the night but stayed only a day or two before catching a boat in the dark, presumably heading for Canada as well. This couple knew to knock on Robert's door; he and Mary Anne took that as a sign that Sam's family had made it across the frozen river that terrible dark night.

Word came of another sort with talk of what everyone called the Erie Canal. Men in New York had the idea to connect those across the mountains in remote places like Buffalo by actually building a canal. Robert could hardly believe it was possible. The builders would have to dig clear through the mountains to reach Lake Erie.

Those in Black Rock were sure the western terminus would be theirs but the upstarts in Buffalo began a campaign to widen Buffalo Creek to make it navigable for the ships they were sure would travel up and down the lakes. With the canal the cargoes would travel much faster from the very interior of the continent all the way to New York City. Robert and Mary Anne could hardly believe the stories.

He still worked at the tannery and another baby had come along over the years. Any day Mary Anne expected a third. More than ever Robert wanted to leave the tannery. Thomas, at six, was a good boy and did all he could to help his mother but, still, as soon as the children were asleep and Robert lit the lamps each night, more often than not, she took one to the bedroom and put it out almost immediately.

Robert sat on by himself thinking. Finally, he decided. Tomorrow on his walk with the children down by the water, he would approach the men digging out the riverbed. He'd seen the workers last Sunday but tomorrow he'd ask after a job. Whatever they had he'd do as long as he didn't have to take a pay cut. He could barely feed his growing family on what he earned now.

He had just decided to join his wife when a quiet knock came at the door; in fact, it was so quiet he thought for a moment he'd imagined the timid tapping. Like a child, he thought, and lifted the curtain. He saw nothing. The sound came again, this time a little louder. He strode to the door, lifted the bar, and pulled the door open. He glanced at the woman, hurried the three visitors inside, and pulled the door closed. The moon was bright this night.

"Someone saw us," the man whispered and the tiny woman beside him whimpered softly as she held a small girl, about five or six maybe, very close as though she'd never let her go. The girl's eyes were wide; her thin body shook. The man stroked the child's head but stared at Robert. "Can you help?"

Sounds in the street galvanized Robert to action. "Quickly, into the bedroom." He led them in the dark into his and Mary Anne's room, afraid to wake his children in the other room, for fear of what they might say.

"What is it, Robert?" Mary Anne's voice was barely audible.

He went around to her side and whispered to her. Then he straightened up. "Sir. Under the bed. Ma'am. Crawl in with my wife, down low. Hide. The girl, too." They all did as he asked and he smoothed the quilt over them. "Leave your shoes on!" he barked at the man.

A loud banging came at the door. The woman whimpered. "Quiet," Robert whispered, hoping his voice was not too loud. He ripped off his shirt and his shoes. The banging came again. "I'm coming! You'll wake the whole household."

He opened the door to two men carrying muskets and looking none too happy even in the dark night. They snorted and sniffed like a pair of running bulls. Robert stood fast in the doorway, his bulk preventing them from going around him. They were out of breath and didn't speak until they saw Robert wasn't going to let them in. That didn't stop them from peering around him into the house, though. Of course there was no light and they couldn't see much.

"What do you mean banging on my door in the middle of the night?"

"Slaves," puffed the larger of the two men.

"We're looking for runaway slaves." The slighter man spoke a little more politely.

"What is this, Virginia, Carolina? We have no slaves here." Robert turned to go back inside.

"Wait! They've run away."

"And we followed them down your street."

The large man had recovered his breath. "And onto your property. You must know where they are." He raised his musket and cocked the lock.

"Keep your voices down. I've got two little ones sleeping inside and a wife who's ready to have another." He waved his arms in the air. "Do you think I've any room for anyone else? Especially those niggers! Wouldn't be lettin' any of them cross my doorstep. You keep 'em down south where they belong!" The more he said the more he mimicked a southern drawl. Maybe that would make his story believable.

The fat man studied Robert. He stepped closer and jutted out his chin. "If you were in bed already why was your door unlocked?"

"I didn't say I was in bed. I was just going. Surely you saw my candlelight?"

Robert talked with the two a little longer. He let them shine their lanterns in the kitchen until they were satisfied. He offered to let them search the barn as long as they made sure the door was fastened properly when they left. "I'm going to bed," he said but from the window he watched until the men took their lights and left the property.

This time he made sure to bar the door and pull the curtains on the window before he took the candle to the bedroom door. "It's safe. You can come out now."

Mary Anne lifted the blankets off the woman and child while the man edged out from under the bed. Robert set the candle on the nightstand and faced the man from the other side of the bed. He was tall, sturdily built, with deep black skin that shone moist in the candlelight, a sure sign of his run and his terror. He wiped his sleeve across his face and reached to comfort the child. His left arm hung at his side but he never once used it for anything.

"What are your names?" Mary Anne had covered herself with the quilt and moved away from the woman and child who now sat as close to the other side of the bed as they could.

"Micah," the man said. "And my woman is Mirabelle."

"And who are you?" Mary Anne reached a tentative hand to the girl who drew back and said nothing.

"She Dolores." The woman spoke but Robert could barely hear her.

"Where did you...?" Mary Anne looked to Micah.

"A woman drove. Told where you live."

"What woman? How far did she drive you?" asked Mary Anne.

Micah looked confused. "She said you help us. Mrs. Greenback, I think."

"Greenstone?" Robert blurted.

"Sh, Robert. They could be outside listening," Mary Anne said.

"Yes, Greenstone. She not want to tell us but she did. Your sister?" His eyes rested on Robert.

"But why didn't she bring you here? I..."

"Bad men would know you. We jumped from wagon. She slowed, we jumped and ran to trees."

Helen had helped the family by bringing them from her farm and into Buffalo but she didn't dare lead the men who caught up to them as they neared Buffalo to Robert's home. She'd given Micah the directions and sent the family on their way while she drove on as though nothing had happened. Micah and Mirabelle told the story together while little Dolores glanced fleetingly at both Mary Anne, who smiled at her, and Robert. Mary Anne dragged herself out of bed and set about finding sleeping places for the three.

They used no candles and put out the one in the bedroom as quickly as they could. Back in bed the two of them soon fell asleep holding each other.

Heavy pounding woke them before the neighbor's rooster even crowed. Robert raced into the main room, Mary Anne with him, and pointed the family into the bedroom just as Thomas appeared at his door rubbing his eyes and staring at the people in their home. Mary Anne sent him back to bed. "Do not come out, Thomas," she warned. They grabbed the extra bedding from the floor and stuffed it in their bedroom. "Get back in the bed," he told their guests. "Like last night." The knocking got louder and louder. Mary Anne took one last look around and ran to the bed. Robert pulled the bedroom door closed and pushed his hair back off his face as he walked slowly to the door. He grabbed his musket from overhead.

He lifted the bar awkwardly as he did not want to drop the musket. When he pulled the door open just a crack the pressure from outside was tremendous. He jammed the musket into the space and by sheer brute force slammed outside into the same two men from last night and a crowd of neighbors and onlookers. Some he recognized and some he didn't but he certainly knew the two before him.

For a moment all was silent. A few people had stepped up onto his porch but most were in the yard rustling the fallen leaves and holding their coats and shawls over hastily donned clothing. One woman still had her nightcap on. Robert felt the cold and wished he'd taken a moment to get his own coat.

"Where are they?" Spittle from the man's mouth dropped onto his beard, already frosty with frozen bits from his shouting. He held a club now. Last night he'd had a musket. His partner, however, still carried his musket but now it was pointed right at Robert. He raised his own. "I do not know who you mean." He spoke slowly, tried to keep his anger in check, and hoped the family had enough time to hide. This crowd looked determined to search his home.

He raised his musket and his voice. "I don't know what you want but I have the right to protect my property and you are all, every one of you, trespassing on my land."

"You can't shoot us all," someone in the crowd shouted.

"No, but I'll shoot one of you. Who wants to take the chance?"

The yard was so silent Robert thought he could hear the few flakes of snow in the air hit the ground. Neither man in front of him moved. No one in the yard moved. He gripped the musket harder and raised it to sight along the barrel. Suddenly the door opened behind him.

"Ooh." Their next-door neighbor, Mrs. Gladstone, put her hand to her mouth as Mary Anne squeezed in beside him.

"She's in her nightgown."

"...not dressed."

Everyone talked at once and pointed at Mary Anne. He chanced a glance at her and couldn't believe what he saw. His very pregnant wife stood beside him in only her nightdress, stretched tight over her abdomen and anyone could see she could give birth any minute. Those closest might even notice her nightgown move as the child kicked. Robert certainly did. "Go back inside, Mary Anne," he whispered. "Cover yourself."

But she did not heed his words. Rather she smiled at the crowd. "I have tea," she said, "and a few biscuits. It's early, but...come inside if you like." With that she turned and slipped behind Robert and back inside.

For a moment no one moved but gradually people drifted away, shaking their lowered heads and saying very little to their neighbors. Robert lowered his musket a few inches as the two men in his face backed off. Obviously there was no one in the house or Mrs. Garner wouldn't have invited them in for tea. He could almost hear their thoughts. He stood firm until every last person had left his yard and then he breathed a sigh of relief, lowered the musket and went back inside.

Chapter Fourteen

Nissouri Township, District of Oxford
September, 1824

"I'm just that tired of these roads, Catherine."

"You've done well with our section, dear." She was used to these outbursts and her fingers kept on kneading. William pulled out a chair and sat facing her as she stood at the table preparing the week's bread. "We can't seem to change any of the rules, can we?"

He shook his head.

Bishop Strachan's plans to keep all the church lands for only the Anglicans meant their own Methodist church congregation had to meet in parlors. And that meant these vacant clergy reserves all up and down the concessions had no one to help keep up the roads. With reserved lands on both sides of their two hundred acres, William did what he could to keep up the roads himself. South of the clergy reserves were military reserves, which had not been designated, or if they had, the owners had chosen not to accept the grants so far out in the wilderness. William and Catherine had almost six miles on either concession fronted by military or clergy lots.

"I'm sick of it, Catherine."

"I know you are, but now Will and John can help. And Mr. Dickson has done his part, hasn't he?"

"Yes. Dickson is a man to do his duty. Even if he is a little testy at times."

She smiled at him but said nothing. Instead she turned to Eva at the end of the long table working with her own bread dough. "You'll not want to work the dough too much."

"I can't shape it." She slapped the dough onto the floured table and flopped into the chair behind her. "No matter what I do."

Catherine remembered her own mother telling her the bread recipe and leaving her at the table all alone to figure out the secret while she milked the cow in the barn and did all the outside chores. She remembered smacking the dough on the table, adding water, adding flour, and adding water again until her dough was hard and barely rose in the warmth of the stove. That bread her mother had thrown out and the next day they fashioned beautiful brown loaves together. William rose from his chair and slipped outside.

"Put your hands on my loaf," she said to Eva. "Gently but firmly shape it into the pan. Trust that it will rise and fill in the empty spaces."

"But my fingers don't work like yours do," Eva said.

"They will, my daughter, they will."

"I know. I just need to practice, don't I? That's how you'll get me to make the bread from now on."

Their laughter filled the cabin, which had an extra two rooms added to the north side and actual smooth walls plastered inside over the pine logs they had started with. William had cut a door into the road side of the house with a narrow window beside it. Mother and daughter shaped the loaves in the pans and set them to rise. As they washed up the table and tidied the mess, a horse neighed from the road. Eva ran to the front door.

"A wagon, Mama," she called. "Full of people. Should I get the rifle?" Even though the girl was just learning the fine points of baking bread she had spent hours practicing her shooting. Her mother made certain that not only the boys could shoot but her daughter also.

Catherine thought she knew the man, but the woman and the children were strangers although they all wore wide grins and

....

waved as William ran around the house toward them. "No. No rifle," she managed to sputter before throwing open the door and then stopping. "Mother. Come see." She went into her mother-in-law's bedroom and helped her out of the rocking chair by the blue-quilted bed. Her hair was completely white but still curled tightly wherever it escaped its bun at the back of her head; long white tendrils curled around her ears. Her freckles were almost gone, her lips thin but smiling. Brilliant blue eyes still took pride of place over her wrinkles.

Her gravelly voice began, "Who—?"

"Come. You'll see." Catherine hurried out the door.

She did know the man. He looked like William and she remembered his visit to their farm so many years before. Six, she thought, although it seemed longer. He was broader across the shoulders but he still moved like a young man as he climbed down from the wagon seat and turned to help his wife and a small child hiding his face from all the new people.

"Come, Russell," his father said, as he lifted the boy and held him in one arm while giving his wife the other. Two other children jumped off the loaded wagon and edged toward William and Catherine.

"Robert," William whispered as he shook his brother's free hand. Neither could say any more. Catherine moved to Mary Anne and embraced this woman whom she had never met but about whom she knew so much. And then the brothers and the sisters-in-law and the children were all talking at once, but one person stood alone on the porch just outside the door. Robert thrust little Russell at his wife and rushed toward the porch and his mother. Everyone went silent—even the children—as Robert ran up the steps and Lucy hobbled to him.

ROBERT HAD SENT A LETTER but before it had time to reach his brother's farm he sold up his home and crossed the Niagara. He planned to buy land nearby. Mary Anne had agreed they needed to get out of Buffalo before it was flooded with activity now that the new canal terminus was opening. They both longed to raise their family away from the hustle of the burgeoning town. Luckily, their land sold at a huge profit; Robert thought this was his chance to establish himself and his family in Nissouri near his brother.

"We're just worried about that business with the jail back in Niagara," Mary Anne said. They had gathered for the evening meal, a feast Catherine and Mary Anne had joyfully prepared for all twelve of them, the most that ever sat around the long table.

"What do you mean?" William asked.

"When we took father from the jail. Surely you remember." His face was sombre as he went on. "I wanted to come back years ago. Didn't think we'd be welcome here...after that business." He twisted his fork around and around in his hand.

Catherine looked at William whose wrinkled forehead told her he was as confused as she was. She couldn't wait for her husband. "But William fixed all that. Didn't you know?"

"No...fixed all what...how?" Robert's brows wrinkled over his brilliant blue eyes.

"He spent years on it...didn't you, William?" She turned to her husband.

"I wondered why you never answered my letter, Robert." The children stared from one adult to the other sensing something important was happening. Before his brother could answer William went on. "We found a way to fix everything. Eventually." He glanced at Catherine and back to Robert. "Mother made a friend with the right person in York."

"You mean we're not going to be arrested? Why didn't you tell me?"

"I did, Robert. In a letter."

"That's easy to say now, isn't it? I've watched that shore for all these years afraid to go home—"

"Of course we sent you the news, Robert," Catherine said. "We were surprised that you never mentioned it. William felt a little slighted." She gestured toward her husband.

"It's all done now. You're safe here, just as I am, as we are." He sat back and rested his hands on his rounded stomach. "What have we got for pie, Catherine?"

Eva slept with her grandmother, leaving her bedroom for Robert and Mary Anne. Thomas and Russell slept in the parlor although wee Russell snuggled in with his parents partway through the night. Elizabeth squeezed happily into the trundle bed on the floor beside her parents, ready to sleep in a real bed after so many nights on the road.

In the morning the men and boys wolfed their breakfast and hurried to the cornfield. William thought it providential that Robert had come in time to help him and his boys pick the corn. Once the cobs were picked, the men scythed the dried stocks and stacked them for winter feed for the animals.

Meanwhile inside the cabin Catherine and Mary Anne organized their own work team. Eva made all the beds although Grandma Lucy insisted on doing her own; her cousins gathered up their bedding from the living room and piled it beside the bed where their parents had slept. Even little Russell dragged his blanket which had followed them all the way from Buffalo and put it with the rest. Four-year-old Elizabeth sniffed and set her nose in the air as if to say he was a baby. She was certainly too old for that.

When the corn was all picked and hung to dry, for several days in a row Robert and William disappeared but wouldn't say where they were going. Mary Anne became quite tense about the whole thing but Catherine knew her William wouldn't be doing anything wrong. One cool evening after the sun had set and the rest of the two families were sitting at the table eating, the two men reappeared wearing broad smiles and looking for all the world as though they had found the golden goose.

They sat and picked up their forks with no word to the waiting women and excited children; Eva could wait no longer. "What is it, Father?" The table erupted and William had to raise his hands for silence.

"It's Robert's news, I think." He nodded at his brother across the table.

"I've bought a farm." He looked around the table but settled his glance on Mary Anne. "I think you'll like it."

Again everyone talked at once and Mary Anne jumped up from the table and ran to her husband where she threw her arms around his neck.

"Sit, sit, my dear," her embarrassed husband said but laughed with everyone else and held on to her hand as long as he could before she moved back to her chair.

Of course they all wanted to know the details and the men slowly answered all of their questions.

"But, it's September." Lucy rapped the table for silence. "You have no time to plant a crop before winter."

Even the children quieted. Having food to last the winter was something they knew about.

"We signed the papers and paid the money. We take possession immediately."

"And the crops need to be harvested but they are all Robert's."

The brothers spoke almost at once, their faces bright and their voices drowning out the others.

"But where is it, Robert?" Beside Catherine, Mary Anne leaned into the table.

"It's just a few miles south of here." Robert grabbed his wife's hand and pulled her from the table. They danced around the room laughing and singing out their own dance music. All of the children joined the dancers. Catherine looked at William and nodded toward Lucy. He rose and extended his hand to his mother but she insisted Catherine dance with him. In the end he danced a sedate trio with both of them.

The next morning the families loaded two wagons and everyone headed out to the new farm four miles south. Catherine and Eva helped Mary Anne scrub everything clean but left the new lady of the house to place her possessions where she would. After a big midday meal they took Mary Anne's three children back home for a few days to allow their mother time to settle in and cook for the harvesters. Of course Catherine's boys stayed to harvest.

Home again, Catherine herded the tired children to the table but they barely finished Lucy's lovely meal before their eyes drooped. Little Russell even pushed his bowl aside and laid his head on the table without quite finishing his stew. This night Catherine organized the beds, washed faces and hands, and sat with Eva and Grandma Lucy reviewing the day but none of the adults lasted long either.

CHRISTMAS WAS JOYFUL THAT YEAR for everyone but especially for Lucy who hadn't had two of her own children and their offspring in the same place for years. John would have been so proud of his tall sons. If only Helen were here, she thought. At least she had the letter Robert had brought. Helen would be making Christmas for her own family; she smiled to think how much of herself came out in her only daughter. *The apple doesn't fall far from the tree.*

"Grandma." Little Elizabeth poked at her knee. "Story?" The child held up a book.

"Of course." She pulled the child into her lap and began to read the story of the first Christmas. Pictures of the Christ Child and his haloed mother kept the girl enthralled as Lucy read. They had few books; this gift to Robert's whole family from William's family was a treasure. Elizabeth ran her just-washed fingers over the pictures as Lucy read on.

Her mind wandered to that Christmas when her first child was just born. John had returned from the war and as they ate their Christmas meal a loud knock had come to the door. She smiled. She had not thought of Frank in years. He was John's best friend and had shared Christmas and his sad story with them.

"Grandma, keep reading."

She pushed the past away and pulled her thoughts back to this child and the book. She smoothed her fingers over a new page with wise men and camels—whatever they were—and even a young boy holding a lamb.

"Grandma!" Elizabeth jerked the book out of her grandmother's hands and fixed her with a frustrated glare. Lucy cuddled the girl on her lap once more and reached for the book; she held her memories at bay for the rest of the story. Soon Elizabeth slipped off her grandma's lap and reached for the bowl of roasted chestnuts on the table.

"You can have one," Mary Anne said, holding up a finger.

A loud banging sounded on the door. Lucy took Elizabeth's hand and pulled her close. William and Robert rose from the settee. Robert reached for the rifle and nodded at William who opened the door leaving Robert peering through the crack.

Lucy couldn't see the porch, only a narrow strip of snow-covered cornfield. A sudden gust of icy air invaded their cosy home; she pulled her shawl around herself and Elizabeth, too. William stood like a statue, his hand on the door and his hot breath steaming into the open doorway. Finally Catherine stepped forward and the rest of the family followed. Lucy gentled Elizabeth down and pushed out of her chair, holding on to the table for just a moment while her legs steadied.

A boy almost her height with dark eyes that looked somehow familiar stood rooted to the snowy porch, his eyes riveted on William with a look of fear and bold defiance. His head was scarved in folds of gray dotted with snow and his black oversized coat reached almost to the ground.

Catherine pushed between her and William, a flurry of skirts and flying hair dashing onto the porch. "Solomon!" She pulled the boy inside and began unwinding the frozen scarf while William took a look outside and closed the door. Catherine hung Solomon's wet clothes near the stove. William sat on the settee alone, his hands clasped tightly over his middle.

They pushed Solomon to a chair at the table and the children crowded around laughing and talking as Catherine placed a cup of hot cider before the shocked but smiling boy. She shooed everyone back so that Solomon could pick up his drink. Little Elizabeth crawled back into her grandmother's lap.

....

As the boy thawed out and the excited children quieted, Catherine took his hand in hers. "Tell us your story, dear boy." Marks on his smooth skin had healed over but his one eyelid didn't seem to work right and when he opened his mouth at all she could see a great gap in his teeth where his front ones ought to have been. His clothes smelled. She squeezed his hand again. "Are you hungry, Solomon?"

"Yes," he whispered.

Mary Anne fixed a plate for him and he set on it like a stray dog on a bowl of scraps. Eva leaned over and picked up the empty plate, giving it to Mary Anne for a refill. By now the room was quiet. The boy's fork and knife managed the food almost as quickly as before. When Solomon held out the plate for more, Catherine took it from him.

"No more just now, dear."

The little ones drifted back to their toys but Will stayed at the end of the table. The others drifted off to play Chinese checkers in a bedroom or throw jacks on the bare floor. Baby Russell napped in Eva's room. Lucy relaxed, glad to be relieved of Eva's weight. She didn't have the strength she used to have.

From the settee William's gravelly voice sounded. "Where are Migisi and Kiwidinok?" He gave a special emphasis to the first word as though suggesting the boy had somehow injured them. He had gone willingly with the Indian couple to live in their teepee south of the cabin all those years ago and, Lucy remembered, had begged to go with them when they left to seek out the newly formed reservation.

Despite the warmth of the stove and the Christmas joy minutes before, a bitter breath shivered into the room. Catherine frowned at her husband as she put her arm across Solomon's shoulders. The boy glanced at William and quickly away. The child had a story to tell, it was certain, but getting it out of him would be no easy matter. Lucy got to her feet and hobbled from the table, around the jacks game on the floor, and into her room. She closed the door.

Chapter Fifteen

Chippewa Indian Reserve
December, 1824

EVERY DAY THE SNOW CAME in great blowing belts; up and down the reservation soft mounds piled between the strung out teepees. Poles strapped together and covered with tanned hides and big chunks of bark at the bottom bent in the wild wind. Kiwidinok thought she would choke on the smoke continuously blown back into their cold shelter. Near the sputtering fire her son sat warming his tiny hands over the flames and then stuffing them into his pants next to his skin for a few more minutes before stretching them over the fire again.

The girl child squeaked out a plaintive cry from her cradle on the other side of the fire and Kiwidinok reached her own cold hand to settle the patterned blanket over the child once more. Maybe feeding time? A tremor shook her already shivering body. How could she feed the child with her own stomach shrunk to nothing? The boy's sunken eyes bored into her. She pulled the girl under her clothing against her bare breast and urged her to suckle.

Like a treed polecat the wind howled outside the teepee breathing its icy exhalations down the smoke hole in the top and through the hides covering the sides. Kiwidinok wished for the hundredth time that Migisi would return from his hunting trip with a fresh kill. Solomon had begged to accompany him and, tired of the boy's sullen boredom, she'd agreed. Time he learned to be a man.

Solomon had grown tall this past summer but also restless and full of fire at the least provocation. Migisi wanted to send him on his spirit quest but she had begged to wait another year. He was too young to be a man. The babe gave up sucking and whimpered in her arms, a tiny shiver of life against her breast: she held the child tighter, the only comfort she could offer, and wished her milk would flow as easily as her tears. The boy moved beside her and rested his covered head against her arm. From time to time his tiny hand slid from his clothing to pat her arm. "Where Solomon?" the child asked.

"Hunting. With Migisi." Her scratchy voice surprised her, so thin and small was the sound that slipped into the smoky air. The boy did not answer but snuggled closer to her side as the wind whacked against their shelter. How could the men survive outside in this weather? Maybe they had found shelter. She pictured them stumbling through the storm pulling a giant buck behind them its antlers catching on every stone and branch they snagged under the snow. Or maybe they would bring a doe, glassy-eyed and bloodied, which she would use to feed them all for weeks to come in this biting winter. The fire settled. She pulled away from the boy, wrapped the babe into his tiny arms and pulled herself up to unfasten the ties of the teepee.

Stepping over the protective bark blocking the door she reached for chopped logs and passed them back into the teepee trying to keep the flap closed as much as she could. Wind whipped her hood off and blew against her braided head with such a ferocity she thought it might pull out her hair. She threw more wood inside before following it in and tying the flaps tight.

The boy had moved with his sister to the far side of the teepee away from the tossed wood. One piece had landed in the fire and the boy swatted at a spark on the baby's blanket. She arranged the rest of the pieces in a pile and tried to smile for the boy's sake motioning him back to the heat of the fire. Migisi's old and worn

The Loyalist Legacy

mocassins made of soft deer hide lay against the outside wall of the teepee. She grabbed them and turned them over in the brighter light of the fire. The cooking pot sat empty. Quickly she opened the door once more, filled the pot with fresh snow and tied the flaps safely closed again.

The fire hissed and crackled with another snowy log; she hung the pot, stripped the beads off Migisi's moccasins, and tossed the dried up deerskin into the now-melted snow. The teepee grew warmer and the pot simmered encouragingly over the fire. The boy watched as she stirred the stewing bits that had begun to give off a tantalizing odor somewhat reminiscent of dried bear meat, which was odd. His eyes shone in the light of the flames and the wind settled outside.

Hours later when darkness had plunged them into even more desolation, Kiwidinok dipped into the pot and tasted the strange broth. She had a chip from a salt block which she stirred into the mixture. It didn't taste good but it was warm and perhaps would stave off their hunger. She called softly to the sleeping boy. He took his bowl and drank the cooled mixture. She spooned some into the baby's slack mouth trying not to lose a drop. In desperation she dipped her finger into the bowl and the baby began to suck. This she did over and over. Finally she herself drank a bowlful. Maybe her milk would come for the baby.

For two more days Kiwidinok nursed the fire, stewed the moccasins, and fed her family, all the while fearing Migisi and Solomon would never come back. She was quite worried by now both for the storm and for the time her men had been gone but her features were rigidly composed before her children. The baby suckled now and the little boy bestirred himself to play with his sticks and marbles by the fire. He still whined about his hungry tummy and about relieving himself out in the cold, but the weather had warmed a little and the wind was gone.

On one trip outside the sun shone bright in the azure sky sprinkling bits of its sparkle in the pure snow surrounding them. The boy laughed to see his yellow stream coloring the snow and even took to drawing a circle until the stream ran out. He was just lacing up his breeches when a shout made them both turn. Migisi waved his free arm at them. He was pulling something behind him.

Kiwidinok had to keep the boy from running to his father for fear he'd sink into the deep drifts of snow. She picked him up and held him while Migisi, alone, made his way to them, his strained features becoming more clear the closer he came. Solomon was nowhere to be seen. The boy could wait no longer and squirmed in her arms until she released him to run for his father. She ran, too, and helped pull the magnificent stag home.

WITH THE CHILDREN ALL IN THEIR ROOMS and Lucy long since gone to hers, William watched Catherine's kind eyes as she spoke softly to the returned man-child whose back and curly hair were all he could see as the two of them huddled together at the table. The cold seeped in behind him and he made a mental note to check the chinking in the outside walls on the morrow. Perhaps the heavy winds had loosened it in spots. A soft drone was all he could hear but obviously Solomon was telling Catherine his story. He unfolded his long legs and padded to the table, his heavy knitted stockings making no sound.

Solomon sat at the end with Catherine to his right; William scraped the opposite chair out from the table. He longed to find favor with his wife again; more than that, he was curious. Just what had caused Solomon to leave Migisi and Kiwidinok? Solomon's words ceased and he pursed his thick lips together in that face William remembered so well. The boy was stubborn back then and he was still stubborn now. He looked at his wife, pleading for her help.

A brief glimmer of a smile for her husband broadened into a warmth that covered her whole face when she addressed Solomon once more. She reached for the boy's hand and pulled it across the pine table stripped of its cloth since supper. He watched as the dark brown fingers, now as large as a man's, curled into Catherine's tight grip. He swallowed the bile that threatened and forced himself to speak. "Why are you here, Solomon?" Drat! The words came out harsh. He tried again. "I mean...what has happened?"

He swallowed once more as he studied the child's face. For Solomon was still a child. His height was nigh on a man's, his feet were definitely full size, and his fingers as long as William's own, but Solomon was only in his eleventh or twelfth year. His face was perfectly smooth and still held those frightened eyes of long ago. William pushed those thoughts away.

"He wants to know what happened, child. As do I." Catherine tightened her grip on the boy's hand and drew it closer to her. "Tell him as you've been telling me." Gently she nodded her head when Solomon looked her way.

Still holding Catherine's gaze and her hand, Solomon began his story again. He told of the hunger and the cold on the reservation where he had gone with Migisi and Kiwidinok. He described the temporary teepees constructed by the Indians but far too flimsy for prolonged exposure to this winter. And he told of the dissension on the reservation with Indians long used to making their own way now forced to beg from the British government for their livelihood.

He glanced at William. "I was hunting with Migisi. To feed those in the teepee."

"Kiwidinok, you mean?" Catherine asked.

"And the baby and little boy child."

She nodded. "Go on, Solomon."

He hung his head and covered his eyes. "They hated me." The words came slow and bitter.

"Who hated you?" William was finally drawn into the story. "Surely not Migisi and Kiwidinok!"

"No...the others...on the reservation."

Catherine began, "I don't understand—"

"They called me names, bad names, because of my skin."

"Everyone?" William asked.

He raised his voice and almost shouted at William. "No. The young braves!"

A cold shiver, not entirely caused by the dying fire, started in William's feet and crept up his legs until he reached across the table and clasped both Catherine's and Solomon's joined hands. For the first time he understood the hurt and hate this boy had suffered. A shiver of shame tore at him and he squeezed the hands harder before pulling away. He stood noisily and scraped the chair back against the table.

"But how did the others make you come here? What about Migisi?" Catherine's voice rose. William sat again.

"They followed us. When my father—Migisi—was ready to shoot a beautiful buck, they shouted their war cries and warned the deer." In a rush of words Solomon described the boys laughing and taunting not only him but his father whose pain and disappointment at losing the food for his family had so frustrated him that Solomon tore after the boys for hours but to no avail. When he realized how far he had run with no thought to where he was going and no sign of those he was chasing, he came across a trail that seemed to lead to the northeast. He looked from one to the other. "I thought…I hoped…I would find you."

By now Solomon's voice was shaking and Catherine moved closer to put her arm across his bony shoulders. William patted the boy's other shoulder but said nothing.

"But why didn't you look for Migisi?" Catherine whispered.

Solomon told then of the night coming on, the cold, the trees cracking under the weight of the snow and the moon watching him no matter how he tried to hide his head under his clothing. As the night wore on and the wind picked up he saw spirits in every rock, tree and animal. Manitous that he had only heard about seemed to stalk him the whole night; he even thought he heard the giant Windigo calling his name. At first light he fled along the trail to escape and eventually came to parts that seemed familiar. He met no one and had only his own wits to take him to their farm but eventually he found the road north. He passed the Dickson's farm and trudged on to theirs.

The next day William brought a bowl of hot porridge to Solomon as again the boy sat silent and sad on the same chair as before. Young Will and John came out of the bedroom and stopped midway to the table, staring. Catherine turned back to the dry sink to hide her smile and rattled the few dirty dishes. When Lucy made her way to join the family she, too, missed a step upon seeing William talking easily to Solomon. Catherine grinned at her mother-in-law. Having Solomon back felt good but she worried about his parents. She must talk to William about it.

Will and John sidled in close to Solomon leaving Lucy, Eva, and Catherine alone at the stove end of the long table. More snow had fallen overnight and the window above the dry sink had frosted over completely. Valiantly the sun tried to creep through the patterned hoarfrost but it would have no success until the cold abated. Eva poured coffee for everyone, set the pot back on the stove, and, giving in to the child inside her, tried to thaw the ice and draw letters on the glass.

"Eva, you'll have the windows all smeared," her mother said. "Come back to the table and finish your meal." Sometimes the girl seemed so grownup and other times she was such a child. Her daughter shuffled to her seat, picked up her spoon, and ate but she didn't lift her face from her bowl.

The males of the family talked about their chores outside but Catherine and Lucy had their own work to consider. Even though she was in her sixty-sixth year Lucy still tried to help as much as she could and Catherine loved her for it. She looked sideways at her daughter this morning, though, and decided Eva could take her grandmother's place as they washed clothes and bedding from the holiday gathering. Her suggestion caused Eva to sulk even more.

"I must do my share," Lucy said.

"Of course. You can do whatever you like. Eva, too, will do her full share." Catherine was adamant. "Won't you, my daughter?"

The girl raised her head. "I can make bread," she cried.

"And help with the clothes washing." Catherine's voice was soft but firm. "You can make bread while we clear up." And just like that everyone's workday was planned.

In no time William had taken his boys, all of them, outside to work and Catherine moved to get her chores going. Eva dried dishes for Lucy while Catherine brought water from the well outside, covered over to keep it from freezing. She poured pail after pail into the huge pot on the stove and left it to heat while she stripped the beds and sorted the clothes.

By midday the whole industrious family gathered to wolf down a hurried meal before getting back to work. Eva complained at being sent to hang yet another set of sheets on the frozen line outside but Catherine silenced her with a glance. While the others ate, Eva's dish sat empty until the door flew open and the girl rushed inside. "We have company!" she cried. "Come outside, everyone. Especially you, Solomon."

Catherine grabbed a heavy shawl and pushed past her daughter. She followed Eva's finger pointing off the end of the porch at a horse and sleigh coming around the corner of the house and driven by Old Tom, the peddler. Instead of his usual wagon of wares to sell and trade he had a frozen little group huddled under a heavy buffalo robe in the sleigh. Around and behind Catherine the rest of the family crowded in to welcome Migisi and Kiwidinok. Praise the Lord! Catherine glanced at Eva. How had she known who this was?

She pushed Solomon in front of her and Migisi's face lit up. He threw off the covering and hurried up the steps. His face fairly beaming under his bearskin hat, he stretched out his hand.

"My son."

Solomon sprang forward and wrapped his father in a crushing embrace. Soon they were all inside, the washing forgotten for the moment amid voices raised with stories and joy.

Long after the families had settled into their beds, Migisi and Old Tom still sat with William at the table. This was the first time Old Tom had stopped overnight and the first time Migisi's family had slept inside the cabin. William set aside the deck of cards they had been using and looked hard at the other men.

Migisi's eyes were downcast but at William's urging he told of the hardships on the reservation where the government had not lived up to its promises, leaving the Indians in deplorable circumstances. And he added the general misery on the newly formed reservation regarding Solomon's situation. This tale reinforced what the boy had told on his arrival but William was surprised to hear the severity of the attacks by the boys just because Solomon was dark-skinned.

At last Old Tom, who had listened to the other two, cleared his throat and began to talk, his eyes on the table but his voice rising and falling with his tale. He had been in Centreville when a traveling preacher stopped over at the hotel there and talked to all who would listen about the plight of someone called Gourlay. The man was persecuted by the Family Compact.

"What's that?" Migisi asked.

William and Old Tom told of those closest to the governing bodies of the province who made all the lush appointments, oversaw the legislature and even had their own scallywag groups crossing the countryside to make certain the settlers did as they were told. They favored their family and friends; hence the name had evolved.

"But who's this Gourlay?" William asked.

"A good man. Smart. Tried to challenge Strachan's group."

"How?" William didn't understand.

Old Tom leaned in and whispered to the other two about how Robert Gourlay's reform efforts had led to the loss of his health and his eventual banishment from the province. "Of course this happened a few years ago. Shows the sneaking ways of the Family Compact. Folks are still terrified to say anything against them."

"The roads here are a disgrace. These grant lands that aren't settled are the cause of it. So few of us to do the work."

"Keep your thoughts to yourself, William, or Strachan will come after you. No one's safe, even this far from York."

Migisi had said little but now looked from Old Tom to William. "I, too, have problems with government."

William turned. "What do you mean? They've given you land to live on. What can be wrong with that?"

"Yes, land." He took a deep breath and told about the perfidy of Chippewa leaders who had bargained away so much of their land for the small reservation acreage. They had been promised houses, not teepees, and access to the white man's way of living but instead more and more they were shunned and told to stay on their reserves. Where once Natives hunted wherever they wanted, now they were forced to find food over just a few acres; when the animals diminished and maybe even disappeared they would have no way to live.

"Is that why you've come, Migisi?" William's voice softened as he studied the man but inside his thoughts were churning.

Migisi slowly nodded. "That…and to find Solomon."

Chapter Sixteen

Robert Garner's farm
Spring, 1825

THE FIRE BURNED SO HOT that Mary Anne lifted the burner off the cook top and stirred the hot coals before setting the fry pan back in place and dropping the ham slices into it. She and Robert had enjoyed the first spring weather as they sorted out the plow and the harnesses in preparation for the day when they could get on the land. She'd left Thomas inside in charge of both the sleeping baby and five-year-old Elizabeth for as long as she dared.

Johnnycakes mixed, she poured the batter into her second pan, careful to avoid the hot lard popping in tiny droplets toward the bib of her apron. The children would enjoy the applesauce made from the last bunch of apples she'd found in the cold cellar and cooked up, skins and all, so as not to waste a morsel. In the afternoon Thomas begged to help his father and leave the little ones inside; Elizabeth had Russell in the sitting room, mothering him with tenderness but also the odd bit of scolding. Where did the child learn that?

As darkness descended Robert and young Thomas came inside and washed up at the washbowl she'd already filled. Thomas got his hands in beside his father's and scrubbed himself just like his father. In a few moments they were all seated and saying the blessing. Thomas sat at Robert's right hand and again watched his father's every move.

"Slow down there, young man," she said when the boy took a portion every bit as large as Robert's. "Leave some for the rest of us."

The other children began to complain. Robert shushed them and spooned johnnycakes and ham on to their plates. Mary Anne cut baby Russell's into tiny pieces and then turned to do the same for Elizabeth, who insisted she could do her own. Into the relative quiet of spooning and chewing, Robert looked her way.

"I'm thinking of selling off a few lots along the road."

She stopped her fork in mid air and studied him as he calmly chewed his food. "What gave you that idea?" She needed more information to know whether this was good or bad.

"We need a store. A blacksmith. A mill, maybe, so's people can get their supplies closer."

She didn't answer but helped the baby load his spoon and try to get it into his mouth without spilling everything.

Robert went on. "A couple of the men were by today and we all got talking about it. I thought about it all the time Thomas and I were mucking out the pens." He looked up before going on. "And we could use the extra cash from the sale of the lots."

After the little ones were in bed that night Mary Anne sat at the table beside her husband. He was doing figures on the slate Thomas had been using for his sums. "What is that you're doing?" she asked, and he immediately slid it toward her.

"I've been calculating the lots needed for a village here."

"How much land would this need, Robert?" She knew her worry was obvious in her whiny voice but pushed on. "Don't we need our land for crops? All our land?"

"Well, that's just it. If we sell off lots just along the road allowance with room for stores with living space on the second story, we'll still have enough land for crops." He took her hand. "And we won't have to look after the road allowance where the stores are. The new owners will be responsible." He pushed his chair back and that joyful smile she loved to watch appeared on his face. His brilliant blue eyes shone on her.

His idea did seem clever; she'd give him that. And looking after that road allowance was a thorn in all their sides. This would give him some cash to buy goods and even pay to have the rest of the stumps pulled out of the east field just down the hill. Her face softened and she read his look as she had done ever since they'd met. Almost on its own her head nodded and Robert leaped up, pulled her from her chair, and together they danced around the room.

The very next day, Robert let it be known that he had lots for sale all up and down both sides of the road and he even drew up a notice to put in the newspaper some fellow in Queenstown was printing. Mackenzie was his name. Robert had seen a copy just the week before when Old Tom had braved the late winter thaws to start out on his route. For the moment he used some of the precious paper Mary Anne had bought from Old Tom and made two framed posters for the trees on either side of the road where he thought the lots might be severed off.

Next he rode to talk to William who knew much more about the legal side of things than he did. Between the two of them they came up with lawyer James Logan of Centreville and Robert planned a visit to this man he'd never met. In a very few weeks the lots were measured out and marked with stakes Robert had cut himself. The project was an immediate success as the advertisement Old Tom had taken to Mackenzie in Queenstown drew queries from as far away as York and many places in between. It seemed not everyone was cut out for farming in the bush.

By mid-July three enterprising shop-keepers were well on their way to finishing their two-level stores and Robert rejoiced that the first one to open its doors in a very few days would be a general store. Mary Anne was excited at the prospect of sending her boy to pick up some last-minute item she might need for cooking. The idea of bolts of cloth to touch and feel instead of buying sight unseen had her glowing. The days of getting an order all tumbled into one box, as Catherine had described, would soon be over.

Robert, however, would still be working on the land and she had come to realize farming was not making him any happier than working in the tannery. He really came alive when teaching the children their letters and numbers, or making up games to help them remember and planning yet another scheme. This latest, the stores along their frontage, kept him riding up and down the concessions spreading the word about his village and when he stopped to eat or sleep his mind seemed to swirl with more ideas.

He begrudged the days of going to help William just as much as plowing and planting on his own farm. And yet, he was a hard worker. He would spend any amount of time putting up a clothesline on pulleys which let Catherine hang washing from the porch and push it out to the nearest tree. He ran water along a wooden slide from the well to the porch. To save his wife carrying so much, he said. No one else had either of these inventions.

Once the general store opened folks came clip-clopping along the rough road with more and more frequency until a blacksmith set up shop near the small hotel where two rooms were available to rent and a large gathering room just inside the door attracted passers-by with its cosy tables and chairs. They could get a bite to eat and meet with others out and about on the roads.

More and more people came to refresh themselves on a long journey perhaps to nearby points or much farther afield but many stayed to settle in this welcoming Nissouri Township. They asked about the odd name but the locals simply presumed that maybe it came from an old Native name meaning gurgling waters. Robert didn't know.

One day as fall hung in the air with the crisp tree colors and crisper nights sharpening his senses, Robert heard the dull thud of hoof beats coming fast on the road behind him. He had walked over to the store to pick up black thread for Mary Anne. He shoved the spool into his pocket and stopped to watch the rider come on, expecting the man to just hurry on by. Instead the frothing horse headed for him at the side of the road and the rider pulled up short not a foot away from Robert. He took a step back.

The Loyalist Legacy

"Whoa!" he called. "What's the hurry?"

The rider held his reins in uplifted arms as though the horse might take off at any moment. He held the horse as he studied Robert who simply stood waiting, his fingers handling the thread in his pocket as he eyed the stranger.

"What's your hurry, sir? Your horse looks about done in."

The man lowered his hands and looped the reins on the saddle before speaking. "I have a message," he sputtered. "What is this place?" He pointed to the general store.

"It's Logan's General Store. You can see the sign."

"And you are?" The man didn't even look at the store. Rather he stared at Robert with a shattering look.

Robert stepped back. "Robert Garner," he said and forced a smile to his lips. "How can I help?"

The stranger jumped down from his horse and stood so close to Robert he found himself taking another step backward. "Any kin to William Garner?" the man asked.

Robert explained William was his brother. The man pursed his lips and nodded up and down. "My name is Matheson," he said. "I've come to talk business with you. A bad business."

BACK AT THE FARMHOUSE, where Robert had invited Matheson to accompany him, Mary Anne smiled at seeing Robert and the guest enter the house. She looked from one stern face to the other and realized something was wrong. As they pulled out chairs facing each other at the table, she began to speak but stopped when her husband gave her a sharp look. She turned away to cut the carrots for dinner.

She might offer the man some refreshment if not for Robert's short answers to the man's questions. The knife slipped as she heard the words "arrest you" and she clutched the sideboard while her insides churned. The man scraped his chair back from the table. Robert still sat.

"You're coming with me, Garner." He said in a loud voice that silenced the children playing with their sticks and marbles on the floor.

"I have the proof, Matheson. Just let me get it." She turned from her task to see her husband's face as he pushed away from the table and rushed to the small desk in the corner of the room. What was happening?

"Those papers are worth nothing." Matheson pointed to the crumpled sheet Robert had thrown on the table.

"See this signature here?"

"Yes. And that's an illegal signature."

She felt the blood drain from her face as Robert picked up the paper and peered at it.

"How do you know?" he asked in a much smaller voice.

"Because this man, this Miller,"—he almost spat the name—"is not the rightful owner."

Robert slumped to his chair. A knock sounded on the door. Robert barely stirred. Mary Anne looked at her husband, wiped her hands on her apron, and slipped by the table to see who was now knocking again, louder this time. Surely it couldn't be any worse news, she thought, but all the same her breath caught as the door opened before she even got to it.

William's whole face lit up and, grinning, he slipped off his hat. "Morning, my dear. Is that lazy brother__" He halted and his smile turned to a frown. "Pardon, I see I'm interrupting…"

Robert spoke up. "Here's my brother. He was with me when I bought the farm." He sat taller in his chair and Mary Anne saw his hope. "Tell him, William."

"Mr. Matheson, isn't it?" William sat and faced the visitor.

"Your brother's not the rightful owner, Mr. Garner." He spoke softer now, in a respectful voice. Mary Anne sat at the table with the men as they talked, but she said nothing.

The children's voices rose and fell over their game, a pleasant background to her churning thoughts. She tried to pay attention to what the men said but all she could think of was losing her home in Buffalo and, much worse, clutching her child's lifeless body as she ran from the flames and Robert gone and no one to help her and the hot smell of the fire and wee Mary Anne's smoke-filled body and blanket in her arms and where was Robert?

"Mary Anne...my dear." A hand brushed her own.

Her face was wet. Tears. She shook her head and looked around the table. Her mouth fell open and she immediately closed it. A handkerchief. In her pocket. She swabbed at her eyes and felt the heat of embarrassment. They stared at her, waiting for something, and she realized they knew not what to say. She had slipped back into the old fears. She must go on. With a huge effort she straightened in her chair, breathed a cleansing breath, calmed herself, and smiled. "I was just thinking...."

"I know, my dear." Robert looked around the table before going on in a low voice. "We will be safe. It won't happen again."

Mr. Matheson pulled back from the table and stood. He seemed at a loss and just shook his head. William rose with him and together they went outside leaving the couple in peace. A few moments later William rejoined them; Matheson had left. He would come back once Robert had sorted out the ownership of the land. He believed Robert's story and even thought perhaps he could launch an investigation into who had sold the property to Robert and how it came to be registered with the wrong name on the deed in the first place.

Of course with an official investigation into the land dealings Robert worried that his background would come out. Would he even be allowed to own land here since he had fought for the Americans? Mary Anne went back to her meal preparation and he and William slipped outside to talk about the harvest. They would work together and, since Robert's crops were further along, they planned to start with his farm. Neither of them mentioned the threat now hanging over him but they agreed to get his crop off as soon as they could.

Chapter Seventeen

ROBERT SAT ALONE at the table as Mary Anne rustled about the room tidying the last remnants from their evening meal. She wrapped the hank of ham in its cloth and placed it into the cupboard next to the half-eaten pumpkin tart. None of them had eaten much that night, not even the children, now sitting quiet and solemn on the floor rug. Only Russell poked a chubby finger at a fat marble pushing it closer and closer to Elizabeth, who swept it away with one swipe of her hand. Russell let out a yelp and Mary Anne turned to see what was the matter.

Robert didn't move. He didn't even look up. She settled the children warning them bedtime was fast approaching and sat beside her husband. "How could this have happened?" She put her small hand, still red from the dishwashing, on his hairy forearm. As usual his shirtsleeves were rolled almost to his elbows, the better to wash at mealtime. The curly hairs were soft as she stroked back and forth trying to soothe him as he had her earlier in the day.

Finally Robert shifted his arm and turned to her. He smiled and those blue eyes reassured her. He would solve this. She knew he would.

"We're going to take a day and ride to Centreville."

She nodded but didn't voice her worries. There was no point. Either the men would solve this or…she shuddered and he pulled her against him.

• • •

ON THEIR LONG RIDE to Centreville the next day, William and Robert agreed the Logan brothers, Peter, James, and Andrew who had built the store, were all upright men. Peter had cut wood with William and with Catherine years before; through him they met the other two. Was there something just a little suspect about one brother acting as the lawyer for another brother's land purchase? But wait. He was the lawyer when Robert bought the land, long before he had any idea of breaking off the lots for a village.

"It's true," William said, "but should he have acted for his own brother's purchase of a lot?"

"I can hardly believe he'd cheat me."

William agreed but they decided to get to the bottom of this when they met the man, even if it meant challenging him on his actions. In Centreville they found Mr. Logan's home immediately. Robert explained his visitor's charges of the day before while William kept quiet. Mr. Logan looked at the deed Robert had brought and leaned back in his tilting chair. His hands across his ample stomach, he looked at each of them in turn. The clock on the shelf above him filled the silence with rhythmic ticking that seemed to go on forever.

The man's eyes betrayed an uneasiness that Robert had never noticed on previous visits and his own face crumpled in consternation. The deed lay between them on the mahogany desk, its yellowed appearance marring the pristine shine of the polished wood. He glanced at William.

"Did you do a proper search when you prepared this deed, Mr. Logan?" William's voice was polite but insistent.

The man blustered and sat forward in his chair, glaring. "What do you mean? I most certainly did!"

"Why am I threatened with an arrest warrant, then, for selling land that isn't mine, sir?" Robert jumped up, placed his large hands on the desk, and leaned over Mr. Logan.

William's hand brushed Robert's arm. "Perhaps the mistake is yours, sir?" William said quietly as he stared at Mr. Logan.

"Alright, alright, gentlemen. I'll tell you what has transpired." He stood up and turned his back on them. Robert and William exchanged a look but the lawyer whipped around, a pained expression on his whiskered red face. He stuck a finger into his collar as if to loosen it. "My clerk saw your name"—he looked at Robert—"and seemed to remember it from a warrant years ago. Without my knowledge he contacted his former teacher for information." The man looked around the brothers to the open door. "Close the door, please," he whispered, and William did so. "There is nothing wrong with your deed, sir."

"Then what is all this hullabaloo about me not owning my farm?"

"They ordered me to say it wasn't yours. I'm sorry. You bought the land fairly."

William asked a few more questions and made a pointed reference to the illegality of issuing a false warrant and all the while Mr. Logan nodded his head, such a pained look on his face that Robert almost felt sorry for him. Suddenly, though, he broke into the conversation. "Who was it?"

The other two men stopped talking and turned to him.

"Who?" William asked.

"The teacher!" He could barely contain himself. He had to know.

"Oh, you don't need…I wouldn't think…no…" the man spluttered.

William and Robert each went around the sides of the desk. Their faces pushed almost into Mr. Logan's frightened one. "The school teacher!"

Logan's face was ashen. Even his whiskers seemed grayer and his eyes took on a haunted hunted look. He shook his head back and forth, eyed the closed door, looked from one brother to the other, and let out a long breath. His chin dropped to his chest. He placed his white hands on the edge of the desk, now smudged and lackluster. "I'm sorry. I had no choice." When the brothers pushed closer he dropped his head across his arms on the desk and a soft whisper sounded in the tension-filled room. "Bishop Strachan."

For a moment no one said anything although William moved back to his chair as if in a dream. Robert followed. Mr. Logan's grey serge shoulders stopped shaking and his great gulps of air gradually diminished. Robert's head was awhirl. William was silent beside him.

He became aware of sounds beyond the door. Someone rapped. "Mr. Logan?"

The man sat up and brushed his hand over his hair, hurriedly swiped at his eyes, and tried to speak. He cleared his throat. "Yes?"

The door opened and a primly dressed woman of medium stature edged into the room. She looked swiftly at the brothers and then at Mr. Logan. Her smile disappeared and a look of consternation wrinkled her pretty forehead. She studied the two of them and Robert was immediately sorry for her. "We've just been talking with Mr. Logan, madam." He nodded and added, "My brother and I." He stood up, thinking to leave.

William stayed in his chair scowling at Mr. Logan who waved his hand at the woman, probably Mrs. Logan, until she backed out of the room, closing the door behind her. Sitting ramrod straight William gripped the wooden arms of his chair as though at any moment he might throw himself across the desk at the lawyer. Logan looked beaten. Robert could have pitied the man but remembered his own predicament was because of this man's chicanery with officials all the way up to the bishop.

"You will write out a document attesting to what you have told us, sir." William almost growled, so low and frightening was his voice.

"I...I cannot, sir," the man replied.

"But you must."

"We are not without influence, Mr. Logan," Robert said although he knew what a tremendous bluff his words were.

The man tried to say he would send the document on to them in a few days but neither brother would agree to that. They were not inclined to leave without the lawyer's statement and, even though Robert had some interest in learning why Mr. Logan had done such a heinous thing, William concentrated on righting the wrong, no matter the cost to Logan.

As they rode out of Centreville William hoped Robert's problem was solved and that Logan would make sure the illegal arrest warrant was rescinded. The two rode in silence, allowing their horses to feel the way as the daylight dwindled. They ought to have stayed overnight and traveled the next morning but neither wanted to stay one minute longer anywhere near Mr. Logan. They would stop at someone's farm along the way.

EARLY THE NEXT MORNING the men said their goodbyes to William's friends and continued along the Governor's Road toward home. They veered north under a sunny sky but William felt winter's nip in the air. He rode on from Robert's farm still uneasy about the underhanded dealings of the Family Compact and mulled over what they might do if they realized his brother had fought on the American side in the war. Best they not learn of it. Robert would have to keep his head down.

Clouds of smoke plumed into the blue sky but he thought nothing of it; even now new land owners were always burning off stumps and brush, the battle to clear land in Nissouri far from over. The road was easier for a short distance and he waved at neighbors, known and unknown, along the way but did not stop. The smoke was stronger now. Perhaps the dried leaves had caught and gotten away from someone? He kneed the horse to go faster even though he was traveling a poorly tended stretch of road and he feared for the horse's safety as well as his own.

Wind-whipped sheets of smoke and flame met him as he cleared the tree lot still standing on his own property. Was it his house? Or barn? He pushed the horse harder, a hard knot in his gut. A few hundred feet away he breathed easier. The house still stood. But nearer, his family flung buckets of water on the remnants of the cabin they had built for Migisi and Kiwidinok. Young Will saw him first and waved. Catherine glanced his way but turned back to the smoky ruins. She and Migisi searched the grass for sparks. Kiwidinok kept all the children back.

None of them were fully clothed. Young Will and Migisi wore britches and shoes but not much else while Kiwidinok held the crying children against her night dress. All were red-eyed and smoke-smudged, the little ones with long smears down their sad faces. He jumped off the horse and handed it off to Young Will. All was quiet as though each of them felt they had disappointed him and were afraid to speak. Catherine dropped her bucket and turned toward him her face hard and defeated.

"What happened?" he asked as he held her against him. She said nothing. Her limp body barely leaned into him. "Catherine?" He pushed her back to look at her face, framed with tangled hair, filthy from the fire and singed in a few spots. He smoothed the strands away from her blackened face, its softness turned hard with the heat of the fire she'd fought. Finally, from somewhere deep within, she tried to find her voice but a ragged cough came out instead. He held her.

"They came in the early morning. Before daylight even."

"Who?"

Young Will and the other children stood close; the boy spoke up. "We couldn't tell, Papa."

William cast his eyes to Migisi standing nearby but the man looked away before moving to his own family. "Who was it, Catherine. Could you see?"

Her head moved against his shoulder. "No…I…we had to fight the fire."

Later that day William rode out to his neighbors carrying the message as far as he could before night fell; he needed help building a new cabin and planned a work bee two days hence. Migisi and Will with some help from Johnny cleared as much of the rubble as they could without touching the still-smouldering base logs. Catherine and Eva kept the younger children inside but Eva soon tired of that. When her mother's back was turned she edged the door open and slipped out.

The smell of smoke was still heavy and thick in the air although sun cast its light over the harvested fields. Beyond the blackened gouge in the earth where the cabin had stood, the golden corn stubble showed the fire had not spread out across the land. Everything was dry as the rains had held off for several weeks, just long long enough to get the crops off. A little rain now would wash clean the burned land and reduce the risk of fire creeping across the fields, not just her father's but those of their neighbors and the vast treed lots as well.

Eva trudged toward the place where her brothers, in the oversized gloves their father had given them, pulled and pushed the smoking wood away from the central spot to help stop the burning. A pail lay tipped over on the ground, abandoned. Well she could at least carry water. She seized the pail, rattling the handle as she picked it up.

"No, young lady." Migisi called to her but she took a quick look at him and hurried down the path to the water. He did not follow. Coming back up the hill was harder with the pail full and she lost some of her load as she slopped along but she made it back and slowly dumped the water along a sizzling log Will had dragged off by itself. When she'd emptied the pail she headed back for more.

Johnny for once put his full effort into the work, pushing and pulling right alongside Will and Solomon as they tugged the smoking logs away. She wasn't sure why they didn't just wait until everything was burned up but Migisi must have a plan. On one of her trips up the steep path she saw her mother standing on the porch but didn't go when she called, so focused was she on using her waning strength to carry water. By now the boys and Migisi had cleared the cabin foundations of wood and Migisi was raking away as much smoke and ash as he could. He motioned her over with the water and she poured it where he asked.

She turned and put one foot in front of the other down the path again but this time her brothers came with her, each carrying a pail. For once they didn't tease her but helped her fill her bucket. When they straggled to the top of the hill again her mother took the pail from her and patted her shoulder.

"Inside, my dear. Get some supper. If you're not too tired you might read to the little boy before bed." As Eva stepped away her mother seemed to smile but in the twilight Eva could not tell. "Kiwidinok is sleeping in Grandma's room," her mother called.

Johnny came with her into the cabin; the two of them sat at the long table and shoved food into their mouths. She was starving. A horse cantered along the road and slowed outside. Her father. Back from his errand. In a few moments, he, too, sat at the silent table. When the little Chippewa boy started crying in the corner she took him into her arms and snuggled next to him on the sofa. She read him some of the Christmas book by the dim light of the candle and then snuggled him into a blanket on the couch for the night. In her own room Eva stripped off her smoky clothes and crawled beneath the covers, too tired to even think of braiding her hair or washing some of the smoke smell out of it.

She woke to the low mutter of voices outside her door under which a thin band of light showed. Perhaps her brothers were out of bed already? Her mother's serene voice calmed her as she pulled on her filthy clothes from the day before. Time enough to change after she washed and found out what was happening. She threw open the door.

The room was suddenly silent as all eyes turned on her. Her parents, her brothers, Solomon and one other. Her Uncle Robert. She halted a moment before focusing on her mother. "Did I sleep in, Mama?"

Everyone talked at once ignoring her as she grabbed a plate and sat at the table beside her mother who absently passed bread and bacon grease her way. Of Migisi's family, only Solomon was up. Perhaps they were the reason for the soft voices. Or maybe they were outside already. Eva rubbed her eyes to try to wake herself. She wished her brain would work better this morning but she still felt half asleep.

"We have to know who fired the cabin," her daddy said. Everyone nodded, even her brothers. "I met some stony glares yesterday but mostly people were shocked."

"Will they come to help today?" Uncle Robert's scratchy voice was easy to recognize, especially when he was excited as he was this morning. "I don't know, William. First me, then you." He shook his head but didn't say anything else. What did he mean? Her father nodded and she recognized that cogitating look (as he called it). Something was definitely wrong.

Grandma's bedroom door opened and Migisi led his family toward the table. Solomon stood to let his mother have his place and Eva's brothers moved to the couch where the rumpled blanket from last night lay. Eva kept her eyes on her food but her mother jumped up to find enough for their guests. Funny how uncomfortable it all felt even though they'd known each other for years. Kiwi—they'd all called her that when they were little—made sure her family got enough and then fed the baby from her own plate, her eyes lowered the whole time. Why was she suddenly so shy, Eva wondered?

A short time later the men rose from the table and Will and Johnny followed. "What are we doing, father?" Will asked in his newly deep voice, which no longer squeaked and made her laugh.

"Is anyone coming?" Johnny added.

"Don't know. I asked them for tomorrow but we'll start today."

Eva watched the men all clatter out of the house but no one laughed. There was no tomfoolery as her father called it. And she caught a worried glance between her mother and Kiwidinok. Without being asked she rose and cleared the plates and cups to the sideboard and poured the water for the washing up.

Chapter Eighteen

THE SUN ROSE on frosted fields that next day as the males of the family along with a few neighbors started the rough and tedious work of sawing and splitting, stripping and cutting the logs William had saved from last winter's clearing of more land. Well dried, the wood was perfect. They used the space a little to the east of where the burned cabin had stood as William was afraid the burned smell would be a problem if they built on the old site.

Migisi was strangely compliant given that this was his house but of course it was on William's land and Migisi was one native who had come to terms with the white man's concept of land ownership. Even though he'd been raised to believe that no one owned the land, the crisscrossing of roads and the building of houses and barns over land that his people had previously believed belonged to everyone helped him see the white man's concept. He didn't like it and he certainly didn't understand it but he did appreciate the kindness of this particular family. Since his own people seemed not to progress at all these days, he was happy to stay here. He just hoped his presence would not bring any more hardship to this helpful family.

He and Kiwidinok had now come back to this land of his childhood to be welcomed here when so many others had shunned them. They had tried living on the reservation provided for the Chippewa tribe as part of their exchange for so much land. They would not go back. This fire of three days past weighed on his mind but he tried to push it away. Kiwidinok was content here and Solomon seemed to belong here as did his younger son. Of course the girl child was so young she had no thoughts on the matter. He glanced across the river. That first child was here, too.

Young Will grabbed the other end of the log Migisi was dragging to the site, lightening his load. He nodded at the boy now almost a man and realized how attached he was to all of this family. For their sake he would do his best to live in this white man's world. And for Kiwidinok, also. The two lifted the log into place where William and Johnny chipped away at it to make it fit tight. He felt like that was what he was doing himself to fit in here.

Back to the pile he went along with this boy, now almost his own height, and together they chose another log to strip of its bark and smooth. Young Will took the lead this time, whistling as he worked. By dinner time Migisi was glad of a rest and especially glad for the stew even if it was white man's food. Sitting for the few moments he needed to eat, he glanced around. The main house was in good repair with two additions added as the family had grown. He had helped with one. The barn was small but tightly built and he certainly saw the need to keep the cow and pig and even the horses sheltered in winter and safe from wolves on summer evenings.

Ah, but over towards the river a few of the original trees still stood where he had played as a boy, a tale no one here but Kiwidinok knew. Watching so many of those trees of his childhood ripped from the earth had hurt so much that he and his wife had left for those few years in search of a place like his childhood home. But those days were gone. He finished his stew and used the bread to sop up the last bits in the gravy. It did taste good.

Someone sat on the log beside him but said nothing. Without even glancing up, Migisi knew it was William's brother, a man he didn't know nearly as well as the others but he saw no reason to fear him. Kiwidinok appeared from behind and wordlessly took both their plates. Robert thanked her and Migisi felt the need to do the same.

"I am sorry for your suffering," the man beside him said.

"Yes."

"The walls will be finished soon." He waved his hand toward a spot beside the new cabin where two men were beginning to shape the roof supports, hard to do with no sawn lumber but they hacked at smaller branches to form the base instead. "Lucky Logan came. He's the only one can do that."

"Yes," Migisi said.

"We'll fix the roof in the spring, you'll see."

"Yes." He turned to Robert. "I thank you," he said and rose to work again. Young Will joined him as they headed once more for the log pile, so much smaller now.

As the day progressed so did the cabin. The many hands had almost finished the roof when horses sounded on the road and everyone paused to see who might be coming to the work bee at this late hour. William walked toward the road and recognized the team pulling a loaded wagon with two people sitting high on the seat. He hadn't thought of his mother except to be glad her room was free for Migisi and Kiwidinok but here she was returning from her two-week sojourn with her friends of long ago who now ran a mill at Arva over to the southwest.

William handed Lucy down while the driver unloaded her cases and carried them to the porch. Even though Catherine and William added their voices to Lucy's in urging the man to start back in the morning, he insisted on leaving immediately. Lucy thanked him profusely and he in turn told her how much her visit had meant to his whole family. William wondered at that. As far as he knew his mother was just going to a quilting bee. He carried her bags inside but returned immediately to his own work on the cabin.

Long after Migisi and Kiwidinok's younger children had fallen asleep inside and the neighbors had returned to their own homes, almost everyone else worked by lantern light to sweep out the new cabin and put on the finishing touches. Robert fastened the hinged door with Migisi's help while William climbed down from the roof after nailing the last cedar shakes in place. Young Will and Johnny cleared scrap from the path before the doorway and Kiwidinok carried her few possessions into the tiny cabin and stowed them in the small cupboard Catherine supplied.

In the morning everyone went back to work, this time with Lucy caring for the children and the smell of fresh cornbread in the air. She was glad to be home; sleeping in her own bedroom had been a treat last night. Even learning of the fire had not disturbed her sleep. This morning, though, she was bursting to tell William and Catherine the news from Arva. Such grand ideas filled her head that she hummed as she tidied up the morning dishes and Eva, who was helping, gave her several sidelong glances. They would not get a word out of her, though, until she was good and ready.

By noon Catherine was back inside to help, having done all she could to get Kiwidinok set up again in the new cabin. The woman was content to cook on her outside fire and Catherine had left her there preparing corn and some kind of bread in a huge fry pan. The wonderful smell followed her inside where her mother-in-law set out plates of steaming food. Everyone crowded around the table.

In the sudden silence of everyone finally eating, William looked up at his mother who had not touched her food but sat watching everyone else. "What is it, Mother?" She gave him a broad smile but said nothing. "Are you feeling well?"

"Yes, of course," she began. "I just…" She picked up her spoon, feeling everyone's eyes on her. "I have news."

"What is it, Mother?" Catherine asked.

Now everyone but Johnny fastened their gaze on her and she sensed their mixed feelings. Some were plainly curious but others were just hungry. "Go on. Eat. I'll tell you after dinner." William shrugged and went back to his meal as did the rest of the family.

When the last bit of bread had swiped across the last plate, Lucy pushed her chair back and rose to her full five-foot height before them all. This was her family, or most of them anyway. Her older son, William, the head of the house, her only other living son, Robert, who would leave for home in a few moments, her cherished daughter-in-law and three of her grandchildren, each well on their way to adulthood. She smiled at them, one by one. "We need a school," she said and sat down again.

For a moment no one spoke. Puzzled looks met her gaze. She could just imagine what they were thinking but she pushed on. "More and more people come here every month with families." Her sons looked confused. Catherine nodded encouragingly even though her brow was creased as well. The boys stole glances at the sideboard and the iced cake waiting there. Eva's mind was somewhere else. "We need a school…to teach all the children."

"But we've always taught them ourselves," William began.

"And you've done a good job, especially you, Catherine." She smiled at her daughter-in-law. "But what about all the others whose parents haven't? Those children have suffered and will continue to suffer."

"Mother, you're right." Catherine glanced around the table, looking for support. "Eva, you and Johnny could still do with another year or two of learning."

"But I'm working with the men now," Johnny shouted.

"And I'm working with you, Mama." Eva glanced at her mother and then turned her fiery eyes on her grandmother. "Don't we know enough for you?" She actually shouted.

Immediately William shushed everyone and Eva grudgingly apologized to her grandmother.

"It's mostly for the rest of the children," Lucy said, "but you can show them the way." She paused. "Can't you?" She looked first at Eva and then at Johnny and smiled.

"Where would this school be, Mother?" Robert's gravelly voice cut in. "Close enough for my two to go?" Once or twice before he had told her about Mary Anne's lack of interest in their children's schooling.

Everyone talked at once as the idea took hold around the table. This was just the kind of thing Lucy wanted; she smiled as she remembered her first thoughts about this. She had been quilting with the group at Arva. They had chatted about the newlyweds who would use this quilt and, of course, about possible children. Lucy had kept her school idea to herself but the idea still burned in her mind. This was what she and John strove for all those years. A civilized country with schools and churches and folks living in harmony. He was gone now but she could work to make this first step happen and, God willing, her family would help. She nodded her head. The room was silent and everyone looked her way.

"Do you want our help, Mother?" Robert grinned at her and her face flushed with pleasure.

When he left for home he took with him news for Mary Anne about the school, certain that this would please her and the children who would most definitely benefit from the teaching as well as playing with others. It would be a boon for the community, too. Why, they could build a schoolhouse and use it for meetings and gatherings. He urged the horse on. He could see the traveling preacher holding church services there on Sundays instead of in someone's overcrowded parlor. Maybe they'd even get enough people to eventually build a church.

Of course those church lands were still a problem but surely they could all insist that Methodists be granted permission to build on them. He could see it all now. The children learning day by day, the adults working together to build a better life, and even his little community growing as more and more businesses bought lots from him and built shops and even small factories. He flicked the reins again.

Mary Anne clapped her hands and jumped up to dance Robert around the room and he was more than pleased to let go of his one niggling worry and celebrate with her. Thomas and Elizabeth looked up from their building blocks where a nearly complete village covered the well-scrubbed pine floor and Robert called to them. "Come! Dance with us."

"We're going to have a school," their mother hollered and the baby cried from the bedroom. The older children joined hands with their parents and together they circled the room. They were making so much noise no one heard the knocking at the door.

Suddenly Robert stopped and dropped his hands. "Who's there?" He reached for the door handle.

"Open the door!"

He glanced back at Mary Anne but she shook her head. Neither of them recognized the voice.

"Garner! We know you're in there."

Mary Anne shooed the children into the bedroom and closed the door on them. Robert looked around the room. The table in the corner held his current woodworking project, the beginnings of a crêche which he hoped to have ready for Christmas. His rifle ought to have been on the hooks over the door but he'd left it on the horse so anxious was he to tell Mary Anne the good news. The broom? He took a deep breath, pushed his wife behind him, and threw open the door.

Thoughts of his near arrest filled his head. Had Matheson come back for him again? But no. The men on the porch were neighbors, both of whom had bought land from him. Logan's hairy fist was poised right in front of Robert's head, ready to knock again. His gaunt face was red with fury.

"Good day, gentlemen." Robert pushed right into Logan's face so that the man had to step back. "What brings you calling this fine fall day?"

Logan's hand dropped to his side but his eyes still smoldered bright and hot. The man beside him, Hanson, was not such a hot-head and actually forced a lopsided smile to his clean-shaven face. He made shoes and all manner of other leather paraphernalia from hats to saddlebags and even little leather toys that brought him a fair amount of custom in his village tannery.

"Well, gentlemen?"

The two exchanged glances. Logan was obviously surprised by Robert's calm and gentlemanly manner. Mary Anne's appearance at his side calmed him as well. Mr. Hanson spoke up. "We need to talk to you…please."

Mary Anne leaned forward. "Come inside, gentlemen. And sit at the table with us." She turned to enter and Robert stood to one side. The men removed their hats and followed Mary Anne. As they made themselves comfortable Mary Anne brewed tea and laid large mugs, milk and sugar on the table before them. She cut slices of applesauce loaf, buttered them, and filled a serving plate. Young Thomas came from the bedroom and looked up expectantly but she shook her head and he went to his toys in the corner.

She brought the large teapot to the table and sat waiting for the tea to steep. "Have some loaf, gentlemen." She passed the plate to Logan but avoided his eyes. "The tea will be ready in a moment."

Mr. Hanson took a slice and set the plate back on the table in front of Mary Anne. Still no one had spoken. Robert seemed content to just sit and wait for the visitors but they seemed to have used up all their words on the doorstep and now stared at the table, their hands, the diminishing applesauce loaf in their hands, anywhere but at her or Robert. Finally she opened her mouth but at the same time Mr. Hanson began.

"Sorry we are to bother you, Mr. Garner." He glanced at her. "Mrs. Garner." Long seconds passed while she and Robert stared at the man, waiting.

"Oh, for mercy's sake, out with it, Hanson." Logan's hard voice took over. "We're here about those pesky redskins."

"It's your brother, not you," Mr. Hanson assured them, nodding his head up and down. He looked at Mr. Logan to carry on.

"What about my brother?" Gone was Robert's soft, respectful tone. Mary Anne tried to catch his eye. "Answer me!"

The children stopped their patter and Mary Anne motioned for Thomas to take his siblings back into the bedroom but the boy didn't move. She got up and took them herself.

In a moment she was back but nothing seemed to have happened at the table. Mr. Logan's sneer still filled his whole face and Mr. Hanson's features were frozen. As for her husband, she'd rarely seen such a look from him.

Softly she pulled her chair out again and sat, not daring to speak.

Mr. Logan glanced at her and she took courage from that. Perhaps whatever was wrong could be resolved. Heaven knew she was heartily sorry for all the strife that seemed to find them and would give anything to live in peace.

"Redskins need to be on the reservations." He paused. "Not on our land."

"Or your brother's." Mr. Hanson glanced furtively at Robert whose eyebrows rose, a sign to Mary Anne of what was coming.

"My brother can have whomever he wishes on his land, sir!" He fairly shouted the last word into Mr. Logan's face. Mary Anne felt her gut tightening and gripped the table. Their guests pushed back from the table but before rising Mr. Logan turned to her.

"Thank you for the tea, ma'am." He turned back to Robert. "Next time may be more than a burned cabin."

Mr. Hanson nodded her way and padded out the door after Logan's hulking figure. She closed it behind them. Robert's shoulders and neck were rigid as she placed her hands on him in a calming effort. Back and forth her fingers kneaded but he said not a word. What was he thinking? Was he as worried as she? Or was he just furious?

She left off comforting her husband and walked to the bedroom to allow the children to come out. They hurried back to their game on the floor and she sat on the settee watching them but seeing nothing. She held her arms crossed over her body, the timeless ache of their emptiness from so long ago leaching into her soul. Yet again, she had a new worry, not just for herself or for Robert or their children but also for Migisi and Kiwidinok and William and Catherine.

Chapter Nineteen

ROBERT LAY AWAKE in the early hours of the morning seeing only the moving pictures in his mind. He saw Logan's visit and the other Logan, the lawyer, whose perfidy had almost cost him everything. His life was such a profusion of unlucky incidents. Not as a child, to be sure, but starting with getting caught on the wrong side—or the right side, depending how you felt—in that cursed war. He'd almost lost Mary Anne and they did lose their baby, he lost money in the move back this side of the border and then his name was blackened because of a jailbreak when he was illegally jailed. He shuddered at the thought of that ride to Beasley's farm and his weakened father's death there. Mary Anne shifted beside him. He didn't want to wake her.

His hands clenched at his sides, stiff and straining. He flexed them and carefully eased his shoulder and neck muscles. Turning onto his side he carefully snuggled against his wife needing her but trying not to wake her. She had seemed so frail yesterday. The picture of her walking aimlessly when he found her all those years ago was never far from his mind and he knew that even though they now had three healthy children, that one they'd lost had taken with her a large slice of his Mary Anne's soul. In spite of himself he stroked her bare arm—she hadn't got out her flannel nightgown yet.

She snuggled into him and a soft groan of pleasure floated between them. Turning to face him she stroked his face and neck, the taut muscles of his bare arms, and he felt her hot breath on his chest. He would not sleep now. With every touch of her hand, her breath, her body as she pushed herself against him, his worries disappeared and, if he did think at all, he marveled at his joy in her.

The next Sunday he gathered his family into the wagon, Mary Anne beside him, and drove the team to William's. Several of their friends met there for a service led by one of them each month but this time a preacher would be there. The man traveled from one end of the sparsely settled territory to the other on horseback marrying those who'd had to wait until a preacher might be available and those who'd done their own version of a wedding service and now lived as man and wife until their union could be blessed.

He wondered if Logan and Hanson would show their faces. They hadn't actually admitted setting the cabin on fire but Robert was certain they were part of it. He tried to break off his train of thought. The leaves were almost gone now, with just a few of the hardier yellows of the willows along the way. The oranges had faded to brown but the vibrant reds of the sumac pleased him mightily and he thought for a second about capturing it all with paints. Would that he could.

"You're quiet." Mary Anne spoke at his side. "Worried?"

He smiled at her. "Enjoying the scenery."

"Your mother might talk about a school. Do you think so?"

"I hope she does."

They came upon wagons lined up along the roadway, the horses hitched to the split rail fence and swishing their tails in the dappled sunlight. The yard was awash with multi-colored leaves and squirrels dashing about in their quest for walnuts and acorns. Robert recognized every one of the five wagons; he pulled his horses in alongside and helped his family out. The children ran for the house. Baby Russell tried to follow until Mary Anne took his pudgy hand.

....

Thomas Brush Brown, the preacher was called. A short and thick man, his bald head glistened with sweat as his voice raised louder and louder. His waving hand pointed up to Heaven and down to Hell, out at the small crowd and back to his own cheerful face. Not ordained he had the permission of the Methodist Episcopal church to look after the flock in outlying areas. His smile shone through every happy word and was only gone from his florid face when he broached the sinfulness against which the faithful must surely guard themselves and their loved ones.

When the children could no longer remain attentive and the adults were almost to the same point—those that weren't asleep—Thomas Brush Brown ran his handkerchief over his shining pate, softened his voice, and slowed his delivery to the final Amen. But the service was not yet over. One of the neighbor women rose to lead them all in a final hymn, Blessed Assurance. Mothers kept watch on children and fathers stifled their yawns as they stood for the last bit of the service. Robert thought there must be a better singer than Mrs. Lindsay but no sooner had his mind wandered in that direction than the door crashed open right in the midst of the gathering.

The singing stopped and a shocked silence filled the room. Robert and William, nearest the door, both rushed forward. Standing before them all and puffing like an angry bull whose barnyard has just been invaded was Mr. Logan.

William took the man's arm and led him off to one side. The preacher motioned for the singing to continue but few joined in and those that did soon gave up. He closed the meeting with a hurried prayer and a loud buzz filled the room. Lucy had hoped to use this time for her school announcement but no one could even hear her tentative broaching of the subject with all the talking. Like bees around a honey pot the churchgoers gathered in small groups of twos and threes throughout the packed room and glanced over at those trying to calm Mr. Logan.

Before long that one group was much louder than all the others. Robert had avoided contact with Mr. Logan but now stared across the room to where the man gestured with his long arms and pointed outside. Robert's eyes followed his pointing but he could see nothing from where he stood. He made his way to the door and stepped out. All was calm and quiet, much quieter than inside. What was the man upset about? He glanced south of the house where Migisi and Kiwidinok sat on chairs in front of their newly built cabin. Suddenly he understood. He watched a few moments before heading back inside to confront the man.

William had beaten him to it and now had his arm across Logan's shoulders, a gesture that seemed to be having some effect as the man had lost the fierce red face and nodded almost deferentially as he listened to William's words. The ladies soon shooed the men out of the way while they opened their hampers onto the table and arranged a luscious array of food. Eva stood with her mother helping as though she herself was one of the adults. His niece would soon be starting a home of her own, no doubt. Robert looked around the room but could see no young men of the appropriate age. Ah, well, soon enough she'd find someone.

Once everyone had finished and the women were busy clearing up the leftovers and packing freshly washed plates and dishes into their hampers, the men drifted outside. Lucy's hands weren't needed to clear up with all the younger ones crowding around; she sat in the rocker across the room, glad of the respite but fully involved in listening to the chatter and every so often adding to it. One woman mentioned the scarcity of slates, telling how long she'd had to wait until there was a supply at Mr. Logan's store. This was Lucy's chance.

"We ought to start a school," she said. The talk went on. She stood up and spoke louder. "We ought to have a school right here."

Everyone turned her way, their hands still. For a split second all was silent. What had she done? At once voices rose, a note of excitement in each one.

"Could we?"

"Never thought…"

"How?" This last came from Catherine who beamed at Lucy. The other women began to suggest ideas and places and contacts and fundraisers and on and on until Lucy spoke again. "We need to find a teacher. Does anyone have an idea?"

"We could ask the preacher."

"Where is he?"

"Outside still, I think." Catherine opened the door. "Yes, there he is." She called to him and beckoned him inside where the women set upon him with their excitement and eventually gave him a chance to actually answer their questions. He agreed to look for someone but just to be sure Lucy suggested putting an advertisement in Mr. Mackenzie's paper out of York.

The idea of a school took hold in the fledgling community and though there were a few holdouts most of the neighbors contacted over the next few weeks supported the idea. The old loyalists from years before still remembered their reasons for coming here in the first place and one of those was for the freedom to educate their children as they saw fit. Thomas Brush Brown spoke of the need for schools wherever he did church services. His endorsement went far in convincing the entire community of the wisdom of the project.

Since her children were older now and would soon be past the age of attending school, Catherine offered to have the classes take place right in her own living room. Of course the matter of a teacher still needed settling but in the meantime she and Lucy agreed they could take on the task. After all, only about ten children would be coming and four would be Robert's oldest two and William's Eva and Johnny.

Right after Christmas the freshly fallen snow was crisscrossed with sleigh runners as parents brought their children for their first day of school. Catherine invited Solomon and his younger brother to join the others, a suggestion that caused William to raise his eyebrows but he said nothing as the two came through the door that cold blustery morning. He buttoned on his heavy clothes and left for his morning chores. Young Will escaped with his father, a triumphant smile on his rosy-cheeked face.

Six neighboring children made it that first morning, bringing the total to twelve. They brought from home what slates and styluses, papers and books they had, and settled in on the floor and around the table as Catherine directed them. Lucy took the smallest ones, Migisi's son and a little girl, to her room and settled them on her brightly colored round rug. She pulled out the Christmas story book and began to read to the two who sat with their faces upturned and their eyes wide.

Catherine divided the rest into two groups, her own two and an older boy in one and all the rest approximately the same age in the other. The older ones she set to work figuring while she used the few slates she had to see what each child knew so far. The morning flew by. When William and Young Will came for their dinner the children pulled out their own packages of food and filled the room with their excited voices. At the table William sat with his mother while Catherine shushed the boisterous children and served up the stew she'd made the night before. Eva preferred to help her rather than sit with the little ones and Johnny still wore his forlorn face when he sat next to his father.

The young son of the fiery Mr. Logan had come with Robert that morning. The boy only smiled after great encouragement. He sat beside Robert's Thomas but hardly ate a morsel from his dinner sack. When Catherine urged him he made an effort but she worried about the flash of fear she'd seen in his eyes whenever she spoke to him. Softly does it, she thought, and worried what the boy's father would think if he saw Solomon and his Chippewa brother in the classes with the other children.

At the end of the day horse-drawn sleighs tinkled into the yard full of children playing in the snow, their first day of school over. Solomon was throwing snowballs with the others; his Native brother stood by his side. Mr. Logan had just loaded up Robert's two and his own son when Thomas called out. "Goodbye, Solomon." The tall black boy waved at the child he'd had such fun teaching the finer points of making snowballs. Mr. Logan's sleigh blocked the other parents but he happened to glance around and see the little Chippewa boy a few steps away. He laid the lines across the horse's back so hard it jumped forward and barely missed upsetting them all with its wide turn and careening rush out the snowy laneway onto the road.

"We'll have some trouble there," Catherine said to Lucy as they waved to the children.

"Maybe we could teach the parents?" Lucy chuckled as she walked back into the warmth of the house.

The school met as often as the snowy weather would permit that winter and the children came to know the drills well and enjoyed completing their work. Catherine took to teaching immediately. "It's a lot like mothering," she confessed to William one night in bed. "Of course our two would be much happier if someone else were doing it."

Her husband chuckled but said nothing. She didn't tell him about the Logan boy's problems. The child said very little and even though she coaxed him to read aloud and knew he wanted to, he spoke so softly she could barely hear him. She just couldn't spend all her time with him and her mother-in-law was fully occupied with her charges. Someone else. She needed someone else. Aha! Solomon. She'd seen him with the others and knew him to be kind and fair. He was almost a man. Migisi's influence was obvious in the boy's gentle manner and ready smile.

From that day forward she matched the two whenever she could. The Logan boy now had a friend and protector both during school and at play times outside. His reading improved immensely and she had hopes that he'd soon start answering her questions so that she could actually hear him. The boy's father frowned but said nothing when he saw the two together. Catherine decided he was merely annoyed with the Indians as he still glared at Migisi and Kiwidinok whenever they crossed his path.

When spring came and the longer days meant more time to prepare the land for planting Johnny and Solomon and a couple of the other boys boycotted the school to help their fathers; the little ones still came and that included Mr. Logan's boy. Now, however, he had no protector and while the father seemed happier, the boy regressed and retreated back into his former self. He was so forlorn outside that one sunny day Kiwidinok noticed him sitting alone and spoke to him. From then on the boy followed her around and she took time from her own work to help him. His eyes began to dance again and Catherine smiled.

But it was not to last.

One day Mr. Logan appeared just in time to see his son hand in hand with Kiwidinok as they walked from her cabin back to Catherine's yard. Tying up a young child's bootlace Catherine did not see Mr. Logan stomping her way but from ten steps away she heard his shouting.

"You stop this, Mrs. Garner!"

She straightened up and stared at him from the porch. "Tying shoelaces, Mr. Logan?"

His face reddened and he pointed toward his son. "Letting that heathen touch my boy."

Catherine tried to keep her voice level. She would not be drawn into his anger. "Your boy is happy here, Mr. Logan, and Ki-wi-di-nok—she spoke the name slowly for emphasis—is a large part of the reason. She gets paid nothing but helps the boy out of the kindness of her heart."

"Don't want her touching him…even speaking to him." His face reddened. "Should be on the reserve." He took a menacing step toward her where he stopped, eyes glaring, daring her to disagree. A little more softly, he said, "With the rest of those bloody heathens."

Out of the corner of her eye, Catherine saw the pair approaching and swallowed her anger for the sake of the boy. "Thank you, Kiwidinok," she said as she stepped around Logan and took the boy's hand. The man grabbed his child and dragged the struggling boy to his wagon. Catherine watched them climb into the seat and begin to pull away.

"Wait!" Young Thomas shouted and Elizabeth yelled, too. "Don't forget us, Mr. Logan."

The man jerked the horses to a stop but didn't even look at the two children as they hurried into the back of the wagon. Before they sat down he whipped the team away, jerking Robert's children so hard they fell back onto the boards. Catherine ran a few steps forward but the wagon disappeared around the corner of the house. All she could do was pray the man would calm himself before someone got hurt. Tomorrow she'd talk to Robert.

BUT ROBERT DIDN'T COME the next day and when he did return he had other things on his mind. He handed a letter to William and waited while his brother read it. The children had not all arrived yet so the brothers were alone with Lucy in the kitchen.

"What is it?" She grabbed a towel and dried her hands as she struggled to see over Robert's shoulder. "That's Helen's handwriting, isn't it?"

"Yes, Mother." William pulled out a chair and motioned for her to sit. "Timothy is ill."

"What's wrong." She knew how long this letter might have taken to reach them. "Does she need help?"

Her sons sat with her and together they discussed each word of the short letter but also the things it didn't say. Timothy had a wasting sickness, a malady that came upon him before Christmas but he just couldn't shake it and was not able to work. Helen and her brood had taken over all the chores as well as caring for him. She was just letting them know but stressed they were not to come, especially Robert. She knew how difficult crossing between the two countries could be for him.

Suddenly the door opened and Catherine ushered the children into the house, glanced at the gathering at the table and proceeded to send the children to their appointed tasks. Lucy nodded at each of her sons as they vacated the table and slowly rose to start her day with the little ones.

Outside the two brothers chatted by Robert's wagon. "I forgot this," he said and pulled another letter from his pocket. This one was addressed to Catherine but William opened it anyhow. "It's from a teacher." His features relaxed as he read. "Catherine will want to see this right away." He strode back into the house, Robert behind him.

Catherine glanced over the short letter and called to her mother-in-law. "Mother, come see!"

Lucy looked at the three of them and her eyes went to the page in Catherine's hand. "Who's it from?" Her voice rose and she reached out her hand.

> *Dear Mrs. Garner*
>
> *Pardon my short note but the postman is standing at the door of my room waiting for this; hence, I must rush.*
>
> *I would like to apply for the teaching position you offer in your advertisement in Mackenzie's newspaper. My education has been in letters and numbers with logic and scientific formulae as well, subjects which I have worked hard to learn in the classroom here. I also have spent much time studying writing and poetics. I will send proof of my matriculation as soon as I receive it in a few weeks.*
>
> *Please consider me for the teaching position you so fortuitously have offered.*
>
> *With kindest wishes, I am*
> *Yours most truly,*
> *Reuben Stone.*

The women danced around the table full of staring students and William and Robert laughed and nodded their heads in unison. Within a very short time the teacher would be theirs. Robert was happy but not as happy as the ladies who hoped soon to have their time back to themselves again, and perhaps their home. Out the door he rushed, anxious to spread the good news to Mary Anne and anyone else he met on his way. The next thought he had was a real school building. Perhaps Mr. Logan's other brother would help build it but first a site must be chosen.

Peter Logan, the third of the three Logans lived with his wife and family on the next concession to the east not that far from William and Catherine. He had not yet sent his children to the Garners' school as he and his wife taught their five children themselves. Ranging in age from four to fourteen his family had the advantage of learned parents whose love of reading and rhetoric often led to far-reaching topics of discussion around their supper table; in fact, on many a night the children were late to bed as the talk went on well beyond the eating and the children were not excused until Peter deemed bedtime was nigh.

When Peter Logan heard about the teacher coming and the need for a school building he and his wife decided to pay a Sunday afternoon call to their neighbors to the west. The five children packed into the back and sitting on cushions made especially for the purpose by Mrs. Logan, the family negotiated the couple of miles of improved roads to the Garner homestead. On this lovely late June day Eva had taken all the children outside for a rousing game of stickball.

Inside the adults sat primly on the newly purchased settee and chairs sipping their tea and catching up on what news there was. At a lull in the conversation Lucy mentioned the school and immediately Catherine announced the imminent arrival of the new teacher. He would be there to start classes in a few weeks. "The only problem," she said, "is we have no school house."

"Surely with a full-time teacher we need a school," Lucy said. She looked at Mrs. Logan. "Would not your children come?"

"What about it, Peter?" William asked.

Mr. Logan placed his tea cup on the low table beside him and leaned forward on the settee. His dark eyebrows furrowed. "As a matter of fact, this is why we've come." His wife smiled at him and nodded, her blonde hair wisping around her ears, pretty even while it was unmanageable. Lucy tucked her own curls, now gray but still unruly, back behind her ears. "Well, tell them, Mr. Logan," his wife whispered.

"I'll provide the land for a two-room school." He sat back and crossed his arms over his trim person, a smile dimpling his red cheeks above his coarse beard.

Everyone talked at once. Lucy and Catherine looked at each other with relief in their eyes. They'd get their house and their time back. William spoke first. "Why two rooms?" he asked.

"Thought the teacher could live in one and teach in the other."

When the school opened in mid-August, the community not only had a new teacher but a well-equipped school paid for by the generosity of everyone living within five miles. For some it was a long ride but the parents felt the sacrifice was worth it. The only stipulation was that older boys would miss on the days they were needed at home. Harvest needed hands. The rest of the time the school would be full, now with fifteen pupils. Lucy's plan had happily borne fruit. She was certain nothing could go wrong.

Chapter Twenty

SOON AFTER THE OPENING of the new school Eva stopped complaining and actually looked forward to going each day. Catherine observed the roses in her freckled cheeks and her willingness to do her homework every night. Johnny was a different matter. Even though his figures gave him no problem he still wrestled with reading, saying the letters jumped around on the pages of the Bible. Maybe if they had a different book, Catherine thought, but none were to be had nearby even if they could afford one.

In a private conversation with her husband as they sat on the porch one fall evening, she mentioned her fears that Johnny would never learn to read. William couldn't understand it as he liked to read both for the joy of the words themselves and the new information he gleaned. "He must apply himself. A few swipes of the hickory stick might help," he told Catherine.

"No. That's not it. He tries, I know he does." She sat forward and looked into his eyes. "I think he doesn't see well."

"He sees the numbers well enough."

"I know, but he likes them." She shrugged her shoulders. "He doesn't care about stories, William."

"Maybe the doctor…?"

Catherine agreed and they decided to take the boy to Centreville when the harvest was done.

"You going to see that brother of yours any time soon?" Mr. Logan called over to Robert the moment he entered the store. At least his voice was friendly. As soon as the new school opened the man had actually become civil and even smiled now whenever he saw his neighbor. He no longer had to deal with Migisi and Kiwidinok, Robert figured.

"Why?" He fingered the horse harness lying on the broad counter.

"A letter came for him." He fished into one of the slots behind the counter and handed over a cream colored envelope lettered in black ink.

Robert saw Helen's handwriting and tore open the letter.

"Opening his mail now, are you?"

"It's from our sister. With the sick husband." He scanned the short message and ran for the door. "Got to take it to William," he called over his shoulder as he slammed out of the store and ran to his barn. He was harnessing the horse when Mary Anne came in.

"Where—?"

He fished in his jacket and handed her the letter. "William's. I have to tell him."

She helped him finish, handed the letter back and kissed him. "Godspeed," she whispered but he was already mounted and urging the horse outside.

When he arrived William and Catherine sat finishing their dinner and he noted for a second how strange that they should be alone, but, of course, the children were at school. He shoved the opened letter into his brother's hand. "Pardon me. I opened it." Catherine pulled out a chair beside her and motioned for him to sit.

William's face was white. Catherine grabbed the letter from him. "Oh, my God," she whispered.

"We have to go, William." Robert's voice cracked even more than normal. "She needs us."

"But, the harvest." William's words betrayed his worry, both for his sister and his crops. Both were life or death matters.

Lucy came out of her room. "What is it?" She hobbled to the table and her two sons blanched even more.

"It's Timothy, Mama," Robert began.

"They must go, Mother." Catherine stood a moment by the table as though considering what to do first to help William on his way.

"Dead. Oh, my poor Helen." Lucy dropped the letter on the table and held her head in her wrinkled hands. "Take me with you," she whispered.

All of the others spoke up, listing reasons why she could not go. They were going to ride, not take a wagon, and ride fast. They would travel light, knowing they had a home to go to. Catherine reached across the table and held Lucy's hands in her own. "Your sons will go, Mother. You stay with me." Lucy nodded.

The brothers rushed away, stopping at Robert's home only long enough to tell Mary Anne where they were going and to grab a change of clothes. He borrowed a fresh horse from Mr. Logan. William was surprised to see how friendly the two had become. They took the same roads they'd ridden so many years before but now their father was dead and their mother was safe on the farm with Catherine. The roads had improved so that they covered the distance to Fort Erie much faster than last time.

Luckily they found passage for themselves and their horses on a small steamer plying the Niagara River over to Buffalo and in no time they were pounding down the road toward Helen and Timothy's home. Her letter had been postmarked only the week before, making the brothers hopeful they wouldn't be too late. For the letter had not only held the news of her husband's death but the threat of something almost as bad. A land speculator held Timothy's note and was pushing Helen to vacate the premises. Because of Timothy's illness, payments had not been made. Their bereaved sister and her family might well be homeless by the time they arrived.

Southeast of Buffalo they found the road to Helen's farm by asking along the way. Late on the fourth day they pounded up to her home. All was quiet. Horses tied to the railing by the door neighed a welcome. A window shutter hung awkwardly to one side but through the window a feeble light shone. No face appeared.

They tied up at the railing beside the other horses and, rifles in hand, mounted the steps and banged on the door. For a long moment all was silent. Boots shuffled inside and the door opened but this was not Helen, nor, indeed, any of her children. Had they found the wrong farm? The beefy man blocking the door before them simply stared.

Robert pushed ahead of William. "Mrs. Greenstone here?"

"Who wants to know?"

William answered. "William and Robert Garner, sir." He stretched up to his full six feet. "And who might you be?"

Before the man could answer Helen's voice came from inside. "I'm here, I'm___." The brothers pushed forward at the sound of her cry, rifles in hand, tempers flaring. The cabin was so dark they could barely see but, in the light of the lone candle on the table, their sister's frightened eyes shone bright. Two men had her bound to the chair but her hands were free, presumably to sign the papers spread before her on the table. Pen and ink lay beside the documents.

Robert ran to Helen and loosed her bindings; William pointed his rifle at the men who by now realized they were beaten.

"What are you signing, Helen?" William asked. He picked up the papers.

"Ha! I'm not signing anything for these weasels." She pointed their way and then gave William her steely eyes. "As you well know."

Robert made his way around the cabin peering here and there and even taking a few steps up the ladder to the loft to take a look. "Where are the boys, Helen?" He shook his head at the offered seat at the table. "In the barn?"

The two strangers glanced at each other. They hadn't thought of children.

"Went to gather wood. With all that's gone on, Tim didn't get any cut…" her voice died away and for the first time the brave and defiant Helen of their childhood slipped behind a shadow of pain.

William pointed in the direction of the intruders. "Have these two hurt you?"

"Only with threats and spreading fear. Even before Tim passed." She almost growled. "They couldn't wait to get rid of us all."

Robert pushed his rifle barrel into the back of one of the men. "Enjoy threatening sick men and stealing from widows, do you?" The man shook his head but said nothing. The other, with the neat coat and tidy hair caught in a black ribbon at the back of his neck, attempted to stand but thought better of it when he felt Robert's weapon in his back. "We are owed money." His voice paused with each word but he stared at the table.

"How much?" William asked Helen. When she answered he let out a whistle.

"Timothy..."

"You don't need to explain, Helen," Robert said. "We ought to have been here months ago." He shook his head and glanced at William whose own eyes were bleak as he gently nodded. They talked a little with the better dressed of the two men and came to an agreement. The men agreed to come back in two days' time for Helen's signature but William insisted they would also give her what she was due for the money Timothy already paid for the farm. They agreed.

Just as the tension eased, the door crashed open and Helen's sons rushed to her side. All three boys looked from the two men to their uncles.

"Remember your uncles, boys?" She turned to William and Robert. "This is Thomas. And the twins." Their uncles nodded to each of them. "And these men have bought the farm."

The oldest, Thomas, turned to Helen. "Where will we live, Mama?" That question had not as yet been addressed. Her brothers, of course, wanted her to bring her family to settle in Nissouri but Helen had grown used to her life on the south side of the border and, tempting though it was to be near her family, she wondered what Timothy's wishes would have been. He had never said.

She managed to smile at all these males around the table, yet not answer her son's question. The truth was she didn't know what she wanted. Just at this moment she needed to get dinner on the table for her family, expanded as it was by two extra mouths.

In the end, she agreed to accompany her brothers back across the border and none of them thought for a second they would have any trouble taking her and her family to live with them. When the mortgage holder came back, alone this time, Helen readily signed away the land and pocketed the small pouch the man gave her. William and Robert stood on either side as she stood and shook hands with the man but Thomas hung back. His two brothers stayed in the loft where they were tying up the last of their possessions in a large sack Robert had provided.

Helen's wagon was loaded in the yard; with a heavy heart she took her boys on a last walk around the farmyard and stood to one side as William settled the fourteen-year-old twins on the wagon out of the cold. Thomas scowled as he climbed up beside his mother, too proud to be helped by anyone. Robert's last glance as they lumbered down the road to Buffalo was of the money man standing, arms akimbo, on the bare porch now stripped bare.

Finding a boat large enough to take them and all their possessions proved difficult as traffic across the river had slowed with the oncoming weather. Robert's connections helped, though, and by nightfall they were all safely across and unloading at the large loading dock still standing at the tumbledown fort.

Just as they had all the horses settled, the boys in their spots, and Helen ready to crack the whip, the sound of thundering hooves announced three riders on the road who pulled to a stop before the wagon. William and Robert cantered forward. Helen put her arm on Thomas' sleeve.

"Who are you?" The voice pierced the frosty air.

William told their story pointing first to Helen and then to her three sons who stared at the uniformed men with their snorting horses. Thomas stole a glance at his mother but she didn't move. The soldier moved not a muscle but his eyes took in each of them in turn, lingering a moment longer on Helen in her widow's weeds, her fiery red hair escaping around her white face and her shoulders thrust backwards in a stiff challenge.

"What of you two?" He nodded first at William and then at Robert.

"We've come from Nissouri to rescue our sister's family." William was calm and respectful. "William Garner is my name, sir."

The man looked at his companions; one of them pointed at Robert.

"And you?" he asked.

"I am his brother, too. And hers." Robert was loathe to mention his name. The old fear came back to haunt him. But it was no use.

"Name?"

He sighed, looked at William, and answered. "Robert Garner, sir. Also of Nissouri Township."

No one said anything for a few moments. The soldiers simply stared at everyone all over again until finally the leader huddled with his fellows in a close group. Robert thought of kicking his horse forward and outrunning them but one look at William and he gave up the idea. He must not let them know he'd fought for the Americans. The sunlight slanted lower and lower in the sky. A chill reached up his spine and he shivered. The twins talked softly but young Thomas and Helen said nothing.

The soldiers broke their formation and flanked Robert, effectively cutting him off from both the wagon and William, who edged in as close as he could. At least he could hear the leader's words.

"I remember you…from Niagara." He turned to William. "And you were there, too. Weren't you?"

William and Robert looked at each other. Surely this was not their jail escapade coming back after so many years. "I don't know what you mean, sir."

Robert spoke up. "I've never met you. Sir."

The man was not sure. His eyes went from one to the other and Robert's stomach lurched as he thought he did recognize the man who had jailed them with their father. But he had helped them escape, too. Surely he was not carrying a grudge after all this time.

Back and forth his eyes went from William to Robert, his predicament now becoming clear. He could not arrest them, as he seemed to desire, without his own part in the whole scheme being laid bare. And he didn't want to discuss it in front of his two subordinates; that much was clear.

Neither brother had given the man a thought after they escaped with their father. Robert had assumed their ruse locking the man up in the cell had worked but perhaps the jailer's innocence was questioned? Maybe he had been punished for letting them all go? Robert glanced back at the wagon before speaking again. "We must get the lady and her children out of the cold, sir. Her husband has died. She has lost her farm. She must move to a strange place where neither she nor her children know a soul. Surely that is enough, sir." He stroked his restless horse's neck. "Can you not find it in your heart to let us pass?"

"My brother is right, sir. We must go."

The man pulled his horse back and nodded at the other two to do the same.

William spoke. "Once again, we thank you, sir." He motioned to Helen and their small procession started again along the long road to Nissouri and home but before they had gone far a voice called out behind them. "We won't forget, Garner. Better watch your back."

Part Three
The Rising Rebels

Chapter Twenty-One

Nissouri Township
Fall, 1831

LUCY LAID THE NEEDLE AND THREAD on the table beside her chair and with the small scissors snipped the last threads. Her stiff fingers smoothed the soft wool of the prettiest dress she had ever made. High-necked with long sleeves, it had so many tiny white buttons up the back she had struggled to get them all sewn on. Eva had insisted on a pale blue although both Catherine and Lucy warned she'd never get the wear out of it. Now that it was finished, however, Lucy thought the girl had chosen well.

Over the years she'd learned to take more pleasure in her sewing but in the early days with John, milking a cow had suited her better. How she missed his dimpled chin and his ready smile always on hand to brighten even the worst of days. He would not see this granddaughter married and, indeed, had missed most of her growing up. A tiny surge of pain plagued her side and she took a tortured breath.

"Mother?" A knock came on her bedroom door.

"Yes, Catherine," she answered and laid the dress over the bed beside her. "Come in, my dear."

Catherine's eyes went straight to the dress. "Finished?" Her hand swept over the fabric, fingered the dainty collar, and smoothed the full skirt. "She'll adore it, Mother." She slipped out to her chores.

Lucy smiled. Her daughter-in-law was right. Eva would see the dress on the bed when she came home from helping Mr. Stone with the younger children in the growing school. Once they were married they would live together in the other room there. She said again a silent thanks for the preacher being nearby.

She just hoped her sons would return soon from their trip to York, and with good news. Why could the two of them not agree? Robert's difficulties had been many, she knew, especially during the war. Why, though, could he not forget it all and settle down to farm with Mary Anne? And William, always the good son. He went his own way measuring himself against his father's worth years after John's death.

She followed Catherine to the kitchen and began to place dishes on the worn pine table. Suddenly the door flew open and in walked her son, and if his broad smile was any indication, his trip had been fruitful. Catherine ran to him and helped him remove his muddy boots. He must have been anxious to get home to ride all that way in the drenching rains.

No sooner had they got William settled than Will and Johnny came in with Eva from her day at the school. Her brothers, both still single and a little envious of their sister's impending marriage, missed no opportunity to tease her, in spite of her ability to give back as good as she got.

"OUR FAMILY IS CHANGING." Catherine sat on the edge of the bed braiding her graying hair and thinking of Eva's wedding gown. Tears came to her eyes just as they had to Eva's when she'd seen her grandmother's work. Soon she'd be a married woman.

On the other side of the bed William dropped his trousers and pushed them under the bed, a habit she hated. He turned toward her. "Does it worry you?"

"No…yes. I don't know."

"It's just different." He crawled in beside her and pulled her to him.

"Soon we'll be the grandparents." She looked back at his crinkled eyes and thinning hair. "And your mother a great grandmother." She snuggled against him. He didn't answer. "William, what happened in York?" He cleared his throat.

He and Robert had made the trip to put forward their case to the government representative because Robert's land still did not seem to be his own. Whenever he tried to sell a plot or get a boundary line changed or get help with the road maintenance or do anything that involved the powers higher up, he ran into roadblocks. Mr. Logan, the lawyer in Centreville, now did everything he could to help them but his hands were tied. There was nothing for it but to have a meeting with Strachan and have it out once and for all. That was what he had persuaded Robert to do.

And that was why Robert was still in York. The man had refused to see them, even though they had an appointment. When the time came, his minion ushered them out the door and gave every indication they would not be welcomed back. Robert had exploded.

He'd tried to calm his brother, William told Catherine, but his temper was unstoppable. Always had been. The clerk finally had to call in the guard and the whole thing ended up with Robert in jail.

"Where is he now?" She'd get no sleep this night, Catherine thought. "He came home with you, did he not?"

William said nothing.

She threw off the quilt and jumped out of bed to stare at her husband in the dim lantern light. The silence stretched. She put one knee on the bed. "He's still in York! In jail! You left him there." In all the years and through all they'd suffered, she had never thought to see this day when her husband would simply abandon his brother far from home, with no help and no hope.

He started to speak but her hands flashed up between them. She would not hear him. A look of amazement stole across his face. He pushed the quilt away, eased his legs out of bed and stood with his back to her. His whole body seemed to sag as he inched around the bed and headed for the door. He was leaving, dodging the argument. Again. His eyes avoided her but his sloping shoulders and utterly desolate face so softened her heart that she reached out to him.

"What can I do?" she whispered.

"Talk to me," he said and she pulled him back to bed where they talked half the night before finally slipping into troubled sleep.

ALMOST TWO WEEKS LATER, the morning dawned cool but sunny, lighting the fall colors all around the farm. Up and down the road buggies were tied to the split rail fence; this was a celebration not to be missed. The men had rushed through their morning chores so as to be ready for whatever orders Catherine had for them, while she, Lucy, and Kiwidinok labored with the wedding feast, the tables under the big tree—William and his boys set these up—and, finally, to dressing themselves and Eva. Near the time, Helen had come in with her brood and nothing would do but she had to lend Eva her treasured hatpin to fix the veil and its flowered base to Eva's beautiful braided hair. None of these women had ever had such a fascinating piece for their own weddings, a circumstance which only heightened their pleasure as they laughed and talked with the bride.

When all was ready William and Catherine led their daughter out of the house and across the leaf-strewn grass to a small platform built specially for the occasion by Migisi and where the preacher and the bridegroom stood in the dappled sunlight. Eva stepped up beside Mr. Stone and the sunlight sparkled on her headpiece and the bits her grandmother had sewn into the veil. Lucy thought of those Greek goddesses she had seen in a book years before in Niagara.

Most of the guests moved to see better but Lucy had a prime spot. Young Will had brought a chair from the house just for her; she was ever so thankful. She wasn't sure she could stand long today; the pain came and went but she said nothing. This was Eva's day.

The preacher drew the two together to face him and the words of the ceremony drifted out over those assembled there. Her thoughts wandered away from the words to her own day—hers and John's. How she missed him. And her children's weddings.

Well, she'd only been at William and Catherine's. Robert and Helen, both here today, had each married far from home. She glanced off to the side where Robert stood with Mary Anne. She held his arm but his thoughts were so tightly locked inside that only his rigid pursing of his lips, which his mother knew so well, showed his discomfiture.

She did not understand why William had left Robert behind in York. From the look of things since he'd arrived back home a couple of days after William, neither did Robert. So far neither had talked to her about it and Catherine's words had been few for which she was glad. She tried to stifle a groan but Catherine glanced her way; she smiled back.

When the party began Lucy kept her chair until Young Will moved her to the table where she could rest her arms in between bites. People had brought chairs to set at the table so that everyone sat for the wedding feast. Friends and neighbors, those who'd settled back when William and Catherine did and those who'd come later, had all brought food as well so the tables were laden with bounty. A real harvest of blessings, she thought as she watched people around her talking and eating, smiling and licking lips in an endless dance of moving parts.

She ate a little, sipped a little, and listened a lot but the hubbub seemed not to pierce her own private bubble as though her ears were plugged up from some malady. Down the table Eva and Mr. Stone—she ought to start thinking of him as Reuben—seemed to look only at each other. Their plates were heaped with food but not much was going into their mouths. The girl favored her with her auburn hair and freckles. Even her eyes were that special blue passed down from her own father. The Harpers were strong in other ways, too, and she'd needed that back in the day.

But enough of reminiscing. The couple rose to dance in the grass as the fiddler began to play. Everyone circled around and Eva broke from her husband's arms and waved the guests to join them. Lucy's brave grandson supported her as she tried a few steps and marveled at how well her joints behaved.

Soon Robert came to help her to a chair again, sitting by her side for quite some time. Was he using her as an excuse not to be part of the frivolity? She turned to him. His forehead creased over his widow's peak hairline and his square jaw seemed jammed tight. A small tic started on his cheek above his freshly trimmed beard, blacker than anyone's she knew, and she could see what this feud with his brother was costing him. She patted his knee, clad in his Sunday best trousers. His features relaxed.

"Try to forget, my son," she whispered.

His eyes, though lined with worry, twinkled blue at her and his smile stopped the tic on his face. "Mother, you always see through me," he said.

"I don't know about that…but I do know you." Another pat on his trousers. "And you've been such…" she grimaced and tried to continue "a comfort…" but her face contorted. "Ah…" The pain struck hard and she lost her words. Robert's eyes swam before her, concern and worry wiping away anything else. His lips moved but she couldn't understand…

He caught her as she fell.

They laid her on her bed and Catherine shooed everyone away. Too much excitement. She unfastened Lucy's collar buttons. The color came back into her mother-in-law's skin as she bathed the beloved face with warm water from the reservoir on the stove, all the while whispering nonsense under her breath. Lucy had slowed this last year. She and William had mentioned it and tried to make her do less. "Seventy-two…not today, Mother…sons need you…I…"

"You…what did you say?"

Catherine jumped off the bed. The wet cloth flew out of her hands. She grabbed for it but missed. She stared at her mother-in-law. Bright blue eyes watched her. And grinned at her. Catherine's own lips parted but such a feeling of joy and relief and anxiety and she knew not what overtook her that no words came out.

"Cat got your tongue, girl?"

"I…no, you gave us a scare, Mother."

"Didn't mean to."

"No. Of course you didn't." Catherine was back in control. Lucy seemed to be just fine now and even spoke of getting up and rejoining the party outside but Catherine stalled her. "Let me get William, and Robert, first." She stepped into the main room where the two brothers sat together on the settee.

Both rose and came toward her, their features awash with fear which she hastened to allay. "She's awake. Resting. Wants you both." The brothers followed Catherine to their mother's bedside where she lay silent a few moments, staring hard at the two of them. When she spoke she chastised them for their mutual antipathy, reminding them of their familial duties. William glanced at Robert with a sheepish grin; Robert smiled and nodded.

"You thought I was gone. And you remembered you're brothers." She reached to both of them for their hands; they immediately took hers. Watching them closely she drew their hands together so that all three of them joined in a warm and strong knot. "Never forget," she said. "Now I think I'll have just a little nap while you go on with the party outside. I'm fine." She nodded her head. "And you can tell everyone that. Especially Eva."

WITH THE WEDDING OVER and the harvest in, William and Robert went again to York but this time they were determined to see Bishop Strachan. They asked lawyer Logan to accompany them but he declined. The lawyer had his own troubles with Strachan and spent his life trying to avoid Strachan's long reach. Robert should do the same; he couldn't hope to get any help in his legal troubles from a powerful man like the bishop.

This day they were ushered right into the bishop's office almost as soon as they strode into the anteroom, their heavy boots thudding on the polished wood floors. St. James' church had rooms behind the main sanctuary and it was there the brothers found Bishop Strachan. Robert's breathing quickened but he tried to match William's calm demeanor as they stood in front of the man whose actions had so aggravated them for so many years.

Strachan did not look up but went on scratching with his quill pen on a formal-looking document. His hands and his face—all the parts of his skin that showed—were very white, except for the ink rubbed into the heel of his right hand, a necessary evil for those who could write. Robert struggled to soften his breathing. He glanced at his brother who gave him a curt nod and went back to staring at some imaginary spot on the wall map behind the desk. The pen scratched on.

Robert became slightly agitated. Why had the man admitted them? He paid them no attention at all. Robert's nose itched and he scratched it. William glanced at him and frowned. He cleared his throat and looked at William whose eyebrows dipped in disapproval. Just when Robert thought he could wait no longer, the bishop laid down his pen, blotted his work and set the page aside a moment before folding it. Giving them no sign he knew they were there, he dripped wax and sealed the document.

Robert watched to see whose name the man would write but he laid the note on his desk without addressing it. Then and only then did Bishop Strachan lift first his eyes to stare at their waists and then his whole head to study the two of them as though he had a lifetime and didn't mind making them wait. Robert itched to put an end to this ridiculous tableau but forced himself to wait for William. He didn't want the bishop to take too much notice of him.

"Well?" The man's grey eyes flickered over both of them. His pale cheeks each held a spot of red as though he'd painted them. His large head squeezed out of his wrinkled neckpiece and his long sideburns curled toward his cheeks. The shiny hair was smoothed straight back and caught at the nape of his neck. As he studied them his eyes seemed a little darker, certainly more insistent, demanding even. "Speak, sirs!"

"We've come regarding a number of issues, sir," William began.

"Issues? What issues?" He spit the words out and Robert was surprised no sputum came with them.

"May we sit, sir?"

....

The Loyalist Legacy

Strachan nodded and the brothers pulled chairs near the desk. William wanted to clear the air and launched into the settlers' grievances. He mentioned the terrible condition of the roads, which topic led to the clergy reserves and the other lands which had no tenants and therefore no one to care for the roads. From there he patiently talked about the makeup of the landowners occupying the land. They were predominantly Methodist. Hardly any Anglicans lived in Nissouri.

The bishop's eyes narrowed at this incursion into his own policies about keeping the clergy reserves for the Anglicans. William, however, carried on in his clear and concise manner, his words so logical that even the bishop could not object. He ended with a plea that those in government find a way to listen to the settlers whose lives, though much improved now that their lands held fields and they lived in decent homes, could be even better if settlers lived on every lot and not on less than half of the lots in the township. The room was silent again. Robert had noticed the bishop's facial changes as his brother spoke. The man certainly did not look at all disposed to be helpful but silently studied the two visitors, his hands toying with the unaddressed missive on his desk.

"Garner, you said your name was?" He stared at William and waited.

"Yes, sir. William Garner. And this is my brother, Robert."

Strachan's eyes swept over Robert and back to William. "You've a nerve…coming here." He sat taller in his chair. "Telling your betters how to govern." He pushed his chair back and stood. "Perhaps you ought to leave." He motioned toward the door.

Robert sat forward in his chair. He wanted to shout at the man but William's hand on his arm stayed him. William, too, sat forward but he kept his chair and his calm, although his voice turned icy and deliberate. "We are here because we want to help," he said. "We want to see this country grow and prosper—"

"That's not your concern." The man's face was bright red now and his voice shook.

"But it is, sir!" Robert jumped out of his chair to look right into Strachan's fiery eyes. "What you do here affects us all. Your private cronies know nothing of our needs, our concerns, indeed, our thoughts. And you don't care." William's arm pulled him back into his chair but his words just wanted to come out. "You hounded our father to his death! We'll not let you do the same to us."

"Robert! Be silent!"

He glanced at William's shocked face and tried to think what he had just said. The inkwell on the desk caught his eye and he forced himself to study its intricacies, its greenish glass, its smear of black ink running down the outside of the squat round bottle. His breathing slowed, he sat back in his chair. Bishop Strachan sat as well and William removed his hand from Robert's arm.

"I beg your pardon," Robert whispered to the room at large.

"Now I remember where I heard your names before. Your father is John Garner."

"Yes." The brothers answered together.

A tiny smile crossed the bishop's face, thinning out his lips even more. "And you broke out of jail all those years ago. With your father."

William's voice cut in. "We were all wrongfully imprisoned. No charges were brought against any of us." After a moment he added, 'sir.'

A large sense of foreboding in his gut, Robert dared to speak again. "We had to escape. Our father was sick and dying from being in that infernal jail." He kept his voice low but inside his heart was pounding as he remembered.

"Just one of the illegal acts perpetrated by those in power. For their own ends." William's tone was soft. "I ask you, is that any way to start a country?"

"You want me to listen to jail breakers?"

"Who were illegally jailed!" Robert could not abide the sneer on the man's face.

Suddenly the bishop stood and leaned over the desk right into their shocked faces. "Aha! Now I remember. You." He pointed his bony finger in Robert's face. "You're illegal. You blasted American!" The man ranted all around the room, shouting and shrieking, so that the door crashed open and the beady-eyed clerk came running in. "Arrest this man!" The bishop pointed at Robert. The clerk grabbed his arm and shouldered him past the shocked William and out of the room.

Chapter Twenty-Two

HE COULDN'T GO HOME without Robert. Mary Anne would shoot him not to mention Catherine, who would probably load the gun for her sister-in-law. When would Robert learn to control his temper? There was only one way to best men like Strachan. Beat them at their own game. Logic and law were the keys. And now Robert had exploded and got himself locked in a storage room at the church while Strachan figured out how to legally dispose of him.

William sat at the rough table in Montgomery's tavern up Yonge Street. It was not actually in the town of York and that suited him fine although he well knew Strachan's reach extended far beyond York's boundaries. A few patrons graced the establishment but in the middle of the day most men had work to do.

His table was round, though the other two in the place were rectangles of hewn logs sliced to form the table top, glued together with pine resin, sanded and covered with a thick varnish. The round tabletop was somewhat wasteful as the top would be prepared as a square and trimmed of its corners and finished again. Most settlers and tavern keepers had not the time to take the extra steps to make a round table, especially when they didn't fit well into the cramped surroundings. More tables meant more patrons.

This tavern was not as busy as it might have been, and William wondered how long it would take the owner to make a decent wage here so far north of the town. He supposed the man behind the bar who kept staring in his direction was that owner. He didn't feel at all welcome. Why was that? Surely the man needed all the business he could get. "Barkeep," he called out.

"Yes, sir." The man put down his polishing cloth and ambled to William's side.

"What food do you serve?"

A good hour later his stomach full and his temper cooled, William had decided to go after his brother. By now perhaps Mr. Strachan would be civil and together they could come to an understanding. He trotted back down the street planning what he might say. He ought to have saved his time. The bishop was not in his office, nor would he be back that day, and no amount of questioning or of cajoling his assistant could garner any more information than that.

With no other options, William trotted on to the jail where he found Robert had indeed been incarcerated but was not allowed any visitors. He could learn no other information. Dispirited and at a loss he headed back to Montgomery's tavern where he knew he could find a bed for the night.

The next day brought not a little trouble for William but much more for his brother. William had lain awake disturbed somewhat by the raucous carousing coming from below but much more by his own traitorous thoughts. He had made his promise to his mother—they both had—but that did not change the fact that Robert was a hothead and his own worst enemy when it came to dealing with those in power. Of course Robert had been wronged, he couldn't argue, but William's way was to sway with thought and logic whereas his brother...well, his brother's way was anger and shouting.

He went first to see the bishop and managed to get a few moments with him. The man was reasonable and especially receptive to William's promise to take responsibility for his brother. He even mentioned the regrettable imprisonment and subsequent death of John all those years before. The bishop, William was sure, had no stomach for a long court battle over Robert's American background and his questionable land title; he had enough to worry about with trying to get his own college off the ground and his unpopularity as part of the ever more maligned Family Compact. William headed for the jail and, once more, attempted to see his brother.

This time a note from Bishop Strachan worked magic and within a few moments Robert was standing before him, looking exactly what he was—a man who'd spent a night in a cold cell with no chance to wash or tidy himself. Still he had a huge smile for William, who hoped this would be the last time he'd ever have to make such an errand. They struck out for Nissouri, riding the almost completed Governor's Road, detouring to Norwich to pay a call on friends, and continuing on the next day.

When he reached his own home Lucy had taken a turn for the worse but he was able to cheer her up by reporting on his York visit. The details he glossed over.

Robert's conversation with his neighbor, Mr. Logan, was somewhat different. Together they talked over his meeting with the bishop, his utter lack of getting any help from that quarter, and his night in jail, courtesy of Bishop Strachan. He drew the line at mentioning William's feelings on the matter but Mr. Logan brought it up. "And did your brother end up in the jail, too?"

Robert smiled and nodded his head at some private amusement. "No. He did not."

"A bit of a toady, is he then?"

"He does like his way, I'll say that much." He stopped.

"What're you not telling me?" Mr. Logan laid his hand across Robert's arm.

"I promised...I said I'd not fight with him."

"Who're you meaning, your brother?" He squinted at Robert and then suddenly his eyes lit up. "Or Strachan?"

But it was not Strachan whose personality was so annoying to Robert at the moment. William, his older brother, whom he had always revered and still did, wore into his thoughts like a loose nut rubbing a wheel joint. William was the nut, going back and forth, round and round, and never getting anywhere until it so loosened the joint the whole thing fell apart. He gave his head a shake and his face broke into a weak smile for Mr. Logan.

DAYS LATER a rider clattered up Robert's lane and pounded on his door waking them all from a sound sleep long before dawn. Young Will it was, huffing and puffing, his cheeks fiery red and his eyes almost jumping out of their sockets. He could hardly speak. "Grandma…" he gasped. "You must come…Father says."

Robert and his nephew rode the rough road to see his mother; Mary Anne promised to come a little later once the children were up and fed. The two men didn't want to kill the horses so slowed frequently to rest the animals and themselves. At these times talk was possible. Young Will answered his questions but his words were wary as though speaking of Grandma Lucy's illness might somehow make it worse.

When they tied their horses to William's post, the house was black and silent, with a thin strand of smoke spiking into the grey sky. Bare trees, corn stubble across black land, and a rime of frost slicking the porch all foretold winter's approach. Johnny, with a grim face and no words, came from the house and took the horses.

Reuben perched on the settee in the corner, his hat in his hands and his face covered with fear. He nodded as Robert rushed by and into the crowded room where his mother lay, wan and worn, her body barely rippling the blankets over her.

He looked at Eva. And Catherine. And then William, all ranged around the bed. He was too late. His face crumpled, an outward sign of the utter devastation and ruin he felt inside. He swiped at his face, dried his hand on his trousers and reached tentatively to touch her hair. Still curly but not so unruly. She had always struggled to control it. His fingers barely felt its soft texture but he held it just for a moment.

"I'm not dead yet."

He jerked his hand back. Her dazzling eyes were open, looking at him. Now the tears did come and he let them. "Mama." He could say no more.

The Loyalist Legacy

William ushered the others out of the room and gave his brother time alone with their mother. Eva patted his shoulder as she left and Catherine smiled and nodded at him. He sat on the straight chair beside the bed close enough that he could hold both her hands as they talked, haltingly, but the silences were filled with as much love as the words.

She slept and he tiptoed out. Eva slipped back in to keep watch while Robert sat beside William on the settee, his brother's closeness a comfort even though they barely spoke. Catherine puttered at the table, taking special care to work quietly; Reuben sat with her eating his pancake with none of his usual gusto.

"Are you hungry?" Catherine stood before the two brothers, who rose at her invitation and sat before the meal she put in front of them.

The morning tiptoed along as one by one they rose and sat, did some little thing and came back, all the while their senses tuned to the bedroom off the main room. They took turns waiting and watching in twos and threes and the day dragged on. Mary Anne and the children had come in partway through the morning, adding their soft undercurrent to the sad scene winding down in the weathered house above the river, now flowing faster as November's rains threatened to turn to snow.

Robert went in again and stood by Eva whose tears streamed down her freckled cheeks. He went to her and held her, his own heart thumping with fear not only for their impending loss but for what it would do to the whole family.

Her face was white now, her wrinkled skin strangely smoothed and a look of something akin to happiness in the turn of her lips. Satisfaction, at least. She was beyond hearing them but now and again they tried, one or the other, to reach her. Robert's hand stole over Mary Anne's shoulders and he pulled her close. Reuben stood solid and secure beside Eva. Young Will and Johnny tried to hold back their feelings but their rough hair and red faces betrayed them. And William. He stood at the foot of the bed, his face masking his inner torture. He had watched his father die. Now he must witness the rock in all their lives crumble. Catherine held his arm as best she could.

Outside Migisi and Kiwidinok sat before a smoky fire, all of their children with them, their voices keening above the wind rising and falling as the white woman's soul entered the spirit world. The wind whooshed into the fire with a surge of energy that suddenly dissipated until it was no more. It left behind a mixture of joy and sadness in all of their hearts. William and Catherine came out on the porch and stood with their Chippewa friends.

NEIGHBORS CAME from miles around to pay their considerable respects to this lady whose life had touched them all. They gathered by the side of the river and waited their turns to boat across the surging waters and stand by Lucy's grave. Some came from the east and went directly to the open grave, dressed in sober black, their coats and hats solid against the driving wind.

The preacher spoke, the earth bits flew into the hole, and most everyone made the trek back across the river to fill up William's house. With busy hands the women soon fed the crowd and voices rose with stories of the dearly departed, not just of dear Lucy but of all those who'd been lost. The bittersweet tenor of the evening helped but did not assuage the bruised hearts assembled there.

Robert spoke with William just before he and Mary Anne took their exhausted children out the door. As they drove down the rutted road, the extra horse tied on behind and the children safely sheltered in the wagon bed, Mary Anne leaned close to speak in Robert's ear.

"What did he say?"

He glanced at her—she saw the turn of his head in the moonlight—but he just smiled and shrugged his drooping shoulders.

Chapter Twenty-Three

Spring, 1834

WILLIAM SAT ACROSS THE TABLE from Robert and fumed. Their Sunday supper had turned into a full out yelling match between the two as it had so often before. Catherine and Mary Anne scurried back and forth clearing the dishes and talking in tones so low he couldn't hear much of what they said. But he could guess. And he'd hear about it when they went home, he knew.

Across from him Robert's head was bent studying that last fork on the table as though it had some especially important significance. He looked calm but his clever artist's fingers drummed a rhythm over and over, the only sound from either of the two men. William felt that tiny eye movement start, a twitch that he was powerless to stop and that annoyed him more with every passing year. As did Robert.

Every time the neighbors gathered for any reason at all, his brother found an audience for his frustrated complaining. He just did not seem to have in him the ability to forget, let alone forgive and his litany of complaints about the government grew and grew. Far from curtailing him, his brushes with authority and his times cooling off in jail had spurred him on. And that Logan nearby had become fuel to his fire. The two of them found allies in each other.

Today's argument started with William suggesting that perhaps Robert might be better off to spend some time plowing and planting rather than sitting in Logan's store carving before the fire, Logan's hot words flying out with every shaving of wood Robert's knife sliced off. Logan was a blowhard; William had taken the man's measure years ago but, strangely, Robert had not. Their friendship had grown. What's more, they had attracted a few others whose chief topic of conversation was how they were going to fix the many problems brought down on them by the powerful folks in York and across the sea.

And now, rather than look after his land and his animals, Robert planned to take a trip across to Buffalo to sell the tiny trinkets he had made over the winter. How could such pieces, cleverly made though they were, bring him enough money to make such a trip worthwhile? He could no longer use Helen as an excuse; she was safely settled on her own land nearby. But his brother was adamant. He would leave in the morning. What's more, Logan of the store was going with him.

Mary Anne sat again beside him. "You're going to be a grandad, William."

She smiled so charmingly he had to leave off his dark thoughts and turn to her. Catherine slipped into the chair beside Robert and whispered something for his ears only. It seemed the two women had a plan to get their Sunday dinner back on track.

"So they tell me," he said.

"Will is courting a young lady, too." Catherine said. "And Johnny has been driving out with that new girl. Seems her mother goes with her, though." She chuckled softly.

Mary Anne laughed. His sister-in-law joyed in her world, her laugh lines attesting to it more and more each year. Robert could use some of that, William thought. "Yes, both the boys will soon be matched up."

"And high time, too." Catherine's voice cut in. Apparently she and Robert had finished their whispering. He forced a smile for the two women but avoided Robert entirely.

The three of them chatted but William still worried about Robert and what he might be up to. That Mackenzie's printed words struck a chord these days. All up and down the roads neighbors talked about their frustrations, all of it spurred on by Mackenzie's paper and by people like Robert and Logan. William remembered the war back in 1812 and the tensions leading up to it. He did not want to see the same thing happen. How could he and Catherine go through that all again? They'd lost so much.

"William?" Catherine's voice touched him just as he felt her hand on his arm. "Are you day dreaming then, my husband?"

"Just thinking..." He stopped.

"Yes?" Catherine squeezed his hand.

"I, we...should perhaps start for home."

"Oh, there's no rush, William," Mary Anne said. "Stay a little." She motioned toward the parlor. "Let's sit more comfortably, shall we?"

Catherine followed her across the room, as did Robert. William had no choice but to join them and for another couple of hours they talked amicably about inconsequential things such as new neighbors, quilting bees, a barn raising, and the need for another room on the school. The women and Robert kept the conversation flowing with the odd word from William but at no time did the two brothers speak directly to each other.

"YOU'RE NEVER HERE!"

"Of course, I am." Robert brought his warmest smile to his face. "My dear."

"Logan's store. That's where you spend your time. You even have all your carving tools there." Mary Anne's eyes raged.

"I—."

"Don't deny it!"

He didn't. She had some truth in her words, he allowed.

"I saw your shavings on the floor. You don't even have to clean them up!"

"Now Mary Anne," he started, but her flashing eyes and fiery tongue dug deep and his own choler rose. As she threw more words across the room at him he tried to understand her point of view, but he'd never seen her like this. She always agreed with everything he said and did. What had happened? He turned away and paused a moment. He clenched his fists and turned back.

She moved behind the table, her eyes suddenly wide with fear.

He dropped onto the rocking chair, shocked beyond words that she would think that of him. They stared at each other. For the first time in their marriage a great gulf separated them. She slid onto her chair at the head of the table. The silence stretched, broken only by their breathing, his ragged and raging, hers in short gasps, all of it ebbing into the silent room.

A log shuddered in the cook stove. The stew bubbled up under the ill-fitting pot lid. Outside the clouds parted and sunlight streaked through the window and across the smooth grain of the black walnut table, washing over her hands, but still she did not move. He wished she would.

Thomas poked his head around the door. "All quiet here now?" His parents jumped up, Mary Anne to turn her back and stir the stew and Robert to chastise his son for his lateness. The boy—as tall as he was now—stared back at Robert and quietly nodded his head, a question in his eyes. He had heard them.

All seemed normal that night as the family settled after a bustling spring day clearing away the detritus of winter in preparation for spring planting. Thomas would plow this year for the first time and his chest seemed to have grown in anticipation. Russell would be picking stones out of the way and even Elizabeth would abandon her kitchen chores to lend a hand. "We'll start tomorrow, then." Robert looked at each of his offspring in turn, settling on Russell last. "You can help your mama. In place of Elizabeth." The youngest of the family dropped his chin and pouted. His mother's pat on his shoulder couldn't cheer him.

Mary Anne was already asleep when he came to bed that night, stripping to his underclothes and slipping in beside her. Her breath was slow and measured, the way it always was. Their spat today had blown over. Or had it? As he lay on his back thinking again of their angry words, he realized she had not spoken to him or even looked at him the rest of the day. Not like her. Perhaps she was

The Loyalist Legacy

right. He shifted onto his side away from her but still conscious of her every breath. He forced his arguments away and dropped into a deep slumber where no soldiers fought nor lawyers threatened. And where he and his family got along.

ONCE THE CORN AND WHEAT were planted as well as the early garden vegetables, Robert agreed to accompany Mr. Logan to the Centreville depot for supplies for his store. His excitement grew as the day approached and he felt almost guilty at how anxious he was to leave. Mary Ann had frowned and turned away when he told her; whether at his being gone for a few days or spending time with Logan, he didn't know.

They took Logan's wagon, a sturdy contraption with a high seat and large wheels, which seemed to find every rut in the road all the way there. Logan's pair of horses were evenly matched, their collars allowing them to haul a full load with ease. Only once did the men have to stop and walk the horses around a large tree downed right across the road but the walking was a welcome change.

The sun was high in the sky as Logan pulled hard on the lines to stop in front of the supply store. His wagon was next in line for loading and the two hurried inside to place their order. Adjacent to the depot which served much of the area for almost fifty miles in most directions, a small hotel had sprung up with a bustling public house and kitchen attached. Once the load was secured, Logan moved the wagon out of the way of those still waiting with their teams. He would tie off down the street just a little from the hotel.

Robert unwrapped his carvings for the supply store owner who handled each one as though it was a treasure. In the end, the man bought them all at a fair price. With his coins in his pocket he headed to the tavern to wait for his friend. He seated himself at the only table available though it was not empty. The man was old, certainly older than Robert, and wore clothes that had once been very fine. He seemed not to hear Robert's chair scrape as he pulled it close to reach his tankard. His head remained cast down, his rounded shoulders shrunken and lost in a coat sagging open at the neck. Logan came in, and Robert waved him over. Logan glanced at the man and Robert shrugged.

"All ready then?" he asked his friend.

"Seems the whole order is filled, right down to the sewing needles for your sister-in-law."

"She'll be glad. Must do it all now that Mother..." He shook his head.

"Was Mrs. Garner a good seamstress then?"

An odd question from his friend, Robert thought. "She came to be." He remembered how she hated to darn stockings and pictured her frowning face whenever she struggled with it. "Wasn't always, though."

"Your father. When did he die?"

"Years ago now."

"In the war?"

"No, afterwards. He got into trouble with the Family Compact back when it was all just beginning." Robert saw again the jail cell and took a long gulp of the brew. The stranger raised his head. Something in the face, the long nose—Robert couldn't quite make out what his mind was trying to tell him. "Even back then Strachan made his own rules."

Logan started. He glanced at the stranger and then at Robert. "We need to go soon. Drink up."

"Can we make it back before dark?" Robert remembered when this would have been a three day trip and even longer, before anyone had roads, or horses and wagons to drive on them.

"Are the horses rested enough, you mean? We'll take it easy."

"Garner? You said your mother...Mrs. Garner?" The old man, suddenly alert and interested, stared at Robert.

The two men dropped their tankards to the table and beer slopped over the sides and the fresh smell of hops and barley assaulted their nostrils. Both studied the narrowed eyes and the lined forehead of the man.

"Who are you?" Robert seemed to remember the voice. From long ago. "Did you know my mother?"

"I knew a Mrs. Garner. In Niagara. After the war." He nodded a couple of times. "Good woman."

Robert could hardly contain himself. "Did you know her husband? My father?"

"You look a little like him. Just along your hairline. John, his name was."

He had it. "You're the man who helped us. My father died in your house." He thought a moment. "Mr. Beasley. Mr. Richard Beasley." He reached out his hand. "Robert Garner, sir. You saved my father's life." He clasped the man's hand.

The three men talked away a good part of the afternoon until leaving for home was impossible. Robert and Logan readily agreed to share a room in the hotel and, upon learning Beasley had nowhere nearby to go, insisted he share with them. Beasley's lovely property on Burlington Heights was lost. He told them he was tricked by a cousin into signing it all over so that a man named MacNab could buy it. This was the same man who made a good deal of money seizing properties of those dying in the cholera epidemic.

Bishop Strachan did not escape Beasley's wrath as the man had assumed the mortgage on Beasley's tavern and thus profited from Beasley's ruin. Like vultures to carcasses the moneyed had seized opportunities to increase their own wealth at the expense of many who struggled to build homes and businesses in this new land. "I wondered why the bishop wanted a tavern," Beasley muttered, his voice interrupted by his wheezing. "But the man likes his scotch."

"The preachers all up and down the colony are railing against drink!" Robert was almost shouting.

"Sh, my friend." Beasley grabbed his arm. "You never know who's listening."

"And what tales will make their way back to the Family Compact." Logan bit off the last two words as though they fouled his mouth.

Early the next morning Logan cracked the lines and the freshly harnessed team leapt ahead for the long trip home. Neither of the men noticed the short stranger all dressed in black gazing after them. Spurred on by meeting Beasley, the two talked much more on the trip home. Robert shared the story of his father's time in jail and even confessed his own part—and William's—in escaping and hiding out at Beasley's farm on Burlington Heights until his father died. "They killed him."

"What do you mean?" Logan turned to him. "Your father?"

"They threw him in jail and left him there. Yes, they killed my father."

Logan struggled to understand. "Who? And how does Beasley fit in?"

Again Robert explained how it had all come about all those years ago but he didn't go back further. Could he trust his friend with the knowledge that he'd fought on the other side? For the Americans? A flash of memory bubbled up from a place so hidden he hardly remembered it. No, he couldn't tell his friend about Brock, the General, at Queenstown, him shooting, running, escaping with the others across the river, the blood running red down the general's chest, his secret hidden ever since. And he never would.

"Sounds like this Beasley has a lot to complain about."

Robert nodded but said nothing. As the miles clip-clopped by he turned his thoughts to Mary Anne and William. She would be happy to see he'd sold his carvings; at least he hoped so. She could take the money and buy that new-fangled corn popper for a treat. She loved that blue hat in Logan's window. Maybe…his thoughts rambled the rest of the way home.

William and Catherine sat at the table with Mary Anne, their plates empty, each of them wearing a welcoming smile for him as he came through the door. He'd seen their wagon. Was someone sick? Mary Anne rose to take his hat. She led him to a vacant chair. For a moment no one said a word. Smiles, yes, but no words. At least the news wasn't bad.

"The baby, Robert!" Catherine cried. "We're grandparents." William nodded beside her, the largest grin Robert had seen in years plastered across his face. "Yesterday. Reuben came for us in the early morning and late last night the baby came." She clapped her hands together.

"We thought we might just come and tell you," William said.

Robert reached over the table and shook his brother's hand. "You're a grandfather. I can't believe it. Congratulations, both of you."

Mary Anne filled a plate for him and he tucked into it with pleasure, not just at the baby girl but because his brother was here and happy for once. Once his plate was empty he pulled out the money for Mary Anne and everyone congratulated him. Finally he mentioned Beasley. A shadow crossed William's face as Robert talked, but he said nothing.

Chapter Twenty-Four

THE NEXT TIME MR. LOGAN needed to take a trip to Centreville, Robert readily agreed to join him. He had about two dozen carvings completed and hoped to sell them in the supply store as easily as he did the last ones. Even though Mary Anne looked askance when he told her his plans to leave the next day and be back the day after, she could hardly complain about the popularity of his work.

Would Beasley still be in Centreville? He hoped to talk again with the man who had known his parents and who spoke so well of them, especially his mother. The man had mentioned more than once her courage in carrying out the plan to save her husband. Robert hoped to ask him more about just how he had arranged their escape all those years ago.

Logan seemed to have his own reasons for this mid-season trip. Certainly supplies were always necessary but Robert had not seen any empty shelves or lack of goods for sale in his friend's store. Nevertheless, he kept his own counsel as the wagon rumbled along on the hard-packed roads.

Once again the supply store was surrounded by wagons waiting to load while men and women, too, gathered on the boardwalk in small groups renewing old friendships and making new ones. The sounds of laughter and wagon wheels, shouts and cawing crows, whips and horses neighing all gave the scene an extraordinary bustle of life. Robert loved it.

Buoyed up by the price he'd received for his carvings he edged his way into the tavern where, once again, he sat at the round table with his full tankard. This time he was alone. He craned his neck and looked over the whole room but he couldn't see Beasley. He did notice, however, a man who stared at him for quite a long time, not even averting his eyes when Robert's own challenged him.

Logan joined him and he forgot about the short stubby man with the searching eyes. They watched the room fill up even though the hour was early both for drinking and the supper meal. Boots stomped across the wooden floor and chairs dragged out from tables and back in again heavy with eager customers. The barman could not keep up and voices hollered louder to get his attention. Neither Robert nor Logan could understand the crowds.

Someone pulled a chair from their table and sat in it nearby with another group. Barely a seat was left in the room; men lined the walls and still clamoured at the long bar for service. Just as Robert thought maybe they should leave because the crowd was getting uglier by the minute, someone sat heavily on the remaining chair at their table.

"Pardon, gentlemen. May I join you?"

It was the staring man from an hour earlier. Robert was about to decline when Logan spoke up. "Certainly, sir."

"Here for the meeting?" The man's reedy voice was pitched high but one look at his determined eyes told Robert he was not to be mocked.

"What meeting is that, sir?" Logan asked.

"I wondered if you knew." The man squeezed his rotund body closer to Robert. "I saw you with Beasley, did I not?" For once Robert could think of nothing to say and the man continued. "Couple of months back? Sat here for hours. Talked about jails and treason and Burlington Heights."

Robert spit out a mouthful of the ale. "What do you know of it?" He swiped at the foamy ale dribbling down his chin but ignored the mess before him.

"Who are you?" Logan banged his near empty tankard on the table.

"My name is Clark. Henry Clark." He looked from one to the other. "Of course, you don't know me." He glanced right and left and leaned in. "I'm from Norwich."

Neither Robert nor Logan said anything.

"Some call it Sodom?" His shaggy hair fell over his eye and he pushed it back. "The Quakers over there named it in jest and the name stuck."

"What do you want with us, sir?" Robert felt his blood rise but tried to keep control.

"And why were you spying on us?" Logan signaled the barman for more drinks.

Once the drinks were poured and paid for, Clark slowly but carefully told of his own background. He lived near Norwich, sometimes called Sodom, on a farm whose house atop a hill at the corner of the lot gave a good view of much of the surrounding countryside. Most of his neighbors were Quakers and as such were good people and they, too, had suffered under the present government in York. "Peaceful people as they are, they'll not complain," he said, "but many of us have the wit and the words to fight. The question is, will others join us?"

His black eyebrows rose and his eyes bore into both Robert and Logan, who waited to hear what he might say next. Instead of speaking, however, he sat back on the creaking chair and folded his hairy hands across his rounded stomach, content. Robert was for once without words. His eyes darted around the rowdy room but no one took notice of their table. Logan seemed suddenly struck dumb as his eyes flitted from Robert to the stranger, to the table, and back to Robert.

"Quiet, men! Cease and desist!" Someone near the bar struggled to be heard, with no success. The lean man jumped up onto the long bar, much to the barman's consternation, and shouted again. This time he stomped his boot on the bar and the barman hollered; the room went silent as all eyes turned to watch. "Gentlemen." The man's glance included everyone packed into the room. "You've come here today for one reason. One reason only." He paused, nodding his close-cropped head and gathering his thoughts. "You're tired of our government's power over us all. You've had enough. And you want to do something to break their hold on us."

"Whose hold?" A voice came from off to Robert's right, back in a corner, but he couldn't see who it was.

"Ah, you want a name?"

Many voices answered back. The young man raised his rough hands for silence. "Well you know it...the Family Compact." Again he raised his arms and waited. "That group in York and parts east who control everything we do. They only want us for the sweat and toil we give to shape this land." Shouts of agreement broke his stride but soon he continued. "What do they give us, those powerful rich bastards?"

"Nothing!"

"No say in our lives."

"And how do they make our lives miserable?"

"Clergy lands!"

"Empty lots!"

"No help on the roads!"

"Our own preacher can't even marry us!"

"And does this group of rich and powerful men, this Family Compact, listen to us?" He raised his arms to silence the crowd. "No. Our elected members might as well stay home and tend their crops, do their road work and raise their children. Nothing they decide is final. Their votes mean nothing. The Family Compact just do what they want, regardless of the Legislative Assembly." He paused in the ensuing clamor. When the noise threatened to take over the meeting again, he stamped and roared for attention once more and gradually the heated voices subsided.

Robert and Logan looked at each other and at the man with them. His face was beaming as he studied the groups all over the room, even rising from his chair the better to see everyone. Robert didn't know whether to be shocked or delighted that so many gathered here agreed with his own sentiments. He could hear their stories around him as each person shouted out his own troubles with the powerful reach of the government.

"Down with the King!" A voice louder than all the rest temporarily stopped the racket as men looked to identify the speaker.

Into the sudden quiet another voice, high and thin, squeaked out over the heads of the red-faced men. "Rebellion!"

Robert could hardly believe his eyes and ears. Logan slowly shook his head. The two of them edged back in their chairs to get away from the source of their discomfort, for this new voice came from the fat man at their table.

Hands grabbed the portly man and pulled him towards the bar where the first speaker gave over his place to this new voice. The man couldn't get up on the bar. He chose rather to turn and sit on the shiny oak planking. The first speaker sat beside him, his hands in the air for quiet, as the new man spoke.

His name was Henry Clark, and in no time he had the crowd calm and listening to his words. Clark made points which summed up everyone's experiences and men nodded in agreement as the man spoke, his reedy voice forgotten in the power of his message.

He came from Pittsburgh, he said, at his family's invitation a year or more ago, and had settled outside Norwich. Coming from the United States he was used to having a say and to voting for a representative who would have a say in government. "That is democracy," he shouted, "and that is what we all need here." He took a breath. "Whether the highest man in the land or the lowliest worker in your fields," he swept his arm toward them all, "We...need...a...voice!"

THE ROOM EXPLODED. Men jumped to their feet, Robert and Logan with them, fists raised in the air and voices screaming in agreement. They grabbed the rotund man and lifted him to their shoulders. Packed in tight against the crowd who pushed closer and closer, they couldn't move but their smiles showed they didn't have any intention of escaping or stopping the *mêlée*.

When the first drinking glass shattered no one heard it strike the fireplace, but those closest saw and moved aside to get a good shot with their own. Even the tin mugs landed in the fire, some still loaded with ale. The barman shouted himself hoarse and finally a few men with good sense saw the danger and moved to calm the crowd. Robert and Logan, still holding their empty mugs, sat again and the room was almost quiet.

"I can see you're a spirited lot," Clark said. The noise erupted again but Clark raised his short arms and the men heeded him. "We need names, your names, and those of your friends." He looked around the room again, this time studying each face as though he wanted to remember them all. "If the government won't heed us, we must act." Whispering began. For a moment some averted their eyes and studied the floor or, in Robert's case, the table, but almost as one the roomful of men looked Clark in the eye and answered his challenge. Robert and Logan rose with the rest to cheer.

WHEN ROBERT WALKED INTO his home the next day, his pockets loaded with treasures for everyone, Eva's new baby included, he expected smiles and laughter, but the house was cold even in the midst of this sunny spring day, with no kettle on the lukewarm stove. His high spirits dashed, he ran outside to search the barn. No team, nor wagon. Only his horse. Where had they gone? Outside again he scanned the planted fields but saw no one. He ran back over to Logan's store but Logan's wife had not seen Mary Anne or any of his family.

Back inside he built up the fire and made a pot of tea to go with the cold pork and johnnycake he found in the pantry. There was even a slice of pie left from the early rhubarb Mary Anne treasured. When the afternoon wore on and still no one appeared, Robert saddled his horse and headed for William's, watching as he went for any hint of his family.

He rode the miles as fast as he could, thoughts of Catherine's cooking tantalizing him when he managed to stop worrying about his family. When he reached his brother's farm, however, it was as cold and lonely as his own had been. Even Migisi and Kiwidinok's cabin was empty. He stood on the porch scanning north, south and finally east. At first he saw nothing. The late afternoon sun, though, lit up the few trees lining William's east field; a rosy glow edged the horizon with the sun sinking in the west. Slowly the reflection rose but as the darkness increased a spot of smoke remained far in the distance.

He dragged his horse down the slope to the river and forced the frightened animal into the rushing waters, yelling and urging her forward. She reared and he struggled to keep his seat as she kicked and swam her way to the other side. Up the treed hill and onto the old Indian path through William's field, he rode towards the smoke pluming high in the sky; the horse dripped with sweat. Robert whipped the animal forward.

At last he saw the blackened shell with burning bits still flying into the air. The schoolhouse was in flames.

THE FIRE HAD STARTED outside the school along the north wall where one of the older boys shared his tobacco with the others. When the bell rang they stamped out their smokes and ran for the door. Around midday Eva had noticed the smoke billowing at almost the same time as Reuben looked up from his desk, prepared to dismiss the children for their dinner break.

A very few hours later, all had changed. Eva and Reuben took their newborn to William and Catherine's house along with the few bits of clothing they'd saved. Catherine left Eva in the empty bedroom holding her daughter to her breast. The child fed hungrily oblivious to the calamity all around. The desks and tables Eva and Reuben had salvaged in the first frantic moments of the fire were piled back in the schoolyard along with most of the young couple's possessions. Eva didn't want to think of them just yet but Catherine knew decisions had to be made.

Reuben sat with William on the settee and seemed to be listening to his words, but his eyes kept straying to the bedroom door.

Her sons gathered at the table, reeking of smoke. She'd have a time getting that smell out of the house.

"How is she?" William asked as she sat near him. Reuben began to get up but she waved him back.

"Just give her some time." Catherine smiled and nodded. "She's fine. The baby's fine. And in spite of a lot of smoke, we're all fine."

"The children…" Reuben shook his head. "Thank the Lord they are safe."

"Even those boys," Catherine murmured.

"Ought to be horse-whipped." William's sudden anger caught even him unawares and he sat back on the settee with a thud against the wall.

"I'm sure their parents will be cutting switches even as we speak." Catherine raised her voice and turned toward her sons. "Perhaps you might help Migisi and Solomon outside with the chores?"

Reuben went out, too. Catherine moved to her husband's side and leaned into him.

"Robert took his time getting there."

"William. Can't you ever just let it be? This anger has to stop." She sat forward and glared at him. "He's your brother, for Lord's sake."

He reached for her hand and pulled it to his lips. "You're right, my dear."

The bedroom door opened and Eva joined them. Her hair still swirled around her freckled face but she smiled and squeezed in beside her mother. "Where's Reuben?"

"Helping your brothers."

"He is?" Eva's eyes opened wide.

"Seems he'd do anything just to be busy," William said.

"Or to avoid sitting alone with us." Catherine chuckled. "He is still quite afraid of your father and even me," she said and squeezed Eva's hand.

Eva spoke of seeing her family, all of them, coming on the run to help. "Even Uncle Robert who must have been exhausted from his trip—he came to help."

"Yes, he did." Catherine didn't look at her husband. "And don't you worry. They'll all be back tomorrow to help again."

"We'll build another school, bigger and better, for you and Reuben." William paused and leaned forward to look at Eva. "It's only a building. No one was hurt...when I think..."

"Yes, well, time to get some food on that empty table over there." Catherine jumped up and Eva joined her. "I'm sure you've got stew, Mama. You always do!"

"HOW DID YOU COME TO BE AT THE FIRE?" Robert and Mary Anne lay awake in their bed reliving the day's events.

"Looking for you." He whispered to her his growing fears at finding their deserted house and answered her questions about his time with Logan. He glossed over the meeting of the day before and told her only of selling his carvings and Logan's good luck at finding everything he needed for the store. Long after she had drifted off to sleep, though, he saw again in his mind the crowded room with its raised voices and his own thrill at being part of it all. These men thought as he did.

Chapter Twenty-Five

Spring, 1837

FRUSTRATIONS WITH THE GOVERNMENT were on the minds of all and sundry. Wherever people met, different sides in the disagreements became more and more pronounced. Neighbors at church meetings in the new school and parents carrying their young ones to and from that school raged about the events in Toronto, as York had been renamed. In London, Norwich and Centreville, all up and down the back roads and main thoroughfares of Upper Canada, the workings of the Family Compact affected lives both high and low.

Newspapers and fliers published by one side or the other all claiming to be in the right made their way from hand to hand, from house to barn, from tavern to hotel until the actual issues became as muddied as the news sheets themselves. Even Dr. Duncombe, their normally calm and clever representative to the Legislative Assembly in Toronto, was on his way to England with a petition signed by many of the disgruntled citizens of Oxford District.

Robert had heard him speak the summer before to a large crowd in the tavern at Centreville. The man had dared to set up a Grand Lodge independent from British lodges and as its first Grand Master was looking for support. He spoke his mind that day to thunderous applause. When a voice shouted "What about the petty crimes hereabouts? Will you stop that?" Duncolme immediately singled out the man and thanked him for his question. Social injustice resulted in crime, he said, and went on to explain how better laws led directly to contented citizens.

"As long as the laws are fair to everyone!" The man at the back shouted again.

"Yes. And they get passed not only by the Legislative Assembly which you and others like you elect, but also all the way up to our Lieutenant-Governor, Sir Francis Bond Head."

The room exploded. Men jumped on their chairs, then the tables, their shouts rising to the roof and their fists punching up into the smoky air. Robert's throat ached but he didn't want to sit down to drink from his tankard. Besides, these were men who shared his own frustrations and he shouted and pounded right along with them, these men he had come to know in the last two years. Logan shouted too, a voice close to his own, until another noise came from across the room.

Standing on the long bar the red-faced owner held his rifle high overhead almost reaching the tin ceiling as his finger tightened on the trigger. Robert reached for Logan's arm and pulled him down to his chair while all around the room others, still muttering, scraped the floor with their chairs.

For a moment all was silent. Duncolme surveyed the men who showed such fury and frustration on their faces. Robert hoped the man could help them for it was eminently clear that help them he must.

"I can see you like him not," Duncolme said.

Laughter erupted. Not the joyful kind, though. This sound came from desperate throats trying to improve their lot and that of their families.

"I had an idea a few months ago. It will not solve all our problems, but it has helped." When no one spoke up, he went on. He talked about wresting the power of the banks from the Family Compact by starting a joint stock bank.

Questions came fast and furious. What was it? How could it help them? Would those in power allow it? Dr. Duncolme had taken the time that day to answer every last question and allay their fears.

Most of them had immediately seen the value in this new bank system and longed to use it to attack those in power who profited so much from the current system. Robert had even offered up a fair sum to the man in the corner taking deposits. Upon his return home, he had carried the news to William but, once again, his older brother would only side with the current system. He feared any change even if that change was for the good of what could one day become a strong country.

Today he would again talk to William, this time about joining Dr. Duncolme's lodge although he had no real hope his brother would be interested. Many shared William's point of view and Robert worked hard to understand it and, yes, to try to get William's sympathy for his own ideas. Mary Anne told him just to leave it be for the sake of family peace. He had to admit, though, he would be much happier to have William join him rather than fight him, for he could feel the political pot boiling. It could spill over at any time. In the last war he and his brother had been on separate sides. He could not bear to suffer through that again.

Catherine's smile was genuine when she opened the door to find him there, hat in hand. She stood aside to allow him in. "William and the boys are readying the plows and the horses. They're itching to break the land." She carried coffee to him and sat at the table with him. "You're not doing the same?"

He felt a pull of resentment as he always did whenever anyone challenged his farming practices but he ignored it. She meant nothing by it. "Are they across the river, then? I didn't see anyone outside."

"Picking stones and burning downed branches. Didn't you see the smoke?"

Well, yes, he had but he'd ignored it, so intent was he on his purpose. "Are they coming back for dinner?" He glanced at the stove where a large pot was simmering.

"Yes, and soon. Stay?" She looked so hopeful that he agreed, even though he'd hoped to talk and be on his way. This lodge business weighed on his mind. "I've a thing or two to discuss with William."

Soon the clattering of boots on the porch announced it was time to eat. Young Will and Johnny clapped him on the shoulder and even William wore a broad smile, guarded though it was, and they sat to eat. Robert knew he couldn't discuss his business but as soon as was decently possible he asked William to join him on the settee. The boys said their goodbyes and headed outside, their father assuring them he'd be right along.

"I've come to invite you to do something with me," Robert began.

William's eyebrows twisted in surprise and his eyelids dropped a little. "What might that be?"

Robert told him all about the lodge, where its meetings would be, what its purpose was, and why, finally, he was so excited about it.

"A Grand Lodge you say. Independent from the lodges we already have?"

"Our very own one here. A separate lodge in this separate country. Do you not see how it helps us forge ahead?"

"Ah. So that's what this is about. Another way to stick a thorn in Strachan's side." He strode to the door. "Will you never learn? You can't fight them. We can't fight them."

"But this is for us, for our own people." Robert struggled to hold his temper.

"What is best for our people is to get along."

"At any cost?"

"Do you want war again? You of all people must remember how the last one tore families—our family—apart!"

"Oh, I remember. But I also remember our father died because of these oligarchs. Yes, you can look shocked but that's what they are and if we don't stop them we'll be just sheep. Sheep, fattened for the slaughter whenever that Family Compact decides to enact another law punishing us and putting coin in their purses."

William grabbed the door handle but Robert stepped in front of him. Catherine, who had disappeared into the main bedroom, appeared at William's other side, her lined cheeks flushed. She said nothing but laid her hand across his arm to stay him and he dropped it to his side. For a moment they stood in a tight and silent triangle, each of the brothers clutching their disparate opinions as though giving them up would kill them.

Catherine spoke first. "Thank you for coming, Robert." She handed him his hat and pulled the door open. He glanced at William whose whole body bespoke his anger and his defeat. Shaking his head, he headed for the bedroom where he closed the door and shut Robert out.

Perhaps he ought to have told William more, he thought as he rode home that afternoon. If William only knew how dire the circumstances all across Upper Canada actually were, perhaps he would become part of the solution. Did William even know about Bond Head's illegal violence in the recent election? The man had used Orangemen to strongarm voters. His tactics had resulted in a new Legislative Assembly full of Tory supporters, anathema for the Reformers.

Surely his brother had heard these things and more with the unrest all around them, especially after the election, but William was not interested. As long as he had his land and his family, nothing else mattered. Certainly not Robert's need to walk a tightrope in case the government might one day come after him and his family. Strachan knew he was American. He'd even fought on the other side, yet owned land here purely because no one had yet acted on his secret.

In the weeks following last year's election, people learned first hand just how its results came to affect them. Anything the Reformers wanted in the Assembly, the majority tossed out so that effectively the Family Compact held the reins of power with no voice given to those outside their clique. Robert and Logan heard strong talk in Centreville, all of it connected to their lack of power.

At least they had returned their own man in the district, Dr. Duncolme, who tried his best to sway the powerful Compact to listen to reason. Instead they ignored him. That summer he had taken his petition, with thousands of names of people demanding change, far across the ocean all the way to London. When he arrived there, however, he could not get an audience with anyone in power as the Family Compact had effectively closed all doors to him with their malicious letters castigating and belittling him. The man returned, broken and defeated, to learn that his son had died while he was away, a tragedy that almost tore him from public office.

At Logan's store, Robert tied his horse outside and went in. Even though his fields were calling and his family needed him to help, he took his chair by the stove and his fingers began to work out just how to shape the fierce lynx he could see in his mind. The store was busy. No one approached him at first but a small boy who watched Robert flick shavings to the floor as his knife sought to find the shape of the lynx in the wood.

"How did you fare?" Logan, free for the moment, sat opposite him.

"About what I expected."

"Silly bugger. Can't he see the lodge is a step toward freedom?"

Robert looked up quickly. "He just sees it differently." He shrugged his shoulders before turning his attention to the knife again. "What do we want with a lodge anyhow?" His fingers stopped. "Who has the time?"

"Think Duncolme has time? With all his doings? A doctor, our representative, meetings, angry blokes like us to see—think he has time to go to lodge?" The door slammed as a new customer came in and Logan stomped to the counter. The man was right. Robert laid his carving utensils side by side on the small table his friend had supplied just for him and stood. With a nod to Logan he headed out the door.

"WHY CAN'T YOU see Robert's side for once, William?"

"He's going to get himself killed, that's why." He looked across the table. "Don't you think I know he is right on so many of these points?"

"Then why don't you tell him?" Catherine resisted the urge to reach for her husband. Instead she kept her tone strong and her words stronger. "He's your brother. Can't you see how hard all of this is for him?"

"For him? What about me? I had to watch Thomas die right beside me fighting those Americans, ride all night to take his body to my parents, and watch my mother wrap her arms around his mangled body. I tried to free my father and landed in jail with him, escaped with my parents inside a load of straw where every breath filled our lungs with chaff and our heads with terror. I watched him die simply because he wrote letters to help others fight for justice against that Family Compact. Oh, yes. I know." He reached for her hands. "But I want peace. For you, for our children And now for our grandchild."

She watched his green eyes fill up and understood, finally, his pain, but she had to go on. "But peace at what price? He only asked you to join a lodge."

He jumped to his feet, eyes blazing. "Only? It's another way to cross Strachan and the rest of them. Don't you think I know that?"

"I don't see..."

"He's got them all putting money in his new bank. Robert did, too."

"What bank?"

He told her and assured her he had not been tempted. He could see this was another way to fight those in power. "Besides, I'm just too old to fight anymore." He slipped into a chair across the room and she sat close by on the settee. "I want to bounce my grandchildren on my knees and sit in my rocker on the porch," he said.

She laughed. "You've got a lot of years before that!" She patted the settee beside her and he joined her. After a few moments she spoke again in a voice so soft he barely heard her. "Perhaps you could see Strachan again?"

He sat up.

"You got him to release Robert before..." Her voice drifted off to nothing as he withdrew his arm from around her shoulders and stood. He slipped on his coat and his boots. The door closed behind him as Catherine, too, went back to work cutting the last few tired apples for applesauce.

Once the crops were planted William and Johnny saddled their horses one early morning, tied their packs on the back, and rode for Toronto. Will and Catherine promised to keep the chores done up. "We'll have Solomon and Migisi, too, don't forget," Catherine had whispered to her husband the night before. "Don't worry."

The rain had stopped the week before so the roads were at least passable. As they galloped along the Governor's Road, they watched the trees come out in full leaf and the sun light up farmers' fields almost the whole way. Many sections, though, had never seen a plow and most of those held trees sheltering all manner of wild things ready to pounce on the unwary. Ironic it was, William thought, that these unused clergy reserves could pose such a dangerous threat with all the bears and wolves there. Surely clergy lands should offer safe haven.

He stayed again in Montgomery's tavern, the first time Johnny had ever enjoyed such a place so far from home. The next day the two of them headed for Strachan's church but he was not there and his aide wouldn't or couldn't tell them when he might be. For two days they tried again there and at various likely places for a man of Strachan's power to be but had no luck. On Sunday morning they cleaned themselves and their clothes as well as they could and headed for the man's church.

St. James stone church, filled to capacity, held an expectant congregation who knew each other well. Smiles passed from pew to pew before the service started, and more than a few had questioning looks for William and Johnny. When the rector and his acolytes entered, a solemn hush stretching up into the high ceilings above settled on the crowd.

"Don't stare," William whispered to his son who gawked around taking it all in. Chastened, Johnny knelt beside him and, on the pew in front of him, rested his head on his arms like all the other men in the huge place of worship.

For two hours the service went on, most of that time taken up with the bishop's stentorian tones roaring out over the worshippers as he praised God, thanked God and managed to ingratiate himself as God's right-hand man here in the colonies, specifically in Upper Canada's Toronto. His voice was compelling and hypnotic; William wished he'd brought Robert, so convincing was the bishop's whole performance. He glanced at Johnny whose glowing eyes never left the bishop's face.

After the service he shook the bishop's hand outside the huge oak doors and asked permission to see him. The man was puzzled, William could see, so he introduced his son and himself. Strachan suddenly nodded but his brows contracted and his eyes clouded over. They made a date for the next morning.

Chapter Twenty-Six

June, 1837

SOMEHOW ROBERT AND HIS FAMILY got their crops in although the rains that year seemed to come often and just severe enough that the ground hardly dried up before another punishing system was upon them. More than once Robert and Logan arrived in Centreville drenched and dispirited. They went so often that Mary Anne lost her smile even on the days he stayed home and worked their land.

He'd given up talking to her about the Centreville meetings; her face fell and her whole body seemed to shrink into itself whenever he mentioned his worries. Let her concern herself only with the farm and their family. He took the burden of worrying about and maybe even changing their future completely upon himself.

This day, however, his youngest had begged to go with him and Mary Anne, in some clever and desperate plan to keep his mind on their family, had added her pleading voice until he had thrown up his hands in surrender. Russell could come.

The boy sat his horse like a man, a proud man, and though he was only fourteen, Robert saw the change in him. His excitement was palpable. His red hair blew gold in the breeze and his ruddy cheeks fairly bloomed, freckles and all. He glanced over at his father with a large-toothed grin that filled his whole face as he snapped the reins and heeled his horse into action.

"Race you!" He yelled over his shoulder. Robert took up the challenge but Russell was away like a fleeing deer. Robert slowed his horse and hoped Russell would, too. The animals needed their strength for their long trip.

"Why'd you bring him?" Logan had caught up.

"Didn't have much choice. Between him and his mother." He left it at that but his thoughts roamed to meetings they'd attended before. He hoped he'd done the right thing.

By midday the three reached Centreville. Mr. Logan needed no supplies today. Robert took his few carvings and his son to the supply store where Russell marvelled over the shelves brimming with tins of coffee, bags of flour, and quite a selection of ready-made clothes. As usual the owner bought all that Robert had brought.

This time the meeting at the hotel was quietly efficient as Dr. Duncolme reported on rebel activities and brought the group up to date on the bank's progress. Partway through this part of the meeting, Henry Clark slipped in and took a seat at their table glancing in Russell's direction and nodding to the other two.

Men were needed to plan for the Constitutional Convention to be held in December in Toronto. Two of them. And Mr. Logan was picked. The other Robert didn't know but he looked serious and talked with sense. They would be good candidates. Robert was named an alternate.

Once the meeting broke up and Clark had met Russell, the man turned to Robert and began to speak. "Those Quaker boys're angry over in Sodom." He took a slug of ale and paused to let his words sink in.

"That's strange." Robert looked down at the table. "Their elders will stop them."

"Not sure. Elders don't know."

Logan leaned forward. "They're not the only ones. I know some of the names. Smart people. Educated. All plenty angry with the Compact."

"Right." Clark looked left and right and sat forward on his chair. "People are plenty stirred up. Others are talking, too. All over the province."

"What are you saying?" Even though Russell was right beside him, Robert couldn't stop himself.

The men went on to mention last year's crooked election and all the other grievances they had against the Family Compact. None of this was new to Russell, his father knew, but perhaps the excitement of whispering about it in public was. As soon as he could, Robert got Logan's eye and together they rose to go.

On the trip home the three kept their own counsel, even Russell, whose exuberance had changed into thoughtfulness; Robert worried what his son might be thinking. For himself, going off to these meetings and contemplating actions to bring their government to a position more responsible to its citizens was one thing. For his youngest son such actions were quite another.

When the three of them reached their concession road, darkness had almost fallen and, were it not June, would have. Russell rode between the older men, still quiet, but bathed in the last pink rays of the sun. Robert could wait no longer.

"Enjoy your day, son?" he asked.

"Yes, but..."

"You've got questions." Robert finished the sentence for him.

The young man turned to his father and Robert could not see his face. "Are you...are you a rebel, Father?"

There it was. With the straightforward pitch of youth, his son took him by surprise. No preamble. No leadup. Just the heart of the matter. He didn't know what to say. Was he a rebel? Certainly he disagreed with those in power and would do almost anything to fix their little world. His horse trotted along and for a moment he was lost in its sure rhythm.

"Father?"

"Yes, my son. I mean no, I'm not really a rebel."

"Then I don't know you at all," Logan called over.

Robert pulled his horse up and the others stopped, too. "I just want some say, Russell! These Family Compact men have all the power; they can make us do whatever they want. They line their pockets at our expense. Oh, you know what I mean. I've talked about it often enough!" He dug his heels in and rode on. The others caught up.

"Will you fight?"

Russell's words caught him again but this time he kept going. "I don't know. And that's the honest truth, my son."

"I think you should. And I will, too."

"No, Russell, no. You shouldn't." The sight of his twin brother's dead body hanging over William's horse so many years ago flashed into his mind. The waste. No. Not this for his sons.

BEFORE THE PLANNING MEETING IN JULY, Robert received a visitor in his own parlor late one afternoon. "Henry Clark. What brings you all the way out here?" He shook the man's hand and together they sat. Mary Anne hovered at the stove.

"I've brought news, Garner." He glanced at Mary Anne.

Robert hardly knew what to do. Mary Anne simply didn't need to hear this. He rose in his chair. "I've some chores in the barn." He motioned to Clark. "Come with me. We can talk while I feed the animals."

"But I've just made tea for our guest, Robert." She stepped between the men and the door. "Surely Mr. Clark would enjoy some sustenance after his long ride from…?"

Clark's eyes went to the cake on the table, already sliced onto plates. He hesitated.

Robert could see the man's lips moving in anticipation. "If you'd rather…"

The man grabbed the chair Mary Anne offered, pulled a plate over and waited for her to hand him a fork. Robert sat opposite but shook his head when his wife offered him a piece. Mary Anne poured tea and sat with the men. Almost immediately Clark accepted more cake. Robert glowered but he refused to speak of the rebel activities in his wife's presence; he let her make small conversation with his guest.

"And what of that fine young man I met in Centreville?"

"We'll not talk of that." Robert was in the man's face. "I mean,

Russell is too young to be interested...rather, he wants to be a farmer...yes, that's what he said."

"He did?" Mary Anne wore that amazed look she so often used when disagreeing with him. "He said that?"

"Well, yes."

"He liked going to that meeting, I know that. Talked of nothing else for days." She sipped her tea but her eyes stared over the cup right at him.

"You finished your cake, Clark?" He pushed his plate aside.

With profuse thanks to Mary Anne, Mr. Clark wiped his red lips and pushed away from the table. Outside Robert could hardly contain himself but knew he must.

"The wife not too fond of the rebels then?"

They walked side by side to the barn where Robert had nothing that needed doing. He pulled a three-legged stool over and pointed at another one for Clark. The late afternoon sun slanted right in the door Robert had left open and lit the dirt floor across to where they sat. The heat of the day seemed to gather around them, warm but comfortable. Calmer now, Robert smiled at his guest. "What is it, Clark? What brought you out here?"

The man apologized for upsetting Robert. He had not realized how things might be with his wife. "Good cake, though," he said.

"What is it, man?" He stamped his foot into the straw-covered dirt and lost his balance. The stool tipped so fast Robert landed in the dirt. Mr. Clark lost his balance, too, but managed to keep from falling, a difficult thing with his considerable belly. His laughter filled the barn.

Robert did not laugh. He stood facing Clark, the sun burning his back, his temper flaring, barely able to contain himself. Clark blurted out his news. Robert would have to go to the meeting in Toronto; the other man had declined.

Supper was strained. Thomas and Russell both saw the anger in their father's eyes and the pained look their mother wore. At times like these Robert missed Elizabeth's easy ways of making everyone laugh. She'd been married only a few months but it seemed like forever. He passed the creamed peas and beans—a favorite of Russell's—to the boy for seconds. Russell smiled. "Thanks." Thomas took a spoonful and touched his mother's arm with the bowl. She murmured something unintelligible but did not give it to her husband. Robert waited a moment, swallowed the meat in his mouth, and placed his fork on his plate. "Perhaps I'll have some, too." Thomas shoved the bowl toward his father.

She didn't join him on the porch that night. Dark came on as he sat alone, his sons still in the barn, and the first cicadas of the season practising their strident calls. The open window above his head told him Mary Anne was still at the dishes and still angry. There was no singing this night and he missed her tuneful melodies. They had been through so much but they'd faced it all together. This wide gulf between them was new and he knew not how to fix it. His sons clomped up the steps, stood a moment before him, removed their boots and went inside.

It was dark now. No moon, but an abundance of stars. He wished he could peel back the darkness and light up the moon to take its place with the rest of its starry family. Oh, he knew that wasn't how it worked, that the moon had its rhythm and would come again but he needed it now. He sat on, his family settled for the night, and he slid his tired body from the bench to breathe the night air a moment before heading inside.

The hurt feelings and misunderstandings that had simmered for weeks erupted a few days later. Once again Robert had spent much of his day at Logan's store and came home for supper with a handful of new carvings. One he liked especially. For the first time he'd created a human figure. Up to now all his work was of animals; wild or tamed, he'd mastered them all. This time, however, he cut and carved for almost the whole day to get it right. Time had been irrelevant, even unknown, as he poured his heavy heart into a carving almost the length of his hand and with intricate details that had taxed him beyond measure.

He didn't mind. His heart and soul were here in his work for the entire world to see and when he finally set the piece on the counter for Logan and his customers to look at, three people had asked his price on the spot. But he wouldn't sell it. He wrapped it in the soft leather cloth and slipped it inside his shirt, suddenly anxious to get home.

Across the yard and up his front steps Robert hurried. As soon as he pushed open the door, the sound hit him. Sobbing. In the bedroom. He threw off his shoes and ran to Mary Anne. His sons were nowhere to be seen. Was it them? He crept into the darkened room. Her crumpled form was a blur under the quilt. Was she sick? Her sobs pulsed in his ears but as he sat and put his hand on her she shrieked, shocked and frightened by his sudden appearance.

He tried to pull her to him; she pushed back. His voice sounded soothing to him but she covered her ears. He reached up and threw open the heavy curtains. Her face was that of an old hag except that it was redder than he'd ever seen it. Blood streamed from scratches down her cheeks and her hair tumbled through it all. But the worst was her eyes. They were so wide and frightened his gut wrenched for he'd only ever seen her like this once before. Behind him the door slammed but he paid it no heed.

He managed to get his arms around her and keep them there although she pushed and pulled to get free. Nothing would make him let her go. She needed his strength even if she didn't realize it herself. "Sh, sh," he whispered over and over, wondering all the while if she could even hear him, over her own anguished wailing. Such pain. What had caused this?

Gradually she relaxed in his arms and her screams became moans punctuated every so often by sharp little cries. With each one he gripped her tighter, as much for him as for her. When she seemed to have cried her last tears, he held her back from his chest and looked again at her face. The bleeding had stopped, he thought, although the dim light hindered his vision. Still her cheeks were bloody from her eyes to her chin. He took her hands in his and turned them over.

"Oh, God." Cries came from behind. Thomas and Russell had slipped in. He moved to hide Mary Anne from her sons but they had seen too much already. Russell knelt on the floor in front of them, looking from one to the other trying to understand. Robert suddenly recognized the blame in the boy's eyes. Just when Robert thought he could feel no worse, Thomas grabbed at his shoulder and yanked him to his feet.

"No, no," Robert cried. "You don't understand." His oldest son pulled his fist back and, before Robert could react, punched him in the face. His cheekbone on fire and blood now dripping from his own face, he raised his arms in submission but Thomas' fury was not over.

"Come on, then. Fight me. Not my mother!" He screamed the last word. Robert tried to duck out of the way but was not quick enough. His son's furious fist glanced off his ear shooting such pain through his head he thought the ear might be gone. Still he would not fight back. Russell grabbed his brother and pushed him against the bedroom wall. A shrill and shrieking Mary Anne flew at them slapping at all three of them with both hands until at last Thomas checked his fists and Robert turned again to his wife.

He got her back on the edge of the bed, his arms wrapped around her again, his unintelligible words coming from somewhere deep within. His own pain disappeared as he tried to calm her but she shrieked and cried until the sun had disappeared and he could hardly see her, a blessing in a way. He lay on the bed beside her. Eventually she let him pull her close, his arms around her soothing and calming her whole body. Her screams became whimpers.

Russell came back in the room with a basin of warm water and, as Robert held her, washed the blood from his mother's face with a gentleness Robert had not known his son possessed. Thomas held a candle for Russell's task but in its light Robert saw his son's utter shock and confusion. He felt again his own wounds but smiled at his son. "You didn't know. I will heal."

The young man nodded but didn't speak. Instead he motioned toward his mother. "She's asleep."

Robert carefully pulled his arms away. Mary Anne moaned as though she might wake but Russell laid his hairy hand—a man's hand Robert suddenly realized—on her arm and softly stroked her back to sleep. Thomas set the candle on the nightstand but Robert shook his head. They took the candle out of the room, closing the squeaky door behind them.

The three of them sat nearby listening for any sound, all of them too shocked to be hungry. Robert finally told his sons about coming home from the last war to find Buffalo burning and his distraught wife wandering in the smoke amid the blackened shells of homes, his own included, and clinging to the still bundle in her arms. He could never forget her vacant eyes and aimless actions that had taken months to lessen. Mary Anne had never fully recovered.

As he spoke his voice softened and broke as that time came back to him. His sons made not a sound but watched him as though he was a stranger for he and Mary Anne had never told this story.

"We had a sister?" Russell whispered. "Besides Elizabeth?"

"Yes. A beautiful little girl." He could hardly speak. "Mary Anne," he croaked.

Thomas cleared his throat and tried again to apologize to his father but Robert cut him off.

"You thought you were protecting your mother." He reached across to put his hand on his son's knee. "And now you both see why I don't want another war." He pushed out of his chair and moved to the cupboard. "We should eat."

Chapter Twenty-Seven

Toronto, 1837

THE BISHOP WAS SIPPING A CUP OF TEA when William and Johnny entered his office bright and early that morning. Holding their hats, the two stopped just inside the door and dipped their heads toward the man in black before them. His eyes followed their every move. William tried to maintain his composure but the man seemed to have no recollection of ever meeting him before yesterday's church service. He would have to build bridges all over again.

Behind him Johnny shifted from one foot to the other but kept his focus on the stern-faced bishop. The white clerical collar shone against the black shirt and waistcoat declaring his importance for all to see. Not only was he powerful here on earth but his connection to the powers above seemed certain. The man replaced his gold-rimmed cup on its china saucer and leaned back. His delicate hands joined over his slight paunch.

William thought of speaking. Johnny shifted back and forth. A black fly meandered over the saucer on the desk and flitted to the rim of the cup. No one spoke. He could feel the sweat on his forehead but did nothing.

"Mr.?" In a honeyed voice the bishop spoke.

"Garner. William Garner. And this is my son, John. John Garner. We—."

"Ah. I remember him." He lapsed into silence again. "You named your son after his grandfather."

Even on this hot day William could feel the hatred emanating from the bishop. Certainly, he now remembered their family. Seeing Johnny seemed to remind him. "I was here before, you may remember..." he paused, "alone. And you helped me free my brother. For which I thank you again, sir." When the man said nothing, he continued. "I have another subject to discuss, if you will."

"What has your rebel brother got himself into now?"

William swallowed and shifted to a more comfortable position. Perhaps because he had tired of looking up into the faces of the tall Garner men, the bishop pointed toward the chairs. Father and son sat. "You know my family and I came here as Loyalists and loyal we remain. But we cannot tolerate seeing and hearing of injustices, of situations, all of which try the patience of everyone in Upper Canada."

"Watch yourself, sir." The bishop's voice dropped to a deep and foreboding tone but William forged ahead.

"Sir. You and your fellows in government have created a colony out of the wilderness. All of us realize that. Many, though, feel the inequities which your group does nothing to alleviate. Now, I am a peaceful man. I had enough of war twenty-five years ago. I was a young man then and it almost broke me, my family, and most of my friends. Peace is what we want. Peace and fair play." Johnny leaned forward beside him but William hurried on. "Can you not listen to the issues those of us on the back roads and in the tiny villages of the whole of Upper Canada experience each and every day?"

Johnny's hand on his arm stopped him from going further. The young man leaned toward the desk and placed his huge hands side by side on its polished surface. The bishop leaned back in his chair and eyed Johnny.

"These are farmer's hands," Johnny began. "They want to be farmer's hands but God in his infinite wisdom has given them the ability to be so much more." He turned them over and flexed the broad fingers, stared a moment at the hardened lines etched deep into them even at his young age. "They can hold a pen, a child, a spoon, or a gun. Every bit as easily as the handle of a plow or a scythe."

"Are you threatening me?" The bishop jumped to his feet.

Johnny and William stood also and Johnny raised his arms in the air.

"Not at all, sir," he said as he quietly slid into his seat again. William, too, sat. "I emphasize we only want to work the land, to raise our children, and provide for our families in the best way we know. Just as I'm sure you do."

The bishop gave a curt nod, his eyes still on fire.

William took over. "What my son is trying to explain is that we are capable of many things but what we want is peace. And a good life for our families." When the bishop remained silent, William dared to go on. His chest expanded as he glanced at the intelligent and well-spoken young man beside him and back to the bishop. "Those you and so many others call rebels want the same things, too."

"They don't want to fight. From what I see and hear they only want justice," Johnny added.

"Is that so much?" William finished his son's thought and leaned back again. Either the bishop would agree or hustle them off to spend time in the cells Robert had been obliged to occupy.

The man rose from his chair and stomped out of the room, slamming the door behind him. William turned to his son and shrugged but Johnny's face dissolved into a smile so completely disarming he suddenly saw his own father. Of course those had been his father's words he'd heard, too. Not the exact words but the logic, the patient reasoning, the strong position laced with honor and kindness. William would remember that gift no matter what happened now.

When the door opened again they both expected to see the bishop but, instead, his young acolyte marched in and told them their time was up. Like a sentinel he stood to one side holding the door open; all that was missing was his rifle. Father and son left.

• • •

ROBERT LAY AWAKE thinking of his troubled relationship with his brother but could see no solution. Beside him Mary Anne's breathing was troubled. *How can I ever leave her to do my duty?* He had made a commitment to Clark but he had made a bigger one to Mary Anne on the day they were married, and he was incapable of deciding which promise he should keep. His wife meant everything to him, but....

In the morning the answer came from an unlikely source. When Russell took Mary Anne's breakfast to her in the bedroom, Thomas quietly told his father he must go and do his duty. "I'll look after Mama. And Russell will, too. And even Elizabeth will look in on us while you're gone."

And so, when the time came, Robert kissed his passive wife goodbye and left her with their sons who assured him all would be well. And it was.

A week or so later when Robert pushed his tired horse the last few miles, both of them found the extra energy they needed to get home, Robert to ease his mind about Mary Anne and the horse to run free in her own paddock. As he crossed the threshold his wife greeted him from a chair before the kitchen table where she sat scrubbing new potatoes, halving them, and dropping them into the pot before her.

The merry supper with the four of them tired her out and she rose early to pat each of them on the shoulder, drop a light kiss on Robert's cheek, and disappear into the bedroom. Her men cleared up and sat again around the table eating early apples from their own orchard. He supposed his sons wanted the news from Toronto but he waited until he was sure Mary Anne had settled for the night before he spoke.

Most of the rebel activity centered on Toronto but other areas throughout the colony had sent representatives to this planning meeting. He'd met Henry Clark there and a few others who had attended their meetings in Centreville. All the talk was about the Constitutional Convention to be held in December. Speakers outlined their grievances with those in power, many of whom held conflicting positions in various powerful sections of their government. The late King's death demanded by law that the House be disbanded and new elections held, but the Family Compact refused to conform.

"Now they're so strong they're openly breaking the law. Or will be by December," Robert explained. "Many speakers brought news about Quebec."

Thomas' eyebrows wrinkled in confusion.

"Lower Canada." Robert paused. "You know this, Thomas."

"Yes, of course." His son nodded. "But what does it have to do with us?"

"They're in a worse mess than we are."

"With their government?" Russell's face contorted. "Surely not."

"Yes. And what's more they're talking open rebellion. Screaming it, in fact, so the speakers reported." He shook his head and in a moment went on to tell his sons the rebel plans. More meetings would be held all over the district to spread the word about the convention scheduled for December. He tried to downplay the whole affair because his sons, especially Russell, looked altogether too excited about what he was sure was going to be open rebellion here in Upper Canada.

"I just hope all this puts enough pressure on Strachan and his cohorts."

"What do you mean, Father?" Thomas rested his hand on Robert's arm.

"Why, to make them see reason." His voice rose and his fist pounded the table at the last word.

With worried glances toward the bedroom door, Thomas and Russell hushed their father who sagged back in his chair as he remembered again his fragile wife. Later, thoughts of the anger and the reason, the shouting and the calm speeches still pounded through his head and, rather than risk waking Mary Anne, he stretched out on the padded chair, his feet on a small table in front. His sons were long gone to their own beds when he woke with a start and went to to join his wife.

• • •

WILLIAM AND JOHNNY avoided Robert's road as they traveled the last few miles home from their fruitless trip to Toronto. They had no good news to tell and didn't want to risk Robert's ire when he heard they had gone to Toronto without him to try to avert the fight they all knew was coming. Perhaps Strachan would act on their words—he had not said he wouldn't—but neither had he given any sign he heard their point of view.

"He just stomped out of the room," William told Catherine that night at supper.

"Sent his lackey to get us out of his office." Johnny shook his head and his blonde curls flew with the force of it.

Will, slightly put out at being left behind, spoke up. "We had some trouble here, too. A group of neighbors rode up and down the concessions railing at the government."

"Really? Did they come here?" William's tired body perked up.

Catherine spoke before Will had a chance. "I dusted off the rifle and met them on the porch." Will tried to speak but she placed her hand on his arm and cut him off. "Will was across the river with Migisi."

"We couldn't get back. Saw the riders—and heard them—and tried to get here." Will's eyes were on his father who understood his discomfort. The young man felt he'd failed his mother. "I'm sure your mother was well able to take care of herself, son. She's certainly done it before." A look passed between Catherine and himself.

"On another matter," Catherine said, "Solomon has disappeared again. Neither Migisi nor Kiwidinok heard him go a couple of days ago. Kiwi told me she's worried about him. He carries a lot of anger."

William nodded. This was an ongoing problem with the boy—man, now—and he didn't think much about Solomon's disappearance. He'd come back when he was ready. His own son, however, wore a worried frown. Perhaps there was more to this than he knew. They'd have words in the barn later.

Chapter Twenty-Eight

October, 1837

BY LATE OCTOBER word filtered back to both Robert's and William's households about the rebellious activities in Lower Canada where shots had been fired and people killed, all for the same kinds of problems as those in Upper Canada. The rebels met and Mackenzie urged the group to march on the government in Toronto while it was virtually undefended, all the troops having gone to help in Lower Canada. The consensus, however, was to hold back and see what happened. Perhaps the Lower Canada uproar would be enough to make the British parliament act.

Dr. Duncolme, who had lost his fighting spirit after his failed trip to England and losing his son, now turned his attention away from legislation toward the rebel movement. Though he'd not been involved in the various meetings held in the heart of Upper Canada, the news of the uprising in Lower Canada brought him to meetings with rebels closer to his Bishopsgate home. Once more he appeared at the hotel in Centreville. Robert and Logan were delighted to see him.

WINTER WAS COMING. William had to break ice off the water in the bucket three days in a row this week. Early one morning he took Johnny and the wagon to Logan's store. Catherine had given

Elaine Cougler

him a long list for her winter preparations and his own seemed to be growing as he stood in the store fingering the harness and weighing the tools. Johnny had rope in his hands, a long coil of it. He measured the heft of it and considered whether it would be too heavy for tying calves. The smell of fresh cut wood wafted throughout the warm store.

Soft voices rumbled from the back corner of the store but one caught William's attention. He looked to the counter but Logan was no longer measuring sugar where he'd been just a few minutes before. A familiar voice rose above the others. Johnny listened, too, and they looked at each other as the faraway words suddenly made sense.

He motioned his son behind him and edged toward the din. Louder it was, both because William had moved but also because the voices were angry. Or were they excited? From behind a stack of flour sacks, William listened.

"It's in December."

"What?"

"When the six months is up. Since the King's death, I mean." This was Robert's voice.

"Our own government will be sitting illegally. Will we finally march then?" Logan's words rose. "You know what people want. You were right beside me in that summer meeting. What are we waiting for, Robert? Even Duncolme agrees." A fist banged on the table beside Robert, William supposed, and he was just going to step forward and confront his brother when Logan shouted louder than before. "Oh, you've lost your nerve!"

The man stomped around the corner right into William, who stepped aside as quickly as he could but not fast enough. The stack of heavy flour sacks slid to the floor trapping William's feet and tripping Logan, who fell into William's arms and the two sprawled on the floor in a pile of powdery arms and flailing fists.

William pulled himself off the floor and stepped around the store owner but Robert had seen him. His brother glared with a look so intense William expected at any moment he and Logan

The Loyalist Legacy

would gang up on him. He hadn't counted on Johnny, though. Suddenly his youngest son was beside him, brushing the flour from his clothes. Robert checked his fists in mid swing and Logan used the table to pull himself up but he still muttered and mumbled, furious at the mess.

Johnny pulled his father toward the counter where they paid the glowering Logan and got their purchases outside before either he or Robert could say anything else and make the situation worse. Johnny took the lines, a good thing as William's hands were shaking. He'd not been so close to a fight in many years. The feeling was not one he wished to experience again.

The next Sunday the whole family arrived at Helen's house laden with pies and hams, and—the ladies, at least—ready for a quiet afternoon of rocking babies and taking a day of rest. It had been a good harvest and were it not for the political turmoil rousing the whole region all might have gone well.

Helen found her old talents as the family conciliator called to the fore again. She was none too pleased about Robert's glowering looks at his brother and even at his nephews. When she looked at William, expecting an explanation, he glanced away and Catherine spoke up.

"Your garden looks well tidied, Helen."

She saw Catherine's intention. "Yes. The boys have worked hard, as have I. My cupboard is lined with jellies and jams." William and Robert seemed not to have heard. She raised her eyebrows and went on. "They're all lined up together on the shelves and getting along famously, just like family. Or at least like family should."

William still made no sign he was listening. Robert's face went red. "Harrumph," he said.

"Come on, you two. Snap out of it." Helen used the phrase their father had used when they were children, but neither brother obeyed although William's head nodded ever so slightly and Robert had the grace to look a little sheepish. She pounced on him. "Aha. I knew you couldn't stay angry for long. Come on. Help me slice the ham." Robert took her outstretched hand and together they attacked the ham while Catherine set the table. William suddenly became engrossed in his nephew's game of cards.

Neither Elizabeth's nor Eva's family were with them this day, but even without them Helen's tiny cabin was stretched to the limit. Though she'd had offers, she had not married again. Her brothers were united in their opinion that she should, but stubborn she had always been and stubborn she remained.

"What will you do if your Thomas takes a wife?" Robert asked.

"Did you not notice the stakes to the south, then? I wondered why no one asked about them."

William tore his glance away from the knot in the pine floor. "Stakes?"

Helen jumped to her feet, a broad grin spreading across her face. "Yes. Come and see." She wrapped her shawl around her shoulders and rushed outside leaving the rest to follow. Two young men came across the yard toward them—her twins who had been feeding the animals in the barn. They rushed to point out where the new cabin would be.

"Thomas is getting married? Why didn't you tell us?" Catherine held Mary Anne's arm as they surveyed the staked out land. Helen explained she'd only just found out herself and that her Thomas was, even as they spoke, having Sunday dinner with the young lady's family. No doubt the wedding would happen soon. "There'll be a house raising immediately, and that's for certain." She turned to her brothers. "Will you come?"

The day was waning as they trooped back inside to the warm fire to have a few minutes together. The young men sat on the floor, Helen stirred the fire up, and Catherine sat writing out her recipe for corn chowder to leave with her sister-in-law.

"You've a new brooch there, I think," said Mary Anne who had barely spoken all day.

"William brought it from Toronto. I think Johnny saw it and gave him no peace until he bought it." She smiled at the memory but suddenly glanced at her husband. She had promised to keep his trip a secret and wished she had not blurted out where he got

The Loyalist Legacy

the brooch. But it was too late.

"Toronto? You were in Toronto?" Helen raised her voice to reach William across the room.

In the spark of a firefly the secret was out. Robert glared at William who fixed his wife with the most frustrated of looks. Everyone spoke at once. William explained that he and Johnny had met with Strachan.

"Why?" Robert stood before his brother and challenged him. "Checking up on me again?"

William tried to explain but Robert wasn't listening. Johnny's voice entered the fray, too, as the young man sought to make peace. Catherine reached for Robert's arm but he jerked it away. William rose to his feet and raised his fists to his angry brother. Words were flung as hot tempers burned like the fire in their midst until a woeful scream, pitched higher than all their voices, rent the air. They whirled around.

On the weathered settee, her hair loosed and hanging from her head, her eyes red and rimmed with fear, and her white throat stretched long and taut with the effort of screaming out her agony, sat the most vulnerable member of their family, Mary Anne. The sound stopped everyone for a few seconds but when the distressed woman began to scratch at her face, they ran to stop her. It was William who was closest and he grabbed her hands and held them tightly until Robert, a split second later, wrapped his arms around her and pinned her arms at her sides.

William nodded to his brother and stepped back, shocked to the core at seeing firsthand the terrible stress Robert was living under. He glanced at Catherine, nodded in agreement to her wordless tip of her head, and moved toward the door. Before he left, however, he stepped back and put his arm on Robert's for just a moment, though his brother was still trying to calm his wife. Helen made sure Catherine got her dishes, saw them out, and hurried back inside.

WITH NEW AWARENESS of his brother's life, William softened. A few days later, as November edged into December, he took his horse and rode for Robert's house, determined not to anger him but rather to help. Thomas was in the barn and greeted his uncle with a smile, stretched and strained though it was. William asked about Mary Anne and tears filled his nephew's eyes. His parents were inside. A cow mooed and the chickens chosen to escape the axe and live over the winter clucked and clacked underfoot, filling in the silences. Accepting his uncle's help turning the pigs out of their pen, Thomas slapped the last sow on the rump, perhaps a little harder than necessary.

The house was quiet. Robert ushered him in but said not a word. They sat across the table where small carvings faced toward Robert's chair. "Let me see," William whispered. One by one his brother turned the figures toward him. All were good, very good, in fact, but the best was a little taller and certainly more intricate. Robert picked it up with care and folded his large hands around it before passing it to William. He could see it was Mary Anne.

They talked. She was asleep in the bedroom. Robert would not leave her alone, he said. Elizabeth had dropped off a huge pot of stew but as William watched he barely ate. Thomas did his chores as well as his father's. Russell had gone to the store and given Mr. Logan their list yesterday but once he brought the goods home he'd gone back and no one had seen him since. His face utterly drained, Robert spoke. "I think he's gone to Centreville for supplies. With Logan." He almost choked out the last word; fear lit his face but he suddenly looked at William. "Solomon was hanging around outside. Waiting for Russell."

William didn't know why Robert was so afraid. Certainly for Mary Anne, he knew, but his brother held much more inside and William tried to get him to talk. For the first time in years he began to understand more of Robert and his life. He saw the defeat and the terror. Robert picked up his knife and began to shape another carving. Shavings flew over the table and onto the floor around him but he was oblivious to the mess. He bent his head to the task, the only thing that brought him hope, and William slipped away without seeing or hearing Mary Anne. He was strangely glad of that.

On a cold dark morning a few days later William rose from his bed at the rooster's first sound. He thought something else had wakened him but just as he was trying to get his sleep-muddled brain to figure it all out, a furious pounding sounded on the door. Catherine grabbed her shawl while he pulled on his trousers and together they ran to the door. Will and Johnny got there first and pulled the bar across to admit Thomas. Robert's Thomas.

"They've gone to Toronto!" He looked from one to the other and went on. "Russ, I mean. And Solomon. They went with Mr. Logan!" Their young nephew stopped for a breath. "Father says can you come?"

Still fighting to understand why Thomas was so fired up and why he had come so early in the morning—before first light, even—William motioned his nephew to the table. Catherine had already stirred the fire and the kettle would soon boil. The boy needed food. And to take a breath. "Tell me again," William said. "Why have they gone to Toronto?"

"And what's so bad about that?" Catherine asked.

Thomas accepted a mug but before he drank looked at each of them in turn. "You haven't heard," he said.

"Heard what, Thomas?" William raised his voice. "Just tell us what you mean to say."

"They're marching," he cried. "Marching to Toronto where Mackenzie is rebelling against the government, the Family Compact, the whole darn mess of them." He jerked his eyes to William. "Surely you know!"

But they didn't know. And, truth be told, William didn't want to know. Now, though, his own flesh and blood was involved and he saw he must try to avert tragedy. As Thomas calmed down enough to spill all his news, Catherine, her grey hair still in a night braid and her flannel nightgown warm next to her husband, laid her hand on his arm.

"They've gone to Toronto?" Will spoke up.

"Yes. Well, no. The rebels are meeting near Norwich. Duncolme has called them out. To march. They have guns. Neither of them knows anything about shooting men."

"Calm yourself, Thomas," Catherine said. "Where is your father? Did he go with them?"

"No, I told you. He won't leave Mother."

"And the idea is to go to Toronto?" William still couldn't credit the story.

"Yes. They want to take over the government." Thomas drained his cup, hot as the tea still was, and slid his chair back. "I...we... must go. Don't you see that, Uncle?"

Before the sun had any chance to melt the frosty fields Thomas had left and with him, William and Johnny. Once again, Will stayed behind to manage the farm. Catherine packed what food she could and urged her men to take their warmest coats. They left the wagon behind, the faster to travel and pounded down the road to Robert's where they stopped in to reassure him before riding on to the meeting place outside Norwich. When they reached the house on the corner atop a small hill, all that was left of the men were footprints in the snow showing they'd marched east on Quaker Street, probably not long before.

As he stood up in the stirrups to try to look through the trees where the narrow road disappeared, William thought he heard something on the wind from the east but neither of the two with him heard anything. They huddled a moment planning their next move. They would have to follow the group and look for Russell and Solomon with them. He hoped they would come peaceably.

The three men rode side by side, slowly, trying to save their horses both from exhaustion and from catching a hoof in holes hidden by the churned up mud. Even with the slow pace Johnny soon pointed a finger down the road and, while William's eyes couldn't quite make them out, Johnny and Thomas certainly saw the band of men marching up the hill ahead. They pushed on.

As they passed the few stragglers bringing up the rear of the rebel group, William studied each face; he knew none of them.

He edged his horse alongside the main body marching side by side in tight order; the other two kept pace with him. Among the men panting from the steep climb, he searched for Russell and Solomon but could not see them.

"Uncle!" A voice from behind stopped him. He thought it was Thomas. Instead a rider came up behind them shouting and waving. It was Russell and with him rode Solomon. He'd forgotten the horses. Of course they wouldn't be walking. William nodded at his nephew and stopped; the marchers continued and soon left the group to themselves.

Russell's grin slipped as he looked at his relatives' faces, especially his uncle's. With narrowed eyes, the boy squared his shoulders and stared back at his uncle. William could not convince him to return home with them, and Solomon was determined to go wherever Russell went. Finally, William sent Johnny and Thomas home and agreed to ride, himself, with the rebels. He hoped as they traveled to Toronto in the cold and the snow and the mud, the other two would give in.

They rode near the head of the marching rebels quite close to Dr. Duncolme himself whom William had never met but about whom he had heard quite a lot. As he watched and listened he saw an intelligent and forthright man sitting straight in his saddle, his eyes fixed on the road ahead. He looked away only when one of his seconds needed his attention and then he listened, nodded or shook his head, and quietly dealt with the problem. Unperturbed, he was, and full of purpose. William saw why Robert followed him.

They reached the little village of Scotland just in time for Dr. Duncolme to call a halt. The men needed a rest and a chance to eat. William shared his food with his nephew and the ever silent Solomon, who didn't seem to have anything left to eat, and watched the steady parade of men stop by to speak to Russell. Apparently the boy had made his mark here.

Able now to see and hear those who had chosen to rebel, he was surprised at the level of conversation. These men were no rabble. They had a better grasp of the political situation under the Family

Compact than his own sons and nephews did and even than William himself. Quakers marched with them, too, a surprising development, as he knew that group to be peaceful. Perhaps the older Quakers were unaware of the younger men marching here.

A sudden pounding of hooves put everyone on edge and most of the men jumped to their feet, looking to ready their knives and their crowbars or the rifles some were lucky enough to carry. The two riders had messages for Dr. Duncolme. One bounded from his frothing horse and spoke urgently to Duncolme who paused a moment and then gazed around at his men. His hands pointed from one of his aides to another in quick succession. The bugle sounded and William remembered that call even though he had not heard it for over twenty years. Retreat.

All around him men stuffed their pockets and packs as quickly as they could. Duncolme mounted his horse but instead of leading them away, turned the animal toward his men and raised his arm for quiet. For a few moments that was impossible to achieve, but one by one the men noticed and turned to face their leader.

He sat his horse well, his back straight and his gloved hands tight on the reins holding the wide-eyed horse from bolting. From his calm demeanor and the slight smile for his men, he might have been organizing a country pony race, but those closest to him could see the slight jerking of his thumbs and an equally disturbing twitch on the left side of his face. William's lips tightened as Duncolme began to speak.

"The news is bad, men. These riders have risked their very lives to tell us the rebellion is over in Toronto."

A collective intake of the cold December air bespoke the men's understanding and their fear. Some of them shuffled where they stood. William sensed the whole group was ready to bolt but was just waiting for their leader to disperse them.

"Who won?" A voice shouted from the edges of the group.

"They attacked a few days ago but our men lost." Voices grumbled and feet shuffled again. "And that is not the whole, gentlemen." He rose in his stirrups. "Colonel MacNab is just a few miles away, hot on our trail. Somehow he knows about us. We must disperse or we'll be charged with treason." The men began to move. "I release you all now, with my thanks and my best wishes. Go!" He sat a few moments watching his force disperse in a disorderly fashion and then he dismounted. His closest associates gathered round and William glimpsed the man removing a list from his vest pocket. He stepped closer.

"What will you do with it, sir?" Duncolme's second-in-command stayed close.

"Bury it. We don't want MacNab to get his hands on it. Find me something to dig a hole in this blasted frozen ground."

His men produced a small shovel, hardly adequate for the task, and they cleared away the snow before scraping into the frozen ground. A shallow pit was all they could manage in the time they had but into it they deposited Duncolme's piece of paper, covered it with a thin layer of soil and some snow. William climbed onto his own horse and set off with his boys.

They rode for Norwich, stopped to warn the village their men were fleeing, and carried on as fast and as far as they could. At Centreville, the skies turned dark and William took a room for the night that all of them might share. He barely slept. By morning the five vacated the room but Solomon turned his horse in a different direction. William tried to convince him to come with them but Solomon refused.

"Migisi and Kiwidinok miss you, son," he said but the tall black-skinned man before him just shook his head. "Where will you go?" William tried again.

"I go into the wind, Father. There is another who waits for me. I go to her." He bowed his head to William and when he lifted it again bright tears covered his coal-black eyes. William removed his heavy glove and reached his bare hand to the powerful young man who looked at it a moment before baring his own and taking William's.

The blood coursed in his veins; worried at leaving Solomon again, he held on longer than he ever had for any other handshake.

Solomon nodded and blinked his eyes once or twice before gently pulling back. William let him go. "Come visit us, son."

They watched Solomon ride west before heading home themselves, William glad to have his young men with him but worried their names might be mentioned back at Norwich, where MacNab's soldiers would surely go.

Chapter Twenty-Nine

Norwich, 1837

SAM REMEMBERED another night of hiding and fleeing, but then he had Sally and their children with him. The winds across the lake had cut into their warm clothing, pressed on them by the kind white family, and together they had weathered the snow and ice dotting the frozen river, struggling to reach land before the reddish glow edging the bottom of the eastern sky burned forth and caught them in the open.

Sally had clutched the baby in her arms but when he tried to relieve her of the burden for a few moments she had held tight, afraid the child's weight added to his own would increase the constant cracking all around them. They had reached the shore safely and found the farm the man had told them about. Their early morning pounding had brought the Scottish couple to the door. In no time they were wrapped in safety, their travails still foremost in their minds but gradually edged out by hot porridge and fresh-baked bread.

As he ran back to his home this night, his legs threatened to give out and his lungs certainly had not the capacity they'd had twenty and more years before. The young men quickly outpaced him in the slippery mud and ice and many drifted into the trees. He dared not follow. He needed the faint moonlight here on the road to see. In the trees, he'd be blind.

Thoughts flew through his mind: running with Sally, the owner's whip, hounds howling, trees bending low to slap against his curly head, the cold and the blowing snow as they fled north. All of it crashed into his terrified brain even as he struggled to think and to survive.

Morning found him outside his tiny house, collapsed in the snow, with Sally's hands tugging his hair, his beard, his hands, anywhere she could to rouse him. He allowed her to pull him to his feet and into the safety of their home just as the galloping hoofs of horsemen and the shouts of pursuing soldiers woke the village.

His fingers and feet warm again and a steaming cup of coffee hot in his hand, Sam pulled back the curtain and watched with wide eyes as the village woke to soldiers and shouts. Even inside he could feel the tension building and hoped his fellows had arrived home as he had. They would all be safe if they stayed inside out of the soldiers' way. No one in Norwich would give them up.

But Sam was wrong. And while he sat watching the main street from his tiny parlor, bands of searchers systematically turned homes inside out looking for rebels and, once they found them, rounded them up to lock up in London or Hamilton to await trial. When later in the day a neighbor knocked quietly on the back door, Sam and Sally learned that MacNab had a list with all their names on it.

"How'd he get that?" Sam struggled for control but his worst fears seemed to be right outside the door. "I saw Dr. Duncolme take time to bury it. Over in Scotland."

"Found it," his friend said and shrugged his shoulders. "Hide, Sam. Before they come here."

The two men pulled the table and chairs back, rolled up the braided rug, and slipped their fingers into the narrow cleft in the floor to lift up the door to the cellar. Horses neighed in the lane as Sam went down the rough ladder into the darkness below. Before he got to the bottom the door above closed and he felt his way to the damp floor where eventually he stretched out his long legs and said prayers to his Maker.

He imagined the braided rug back over the cellar door, the table and chairs anchoring it, and Sally peeling apples into the big bowl. He hoped she wasn't too frightened but remembered her courage on the cracking ice all those years ago as she clutched the baby and planted one foot firmly in front of the other until they reached the other side. Now their children were grown and Sally spent her days helping Mrs. MacAnally over at the big house while he did what odd jobs he could.

Heavy boots sounded in the dark. Voices, faint but definitely there. Scrapes of furniture. Were they opening the cellar? He stood looking up but could see nothing. Sally's voice, shouting. He put one foot on the ladder but the sounds above died and he clutched the rough wood, uncertain whether to go or stay. In the end he held tight, hardly taking a breath as the sounds dissipated. His imagination ran wild. He couldn't decide which was worse, the fear of the soldiers finding him or not knowing what was happening above.

When he thought he'd been there the whole day and could bear the suspense no longer, scrapes across the floor above sharpened his senses once more and he stood again, almost knocking Sally's preserves right off the shelf beside him. His eyes stretched in the dark and his ears, too. A creaking hinge made him look up again. This time, a crack of light widened as the door lifted.

"Sam," Sally whispered.

He began to climb out.

"Wait," she said. "Stay. I have food for you." She came partway down the ladder and handed him a steaming bowl. "They're right outside." A blanket and a pillow came next and in the pale light of the lantern he stuffed them on the shelf beside the jams. He wanted to talk, to ask questions, to do anything to keep the trap door open but Sally passed him a chamber pot and took back the lantern. For one brief moment he saw her wary eyes before she scuttled up the ladder.

"Do not worry, Sally." He smiled his best smile; she gave him a quick wave and lowered the trap door, leaving him to eat his stew alone in the dark.

Elaine Cougler

• • •

FOR SALLY, the days were every bit as frightening as those of her flight from her owner so many years before. As much as she and Sam and their family had gained, now she was back to terror, but this time her man was hidden below and she could not think of running. She must stay and face what came. From behind her curtains she waited and watched the world outside.

Gone were the children playing in the snow, the neighbors sharing friendly waves, and the odd wagon bringing sugar beets or some such thing into the village to exchange for supplies. All up and down the street the soldiers chased after anyone foolish enough to be out in the cold. Even women with their baskets trudging to the shops up the hill were stopped and searched, although what the soldiers expected to find she didn't know. Nothing could make her step out into that alien landscape.

On the second day of Sam's hiding she had just replaced the rug over the trapdoor and lifted the table and chairs back into place when a sudden pounding on her front door almost knocked her off her feet. She grabbed the table. Maybe they would go away. The pounding got louder and men's voices threatened to break down the door. She checked the floor and the table before hurrying to open up to the soldiers.

Three uniformed men stared at her, speechless for just a moment, before pushing past her into her home. One went into the bedroom, another into the kitchen while the third started tearing books off the shelves, rifling the pages and tossing Sam's precious tomes on the floor. He upended the settee and threw the lace-worked cushion she had completed last winter into a corner. She could hear the other rooms being destroyed in the same way but most of her attention was on the kitchen. She watched the destruction before her, though, knowing Sam's only hope lay in her keeping her head.

"Nothing here, sir." The man from the bedroom came back and very soon the other returned from destroying her kitchen. His uniform was spattered with flour and he dripped her strawberry preserves from a slice of fresh-baked bread onto the floor.

"Clean yourself, man," the leader shouted and turned to Sally who shrank into the corner but the man raised his hands to reassure her. "Where is your husband, madam?"

Her fingers twisted around a scrap of rag she had been using to wipe up the table. She barely shook her head but his eyes darkened as he approached her. "Don't know, sah."

"You don't know or you won't tell me?" He pushed his face right into hers.

"Sah. Don't know, sah." She backed into the cabin wall. She couldn't move. The man's ruddy face spewed hot words; his moustache wriggled with each word. A few crumbs caught in the curved hairs above his lips worked their way loose as he yelled, but she didn't hear what he said, so terrified was she. Not so much for herself, but for Sam. If she could just keep them from finding him.

He didn't touch her and, in a moment, stepped back and smoothed his red jacket with the gold buttons. He motioned to the other two who moved forward. They turned to the door. Just as she dared to breathe again, he jerked back to her.

"We will find him, woman. Be sure of that!"

"And when we do…" The shorter soldier jerked his hand across his own neck in the timeworn sign of slitting a throat. The man's face contorted, his mouth opened to expose his rotted teeth, and she knew the smell would stay with her forever.

They clomped outside and down her porch, leaving her to shut and lock the door, which she now knew was no protection at all for her or for Sam. Sam would be worried but she daren't open the trap door just yet. What if they came back?

When she had righted all the furniture and replaced Sam's books, Sally tackled the tiny kitchen, a much bigger job. Flour, sugar, tea, even salt pooled together off the table and onto the braided carpet below. Their four plates were smashed—she'd heard that—and the kettle had been emptied over everything.

How she would ever get the rug washed and dried in the dead of winter she didn't know but clean it she must, and quickly.

Just as she moved the table to free it, a timid knock sounded on her front door. What now? She dashed to the window, saw skirts and not soldiers, and unlocked the door to admit Mrs. MacAnally.

"I think they've gone, Sally." She looked around the room. "Did they find him?"

Should she trust the woman? Sally hardly knew. Mrs. MacAnally was kind to her, for certain, and always paid her on time, never cheating her or anything like that. Her friends were not so lucky. She led the old lady to the chair and she took the settee. Her hands straightened the book on the small table before her. "No," she whispered.

Mrs. MacAnally reached into her pocket and pulled out a small package which she handed to Sally. "Here. You need these more than I." Two currant buns, freshly baked, lay in her hand. Tears came to Sally now and Mrs. MacAnally patted her knee until she regained control. They talked about the village, the rounding up of those who had marched to Scotland, and the search for those who had fled, some headed for the United States, Mrs. MacAnally said.

"I hope they make it." Sally's words barely touched the knot of fear in her heart. The two women parted with promises to help each other whenever needed and Sally went back to watching out the window.

For three days, the soldiers occupied the village and its surrounding farms, striking fear into the inhabitants not only in case their rebel sons and husbands might be found but also for the paralyzing threat of more reprisals against the whole village. Prisoners were moved to the jail far away in London where family members could not reach them nor know what was happening to them. Soldiers and their Indian allies stole provisions, robbed hen coops, and confiscated whatever guns they found.

One Indian tried to enter a home but was met with boiling maple sap poured from above over his hands and his legs. At another house, a heavy woman of over two hundred pounds sat in a chair over her cellar door, refusing to move. The soldiers declined to try to lift her. Sally laughed to hear from Mrs. MacAnally about Margaret Murphy who stood on her porch, pitchfork in hand and two pistols in her belt defying the soldiers. They didn't dare touch anything on the property.

For those same three days Sam stayed in the dark of the cellar, his only respite Sally's quick and infrequent visits when she thought opening the door was safe enough to hand him food, exchange his chamber pot, and give him a quick bit of news. His eyes hurt now when the light streaked down from above, but he could almost see around his small sanctuary in the dark. Waking and sleeping happened on their own; he knew not what the day was, nor the time, nor anything else. Sally's visits were his only constant.

On the fourth day his wife's face was a blur as he struggled to climb the ladder at her urging. His eyes hurt in the bright light streaming in the small kitchen window and Sally closed the curtain but it was not enough. He squeezed his eyes shut as she led him by the hand to their bedroom, scraped the dark curtains across the heavy rod above the window, and sat beside him in the semi-dark. Only then could he open his eyes and look at her.

Her wide-lipped smile over shining white teeth told him all was well as she described the last three days to him. The soldiers had come and demanded all the rebels be handed over. Those who stepped forward were immediately arrested even though they had done no wrong. The others escaped along the roads and trails to the south and the west, hoping to get across the border into the United States. Gangs of soldiers stripped the community bare of its men, its weapons and even much of its food as they sought to punish the small community for even thinking of rebellion.

"I was thinking," Sam said after Sally's tales had wound down. "Maybe I...there was a man...a group."

"What man?" She stiffened beside him and drew his face to look at her.

"Remember Mr. Garner? Robert, I mean?"

"Yes, of course."

"It wasn't him. In the rebels. Too young." His mouth opened wider. "His son! I think I saw his son!" He stood up as quickly as his weakened legs would let him.

"I...I...don't..."

"With the rebels. I saw him there."

She shook her head and he was sure she thought he was confused after his stay in the cellar.

Sam stayed hidden for much of the next few weeks but the soldiers did not reappear and gradually he felt safe enough to resume his daily chores. To the whites, he supposed, one black-skinned man looked much like another and a number of former slaves had made their way to the area, particularly to the south of Norwich. No one took much notice and if they did they weren't likely to report any news to the departed MacNab whose heavy-handed measures had so incensed the residents, Quakers and non-Quakers alike.

Gradually word filtered back to the tiny village about those who had fled with Dr. Duncolme south of the border. Many reconnected with Mackenzie who, with the help of friends and plenty of good luck, had escaped to a place on American soil just across the Niagara River. More plans were hatching there but Sam and Sally decided they would not be joining the rebels again.

Those in jail waited for trials in the most deplorable of conditions as reported by one of the Quaker families who had recently returned from attending a meeting in the London area. On one of Sally's workdays with Mrs. MacAnally, the woman insisted on telling Sally the stories she'd had on good authority about the huge vat in the middle of the prison yard. Peeking over the fence, the Quakers could see the filthy pot and unwashed potatoes and vegetables which went into it once a day. And they smelled the bad meat tainting the mixture but when they tried to complain they barely escaped imprisonment themselves. Perhaps the worst picture Mrs. MacAnally drew was of the dogs and cats and even rats licking the unwashed kettle where daily dust settled from the constant digging of graves a few feet away.

Chapter Thirty

William and Catherine's Farm
July, 1838

ON THE NORTH LAWN the sun lapped up what little morning dew remained as the men, still dressed in their work clothes, set up stumps and planks in rows facing the pulpit that had come all the way from the little church two roads over. Along the side, trestle tables waited under the shading maples for the food the ladies had been preparing all week. Plates and cutlery secured the lightly blowing cloth and Catherine was glad the breeze was not stronger.

"You were right." William came up behind her as she surveyed the scene. "Pulling the corn field back and planting this grass has made a great difference."

She smiled and took his arm even though the sweat clung to him after all his heavy lifting. "We must get ready or Will's bride might arrive with us still in our work clothes." A laugh gurgled up from deep within her and she leaned against her husband for just a minute more. Johnny came out of the house carrying a towel and a bar of lye soap. "What—?"

"He's heading for the river." William turned away. "Hold up, Johnny. I'm coming, too." Will appeared at the barn door, saw the males of his family heading down the slope and ran to join them. She watched just long enough to see them all strip to their white skin with their brown heads and hands before she turned back to the house, smiling.

THOMAS BRUSH BROWN held up his arms for silence as he looked over the smiling crowd of friends and neighbors gathered today for the marriage of two of their own. He nodded to the fiddler who began to play a soft and sweet tune that carried out over the seated guests and up into the blue and white above. He cast his eyes toward the house and right on cue Olive and her father walked toward the wedding party lined up in front of the gathering. The fiddle stopped and for a moment only the hummingbirds flitting around the pink and white hollyhocks disturbed the tableau.

"Dearly Beloved. We are gathered..."

Catherine's hands clasped tightly over her new dress and she worried for a moment the heat would spoil it. She resisted the urge to smooth the fabric with her moist fingers. William glanced at her, a question on his face. She shook her head ever so slightly. After so many years together he knew everything she was thinking, sometimes before she did. Her eyes seemed suddenly full but she resisted another urge, this time to dab them with her dainty handkerchief.

"...any man...just cause..."

She thought of her own wedding so many years before. Her own mother's tears. How strange she thought them then. Now she understood and sneaked glances to her right and left. So many people missing. Not just their parents but friends, Migisi, Kiwi—so many. She wanted to reach for William's hand lying there so strong and firm on his lap.

"With this ring I thee wed..." Will's voice was strong and sure. So like his father, he was. She didn't hear her new daughter-in-law's words but saw her warm smile as she stole a glance at the man she was marrying. They had love. And family. Farms carved out of the trees. The land was cleared now and wheat shone golden down the hillside and across the river.

William leaned toward her just as her son kissed his new bride. In moments the cheering began and rice flew over the young couple's happy heads, everyone joining in the celebration. The time had come to feed their guests and Catherine dropped her husband's hand. She gave Will and his new wife quick kisses, afraid to linger and let her emotions out, before gathering her ladies at the food tables. William did his part as host and in no time guests and wedding party alike sat before the feast.

Once the preacher had said the grace, everyone tucked into the cold sliced beef and new potato salad, the fresh garden peas and beans creamed in a well-flavored white sauce, and tiny new carrots scrubbed so their purples and yellows and oranges shone. People passed sweet pickles and sipped spring water iced with a big block from the icehouse. A comfortable stillness settled over them all.

A sudden galloping on the road to the south made everyone pause. Who might be coming? Wasn't everyone here? When the horse slowed, William stood up, swiped his napkin at his lips, and, motioning everyone to carry on, walked to the front gate.

Catherine tried to concentrate on her food but kept stealing glances at her gesturing husband and their untimely guest. He looked familiar but she couldn't see as well as she used to. William led the man into the house and came back out alone to take his seat beside her.

"Who is that?"

He gave his head a slight shake and popped a forkful of beef into his mouth. He seemed to take forever to chew it but Catherine waited, convinced something bad was happening. Why else would William leave a stranger in their house? Robert, seated down the other side of the table, kept his eyes on them. He suspected something, too.

"Please, William. Who is in our house?" She tried to whisper but her words betrayed her worry and eyes all up and down the table turned toward them. She forced a smile and she glanced right and left before concentrating on her husband again. He seemed not to have heard her and she resisted the urge to kick him under the table. When he lifted his fork again, she put her hand over his to stop him. "Who is it?" Near his hairline his "worry" vein pulsed blue under his white skin. As people talked all around them he leaned her way.

"It's Matheson again."

She took a quick breath. "What does he want with you?"

"Nothing," he whispered. "It's Robert he wants. Again." He turned to answer a question from Eva on his other side.

Throughout the rest of the wedding feast with its laughter and voices raised in happiness, Catherine smiled a brittle smile and tried to forget the bile rising inside her. Her two grandchildren, just down the table, kept William laughing with their childish antics and she, too, almost forgot the nugget of fear swishing inside her along with her food.

As the sun slid over the trees across the road the party began to come to an end. The young couple were loaded onto their wagon and waved off down the road to a new house the bride's parents had provided for this first night of their marriage. Once they were gone guests seemed to remember their own duties and a string of wagons rattled up and down the road. Catherine hoped those going south would leave the young couple to themselves.

William stood with her through the waving and the leaving, Mary Anne and Robert close by, along with their children. "I'd best get the wagon," Robert said, and his tired but happy wife nodded. William raised his arm. "Just a moment, Robert." They all looked at him and Catherine felt her stomach lurch again.

"Come, Mary Anne," she said. "You must see my garden. I've so many baby squash blooms you must see." Arm in arm the two ambled off to the garden; William led Robert inside.

"YOU'LL NOT GET ME on that phony land charge again, Matheson," Robert shouted. "I've got the deed that's signed with Strachan's own hand." He jumped to his feet. "Let me take you to my house and I'll prove it."

"No, Robert. It's not that." William glanced at Matheson sitting in the rocker. "He's not here about the deed."

The Loyalist Legacy

Robert looked from one to the other. "Why is he here? Surely you've not become friends." He edged over to sit by William on the settee, careful not to smudge his boots into Catherine's new braided rug.

Matheson pulled a wadded sheet of paper out of his coat pocket and quietly unfolded it, all the while watching Robert as though at any moment he'd bolt out the door. But Robert was curious. What could the man want now? Surely not his thoughts? For that's all he'd done—think about joining the rebellion with the other lads. At his side William clenched his hands in his lap.

"I have your name here...on this list."

"Why would you have my name?"

"On this list of rebels." He shook the paper in front of him and glared at Robert. "You rode with Duncolme, sir, and we can prove it. What's more you'll pay for it, this time." The man sat back in the chair, nodding.

Robert hardly knew what to say. If he told the truth he might endanger Russell and Solomon. And even William. If he didn't, perhaps Matheson would take him and leave the young ones alone.

William reached for the list and Matheson slowly handed it over. Together the brothers read. Robert's name was there but not the young ones. And not William's. "What is this? Where did you get it?" William handed the paper back to Matheson as the door opened and Catherine came in with Mary Anne. Their smiles disappeared as soon as they crossed the threshold.

"Answer me," William said, his voice soft but steady.

Matheson swallowed. "It came from someone who sat in on your meetings in Centreville. You can't deny you were there."

"Of course I was there. Let me have that list again." He grabbed the paper from Matheson. Logan's name was there. And the names of many others he'd met over the past year. "Surely you can't arrest us for being in a public hotel?"

William relaxed his hands. He let out a deep breath and nodded a few times before opening his mouth. "My brother is right, sir." He passed the list back to Matheson. "You have no proof of anything illegal on my brother's part. And you won't find anything either. Robert is a solid citizen of this province. He's proven it over and over." He turned toward the ladies. "Come, now, and sit with us. Ladies, tell us your thoughts about Will's wedding."

The brothers made room for their wives and listened to their tales of Mrs. Logan's large hat and wee Charlie Simmons messing his first pair of short pants. Eva had supervised the cleanup outside ordering her brother and her husband around as though born to it, and not resting until all the benches were disassembled and the planks piled ready to go back to the sawyer's on the morrow. The men had piled the stumps on the woodpile.

Through all this talk Robert watched his wife. She seemed to have recovered completely. His glances toward Matheson were quick and infrequent. The man nursed a perplexed face and though he tried to look interested in the talk of the wedding his mind was obviously elsewhere.

When the lamps were lit to ease the crowding shadows of night, Matheson rose. William went outside with him and Robert heard them talking on the porch a few minutes before the man rode off. William came back inside. "Does he know?" Robert whispered.

"No. I didn't tell him I was there. I did tell him why you didn't join the rebels for that fateful day."

"You mean about..."

"Yes." He glanced at Mary Anne. "We won't hear from him again." He raised his voice and motioned for Robert to sit by him at the long table spread with food. "Tell me more about the new Governor. Will he be able to correct all the mistakes made here?" Catherine and Mary Anne joined their husbands at the table.

"They say he is the first one to come from England with the express purpose of addressing the discontent here." Robert's voice quickened. "I hope he follows through."

William studied his brother a moment, nodding. "Maybe with this Lord Durham our lives will be better."

"And our children's and grandchildren's lives," said Catherine. The four of them loaded their plates from the wedding leftovers and ate in silence, a shared vision of the days to come filling their thoughts.

Afterward

THE LOYALISTS FIRST EMERGED as a group during and after the American Revolutionary War when they wished to remain loyal to Britain, a stance that angered the Patriots greatly, and led the Loyalists to flee. Those who came to Ontario through present-day Niagara-on-the-Lake are the subjects of this trilogy. The three books follow the journey of the Garner family who are representative of the many families caught in these two wars and in their aftermath in what is now Ontario, particularly southern Ontario.

Loyalists also settled further east in Ontario, as well as in our Eastern provinces and I have left these stories to be written at a later time by myself or others.

IN THIS BOOK I'VE CHOSEN to show the discontent in Upper Canada that led to the Rebellion of 1837; in so doing I've portrayed the Garner family as being divided in their loyalties, a circumstance which was quite prevalent at that time. Robert and Helen had lived across the border. William had not, and neither had John and Lucy. This allowed me to show how hard it was for those who came to Ontario after the War of 1812 and also to show the staunch support for the British Crown still among many of the Loyalists. Even though life in the colony was very difficult under the Family Compact, many Loyalists did not want to rebel. Others were driven to it.

Elaine Cougler

   Whichever side our ancestors took, these are the people who settled and seeded this land, a land which has grown and evolved into the thriving center of industry and agriculture, innovation and technological knowhow, multiculturalism and tolerance which we enjoy today. May our own progeny down through the ages have the same reverence and respect for our efforts to build lives through work and wit.

More Information About the Loyalist Trilogy

More about the Loyalist triology at: www.elainecougler.com

Elaine on Goodreads: www.goodreads.com/ElaineCougler

You're invited to join Elaine's email list to get updates and special extras: http://eepurl.com/FCKL1

Notes Re The Loyalist Legacy

MY USE OF BUFFALO is not historically accurate as Buffalo, much smaller at that time, was farther south along the lake and my characters would not have been able to see the mill near Fort Erie on the Canadian side. New Amsterdam was closer to the Niagara River but I've chosen to have Robert and Mary Anne live in Buffalo across the river from his parents' former home.
   The historic mill which still stands today at Arva, Ontario, north of London, was at St. John at the time I have Lucy visiting it. To make matters clearer I've used Arva instead of St. John, the name when the mill was started in 1819.
   Bishop Strachan did not actually receive his bishopric until 1839 but I have called him bishop throughout the novel for simplicity's sake. While he undoubtedly deserves a preferential position in Ontario's

The Loyalist Legacy

history, he caused much dissension during his lifetime, particularly for his views on the common people and the Anglican Church.

For purposes of my story, I have not been particularly kind to the Family Compact but readers and students of history will know this group played an important part in creating the country we know today. Though I have used actual historical fact in many of the incidents reported, the whole story of John, William, and Robert Garner being incarcerated is fiction. The real John Garner, however, was often called upon to help his neighbors with legal problems.

The village known today as Norwich was often called Sodom in the 1800's and sometimes Norwichville, but I've chosen to use today's name for clarity. Not only was Norwich known far and wide as Sodom, Gomorrah was used for the village nearby although opinion varies on just where that was. The early Quakers of the area would not have countenanced sinful ways gladly; hence, the biblical names.

At the time of this novel Centreville, which today is a small blip on the road connecting Woodstock and Ingersoll, far outstripped in size these two centers in modern-day Oxford County. I have chosen to honour Centreville's part in Oxford's history.

My beta readers noted my used of "receipts" instead of recipes, causing me to explain this word actually was used instead of recipes at the time.

Dr. Charles Duncolme tried all legal ways to improve the government for his constituents up to and including traveling all the way to England to put the reform case before the British government. For the most part he was unsuccessful. In December of 1837 he finally joined the rebellion and tried to take part in Mackenzie's march in Toronto (York) with his group which marched from Norwich to Scotland. For the sake of my story, I have implied he was involved with the rebels earlier.

Because of my characters living in Nissouri and other nearby places far from Toronto, I have not used the march of the rebels down Yonge Street in Toronto from Montgomery's Tavern. None of my characters would have made it to Toronto. Instead I have them joining the group who marched from Norwich. I did, however, have William stay over in Montgomery's Tavern.

Lord Durham only visited Upper Canada and its counterpart for four months in the summer of 1838 but his report, which he finished in 1839, recommended responsible government and was the beginning of the end for the Family Compact. It would take another thirty years before the basis of the Canada we know today actually was formed with the British North America Act on July 1, 1867.

Some of the Sources Consulted By The Author

The Loyalists: Revolution, Exile, Settlement, Christopher Moore, Macmillan of Canada, a division of Gage Publishing Limited, Toronto, 1984.
King's Men: The Soldier Founders of Ontario, Mary Beacock Fryer, Dundurn Press Limited, Toronto, 1980.
Joseph Brant and His World, James W. Paxton, James Lorimer & Company Ltd., Publishers, Toronto, 2008.
Loyal She Remains: A Pictorial History of Ontario, published by The United Empire Loyalists' Association of Canada, Toronto, 1984.
Much To Be Done: Private Life in Ontario from Victorian Diaries, Hoffman, Frances, Taylor, Ryan, Natural Heritage/Natural History Inc., Toronto, 1996.
Historical Atlas of Canada, Derek Hayes, published in Canada by Douglas & McIntyre, 2002.
The Family Compact: A Chronicle of the Rebellion in Upper Canada, W. Stewart Wallace, Glasgow, Brook & Company, Toronto, 1915.
From Bloody Beginnings: Richard Beasley's Upper Canada, David Richard Beasley, Davus Publishing, Simcoe, Ontario, 2008.
The Blacks in Canada: A History, Second Edition, Robin W. Winks, McGill-Queen's University Press, Montreal & Kingston 1997.
Flint & Feather: The Life and Times of E. Pauline Johnson, Tekahionwake, Charlotte Gray, Harper Flamingo Canada, 2002.

Autobiography of Thomas Brush Brown, Reprinted 1967 by Isabel Grace Uren with additional notes, 1967.
Through the Years in West Nissouri, Ila Logan, 1967.
West Nissouri Township, vol. 1 & 2, J.J. Leverton, ed., The West Nissouri Historical Society, printed by The Aylmer Express Ltd. Limited Edition of 1000 copies, November 2003.
I Came as a Stranger, Bryan Prince, Tundra Books, 2004.
The Backwoods of Canada, Catherine Parr Traill, McClelland & Stewart Inc., 1989.
The Family Compact: A Chronicle of the Rebellion in Upper Canada, W. Stewart Wallace, 1915.
Frederick H. Armstrong and Ronald J. Stagg, "MACKENZIE, WILLIAM LYON," in *Dictionary of Canadian Biography*, vol. 9, University of Toronto/Université Laval, 2003–, accessed December 1, 2015, http://www.biographi.ca/en/bio/mackenzie_william_lyon_9E.html.
To Stand and Fight Together: Richard Pierpoint and the Coloured Corps of Upper Canada, Steve Pitt, A Sandcastle Book, a Member of the Dundurn Group, Toronto, 2008.

An Invitation to Book Clubs and Other Groups

VISIT ELAINE COUGLER'S WEBSITE to connect with her for speaking and workshop opportunities. She is available to speak on many subjects ranging from book club discussions to the impact of the Loyalists, the birth of both Canada and the United States, and writing a novel, historical or not. Skype makes inviting an author to your meeting very easy all over the world, really.

To contact Elaine, email her through the Contact button on her website at www.elainecougler.com. Goodreads and Amazon both have Elaine Cougler author pages where readers can interact with the author as well as write reviews of her books. Come put in your own two cents worth.

Elaine Cougler

The First Two Books in The Loyalist Trilogy

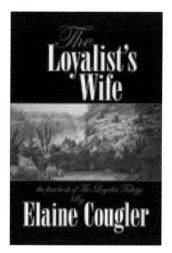